THE PATRIOT

BOOKS BY NICK THACKER

JAKE PARKER THRILLER SERIES
Containment

NICK THACKER

THE PATRIOT

bookouture

Published by Bookouture in 2021

An imprint of Storyfire Ltd.
Carmelite House
50 Victoria Embankment
London EC4Y 0DZ

www.bookouture.com

ISBN: 978-1-83888-718-6
eBook ISBN: 978-1-83888-717-9

This book is a work of fiction. Names, characters, businesses,
organizations, places and events other than those clearly in the
public domain, are either the product of the author's imagination
or are used fictitiously. Any resemblance to actual persons, living or
dead, events or locales is entirely coincidental.

CHAPTER 1

"I can help you find the man who killed your wife."

Jake Parker stared straight ahead, into the eyes of the man seated across the table from him. He didn't move, and neither did Jake. For a moment, time stood still.

He had known this man for over fifteen years, and there had never been a time when Jake doubted him. But he had to be lying.

The newly minted Lieutenant Colonel Douglas McDonnell was an old friend from his West Point days and they were meeting at the same hot dog restaurant he and Jake had often visited after a game back in college—*Pete's Hot Dog Stand*, a no-nonsense family-owned restaurant that had been serving tube steaks for longer than Jake could remember. Today, it was a traditional Chicago-style dog, done up right and served with a steaming pot of coffee. The coffee was good, with just enough heat to tickle the back of his throat without being overpowering.

McDonnell had sat perfectly still while eating and while he spoke, though not many words had been exchanged thus far. They'd barely gotten through the pleasantries when their food was ready, and neither man seemed to be interested in discussing anything over a mouthful of food. He had already finished his dog and now had his mug of coffee in front of him—black, a requirement for any career Army man—which he held with two hands, watching Jake. No doubt measuring his reaction to his statement.

"Tell me more," Jake said quietly. He pulled his own mug up to his lips and took a sip. It was a larger sip than he had intended, and the hot liquid stung the roof of his mouth. Still, he didn't flinch.

McDonnell finally moved, shifting in his chair as he began to speak once again. "It's been a long time since we've talked, Parker," he said. "You look like the same man who walked off the ice after that last game junior year."

"You mean *hobbled* off the ice," Jake said. The last college hockey game he'd played at West Point had ended in disaster for him. Just short of needing a full knee replacement, Jake had never fully recovered from the injury. While he no longer walked with a limp, his hopes and dreams of going pro had been dashed by a single dirty hit on the ice.

"I bet you still have it in you, though," McDonnell said. "I bet you could take me one-on-one right now—"

"What about my *wife*," Jake said, the words stilted and forced, and sounding slightly more intense than he had anticipated. But he didn't try to retract the statement. He'd meant it, tone and all. He didn't want to offend McDonnell, but he also wasn't going to pretend that he hadn't heard what his friend had said.

He took a breath and tried to calm himself down. McDonnell was a friend—he needed to remember that.

Like Jake, Douglas McDonnell had entered the Army after college. There, however, their careers branched apart as the two men became successful in their respective fields: Jake in international military intelligence and McDonnell in computer information systems, specifically defense hardware and software.

Jake had heard McDonnell's name mentioned a few times since then, most notably for his recent promotion to Lieutenant Colonel, as well as for stepping into a new role with the United States Army's new counterterrorism division based in Washington, DC.

Jake hadn't realized, though, that McDonnell knew of his wife's death. So many people had written cards and sent flowers when she had lost her life in the aftermath of a terrorist attack on the city of Boston that he had never bothered to pay attention to who was sending them. If McDonnell had in fact reached out to him three years ago, Jake didn't remember.

The wound from his wife's passing was no longer fresh, but it certainly had not completely healed. He wondered if McDonnell thought otherwise, or was somehow trying to get a rise out of him.

"I didn't know you knew," Jake said.

McDonnell nodded. "I'm sorry I never met her. She sounded incredible. I was devastated for you when I heard about it."

"Thank you," Jake replied automatically. "Now tell me what you think you know about Mel's death."

McDonnell shifted again as he took a sip from his mug. He swallowed, then looked back up at Jake. "I'm on a new project. It's related to fighting terrorism—tracking gang-related activity—and there's a little bit more I can tell you about it, but…"

Jake nodded. He knew the drill. Agree to the terms, accept them—*then* they would bring him into the fold. Refuse, and he would be left wondering what exactly McDonnell's project was all about and what this man knew about his wife's death.

McDonnell continued. "You remember the trial after her death?" As soon he said it, he winced. "Sorry, of course you do. What I meant was, do you remember that it was not really the Boston Police Department itself the state was trying to go after for mishandling the terrorist attack? Because of the nature of it—it was a bomb in Boston, but linked to an *international* terrorism cell—it was specifically the counterterrorism unit *within* the department the state wanted raked over the coals."

"Yeah, but they had trouble drilling down to them specifically, so the entire department was laid bare and on display, just like I was. It was a public massacre, McDonnell."

"I know, I know. And I promise I'm not trying to dredge up old memories for the hell of it. Jake, the reason the counterterrorism unit was the target of the investigation was that, at the time, my project was investigating a gang based in Puerto Rico called Dominguez that we thought was beginning to operate inside US borders."

"And were they?"

"Yes, we are now one hundred percent sure that they were. At the time, we didn't know that for a fact; we didn't even know where they were based. I've been tracking them since I took over the project two years ago, so I wasn't around when the trial was happening. I know the state paid you two million and called the trial a victory, but…"

"But you think it was a little 'shut up' money? That it was meant to silence me?"

McDonnell arched an eyebrow. "Did it?"

Jake took a moment before he responded to the question. He knew what McDonnell was implying—that the state had awarded him money not simply because his side had won the trial, and not simply because reparations needed to be made for Mel's death, but because they *also* did not want Jake investigating further into the matter.

"I see," Jake said. "You think the state wanted to keep me quiet?"

McDonnell shrugged. "You'll never see it written anywhere, and anyone you ask will deny it point-blank, but, sure. It's how these things work, Jake. I mean, in your detective career, you know that. Hell, you saw a bit of it during your stint as an intelligence officer."

"Okay," Jake said, "I'll bite. So the gang you are tracking now is the same one you believe had something to do with the terror attack that led to Mel's death? That she was some sort of collateral damage?"

"Exactly, yeah. Boston PD's counterterrorism unit, in my mind, should have been charged with criminal negligence. That bomb would not have gone off when it did if the department hadn't rushed the operation's intelligence-gathering. I know the unit's lead got a slap on the wrist, and a few others were put on probation, but my project simply could not allow all of the information to go public, so our hands were tied. If the cell we are tracking knew how much we actually have on them, the case would be open and shut—and not in a good way. We think there's another attack coming in a few days or so—a big one. I want your help preventing it."

"Okay, so what you're telling me is that Mel was accidentally killed in the explosion, but that the explosion itself was not an accident."

McDonnell shook his head. "No, Jake," he said. "I don't think it was an accident at all."

CHAPTER 2

McDonnell continued after a final sip of his coffee. "On March second of that year, the team got word that a high-profile member of the gang was on US soil. I can't give you any more than that at this point. Rest assured, we believed the intelligence, and we acted on it."

McDonnell's eyes fell quickly, then lifted back up and pierced through Jake. Jake knew what was going through the man's head. Still, it hurt him more than McDonnell could ever know. More than the man could ever understand.

"McDonnell, are you telling me it could have been *prevented?* That Mel may not have—" He stopped, then tried to collect himself. "Sorry. You weren't even on the case at the time. There's nothing you specifically could have done."

"I know, but *dammit,* Jake, if we weren't close. My predecessor on the project—now my boss—had everything in the bag. The case was easy—we were tracking this guy from the moment he stepped off the plane. We had him pegged and ready to go all week, it was all lined up, and then…"

"And then you lost track of him," Jake said, filling in the blanks.

McDonnell nodded. "Yeah. About three hours before the explosion at the café. Jake, we *had* him. We were moving people into position, ready to bring him in, and then he just… disappeared. And when the explosion happened, it threw everything off. Naturally, it got a little out of control and my project team was no longer the only investigative committee interested in this cell. The rest, well, you know most of it."

Jake nodded. "Nothing ever goes according to plan, I guess?"

McDonnell cracked a smile, but his eyes remained solemn and steady. "No, nothing ever goes according to plan. But guys like you and me—you know how it is. We never stop planning anyway. There's always *one more thing* we can try. One more thing we can do."

Jake felt the shift in the conversation, anticipating it. The ask. "All right, what's the one more thing? I want to know *everything*. Whatever it is, bring me in. Whoever you need to convince, just tell them my name. Recent events have made me sort of a public figure again, and I have a feeling my reputation's value is high enough that I can get whatever clearance I need. I used to have it, and after the mess with the virus and ICE I just helped sort out, I think I've got a little sway."

"Well, that's true, but there's no convincing I need to do. It's my call to make, and I've made it. And you won't need a higher clearance."

"Okay, so what is it, then? What do you want me to do?"

"Parker, I need your help with something. I need you to figure out what the attack's going to be, specifically. We have some rough details based on previous attacks. I want you to figure out *when* it's going to happen, and then help my team on the ground stop it. Like I said, the decision's as good as made. You know how things work, though—we'll have to get you through some of the red tape and officially onto the project before I can give you actual details to move on, but that's the gist of the mission."

Jake frowned. "Why can't you do it yourself?"

"We can, Jake. In time. But I'd rather do it sooner than later, and I've got two really good reasons for bringing you on, specifically. Firstly, this is what you *did* after West Point. This was your job—international intelligence as it specifically related to terrorism.

Your career after that in Boston as a detective is just icing on the cake. You were an exemplary officer, and with your recent success bringing down Derek Briggs, there was absolutely no resistance to bringing you onto this case."

"Okay," Jake said. He shook off the pang of anger as he remembered the ex-director of Immigration Customs and Enforcement, and how he had manufactured a virus that nearly wiped out thousands of Americans. "And what's the second reason?"

McDonnell eyed his empty coffee cup for a few seconds, then started to speak. "The second is that for you, this is personal. It's about Mel. And I know this for a fact: when things are personal, we make sure they get done. Sometimes when things are personal, it makes it harder to do the job, but somehow I have a feeling that's not going to be the case with you. I can't think of a better person to have on the team. Just what we need to breathe life into the investigation again."

McDonnell was implying that his leads had begun to dry up, or that the terrorist organization they were hunting had somehow given them the slip once again, but Jake knew he'd get all the details later. "Okay, fine. How *exactly* can I help?"

McDonnell nodded a few times, as if physically shifting his mind to the next task on his list. "Well, we know the *what* of it: we know what explosives were used, and we've traced them back to Dominguez. We know the *how*: again, we've got surveillance tapes and credit card statements, plane ticket purchases, the works. We even know the *who*—"

"You know specifically who did it?" Jake asked.

McDonnell shook his head. "No, we need you to find that out. But we do know who they were targeting in Boston—sort of. We have video of a man entering the café. It's the only person not found in any other records. We couldn't cross-reference him anywhere. No credit card transactions from him from the café's books. But we think he was the target of the bombers. We think he was the person the terrorists were going after in their attack. We've got a grainy picture of him, but other than that, he's a ghost." McDonnell paused. "We had a way to figure out this attack in Boston three years ago was related to Dominguez—a deal that soured, for whatever reason, and Dominguez wanted to take this guy out of the picture, and we *also* just found evidence to suggest there's going to be another attack. We need to know if this ghost was really their target. How exactly he was involved in this. We figure that out, we understand a lot more about the case. If we can understand more about the case, we are that much closer to taking these guys down and preventing the next one."

"So you have a motive," Jake said.

McDonnell nodded, then waited for Jake to meet his eyes. "So that's it, then. That's the whole story, at least the bird's-eye view. Come in tomorrow and I'll fill you in on the details and you can meet some of the US-based team. Right now it's only three of us, but we do have operatives in a few spots around the world."

"Okay, I'm in," Jake said. "I'll do it. I'll figure out who's behind these attacks, and who's pulling the strings."

McDonnell nodded once and started to rise from the table. All army, all business, all the time. He hadn't changed a bit, and Jake appreciated the man's ability to maintain his calm, collected exterior. It was a trait he appreciated in all of the military men and women he had worked with.

They shook hands, then Jake brought both mugs to the counter at the front of the coffee shop. The hostess who had served them smiled at him as she set the mugs into the basin. He nodded in return, then turned to find that McDonnell had already left the building.

I can help you find the man who killed your wife.

The words had stuck with Jake, and McDonnell had used them specifically to entice Jake to join his project. It wasn't manipulative, it was strategic. He knew McDonnell's mission was slightly different—he was interested in stopping the next terrorist attack this gang was planning. But he'd known how Jake would react to selling it with the promise that he could get closer to those who had killed Mel. He had shown his cards up front, knowing that everything he was about to tell Jake was time-sensitive, and he had wanted to cut to the chase immediately. Jake wasn't angry—he appreciated that about McDonnell, too.

If what McDonnell had said was true—and he had no reason to doubt him—Jake was going to be one step closer to a bit of closure.

He had a job, he had a mission. And that mission began with a single task.

Find the ghost.

CHAPTER 3

Cecil Romero Gonzalez II looked around at the dilapidated building. Nondescript, ancient brick walls framed a mostly empty rectangle, three stories tall with boarded-up windows. He could see the worn, rusted metal rafters of the roof, far above his head.

He sighed. *I thought I was done with work like this.* He had spent the last seventeen years of his life working toward the eventual goal *all* the members of his team aimed for: to retire on the beach, a frozen drink in hand, flush with cash and not enough time to spend it.

But it seemed he had taken a few steps back somewhere along the line. He had joined the gang as a teenager, a high-school dropout with a high-enough IQ to quickly become one of the leaders of the organization's drug-running division. The position had promised a fast-track to success, a route through the winding pathways of organized crime that would eventually end near the top of the food chain.

Eventually.

He was, clearly, not there yet.

Cecil shook his head and turned his gaze back to the workers spread out around the interior of the old building. He was in charge of a group of young men who had recently arrived from Puerto Rico, his own home country. Their job was simple: process the never-ending stream of contraband coming into the United States from their home island. From there, it was Cecil's main task to dole out the goods to local gangs and organizations that would then resell the items and illicit materials for their profit.

It was easy work for the most part, but it lacked the prestige and promise he had envisioned.

Cecil walked past the manned tables, spread out in a grid-like pattern across the weathered concrete floor, where the workers unpacked the boxes and organized the contraband into smaller stacks. The building was once some sort of textile factory, and it still boasted a massive iron machine along the back wall of the room, long since dead and inoperative. Cecil didn't know what the machine was for, but when he had first purchased the old building from the previous owners, there were stacks of cloth and tiny square pieces of fabric strewn about. Nothing had been cleaned up, and now the fabric shards and cobwebs mingled together in corners and beneath table legs.

Cecil had a small office to call his own, but it was still far from glamorous. It didn't seem to give him any elevated authority, as his men would simply barge in to talk with him no matter how small the issue or how long he had been inside, behind the closed door. He had hoped the office would bring him more respect, but so far he had been treated at best like their peer, a man only a few years their senior.

He reached the office and closed the door once again, knowing it would do nothing to persuade anyone to knock. He walked across to the back of the desk—a simple folding table, much like the ones the men were using out on the floor—and picked up his cell phone.

The company that had technically bought the building was nothing but an untraceable umbrella corporation—a typical US-based LLC that captured smaller businesses and tucked them away behind legality and tax codes, safely hidden from the prying eyes of local and state authorities. The company was called—on paper at least—*Integrated Consolidated Holdings, LLC,* a properly vague name that would allow the gang to operate on US soil without trouble, as long as they stayed *out* of trouble. The name was a brainchild of Cecil himself, and he was proud of it.

He held the cell phone up and saw the lock screen—a simple logo featuring the letters of the company, *ICH,* emblazoned on it—and unlocked it. He navigated to his boss's contact information in the recent calls, and pressed connect.

Within a few rings, his boss answered.

"Good afternoon, Cecil." The man's voice was low, lower than Cecil's younger-sounding voice, and he often wondered if the man—only thirty-five, two years older than Cecil—had reached his position just because of his good looks and deep, confident voice.

Cecil cleared his throat and tried to drop his own baritone a few notes. "Hello, Rodrigo. I am calling to update the company on the most recent delivery."

"Everything is in line and as it should be, I gather?"

"Yes, of course. The delivery was late, due to a slower port authority changeover, but it was nothing I could not handle."

"Of course," Rodrigo said. *"Thank you. Is there anything else?"*

Cecil swallowed. *This is it.* The reason for his call. He had agonized over this decision for the past three nights, knowing that the best opportunity he would ever have for advancing his career in the gang would be to take ownership of a project and provide his superiors with good ideas and sound investments.

And he thought he had such an investment.

"Rodrigo—sir," he began, sliding into formality to stress the importance of the conversation, "I have been studying the delivery patterns and I believe I can make some… improvements." He was considered young, but he had been involved enough—and was shrewd enough—to know that any attempt at improving something about his organization could also be easily seen as a way to *insult* the person who had come up with the thing he was improving.

"Improvements? I'm intrigued."

"Well, sir, I have a good understanding of the clientele now, and I believe our location here can be expanded, at little cost to us in the short-term, but at great profit to us within a year."

There was a pause. Cecil knew that Rodrigo had been instrumental in locating and procuring this building in south central Florida, so Cecil hoped the man didn't think he was stepping on his toes.

"Any expansion projects must be approved by the governing clan, Cecil."

"Y—yes, yes, of course," he said. "I was just trying to talk through some of the details. But I—I also wanted to stress that this expansion would be beneficial to us for another reason."

"Oh?"

"There is another building—an old factory, like this one—in North Carolina. Near the coast as well, so there would be little extra land-based transportation from the ships, but—and this is the important part—I believe the factory was once a chemical plant."

Another pause.

"It's not *exactly* what we need, not yet, but it does seem to be close. I found the real estate listing and saw some of the pictures of the interior, and I believe—"

"Cecil, I appreciate your work, but this is a matter best left to the governors."

Cecil felt his heart sink. "Sir, please—I believe there is great opportunity to get a head start on *localized* production, and with only a small investment, we could—"

"That is enough."

There was no more. No acknowledgment, no warning, nothing. The phone simply disconnected.

Cecil slammed the phone back down onto the table. Sure, he was young, but he was driven. Motivated. Consumed by the desire to improve, to grow, to advance—not just by a paycheck. He wanted to be *seen,* to become something in this organization. This opportunity was a no-brainer, even if the old plant needed to be completely gutted. If they could restart production *in* the United States, they could save millions on transportation, security, and personnel costs. They could bring the source much closer to the seller.

It was an easy win, but he still needed to convince them. That was fine, he liked hard work.

He took a breath, calming his nerves, and got to work.

CHAPTER 4

Jake met McDonnell in his office first thing the next day.

"We're wheels-up at 0700 tomorrow morning, flying out of Reagan."

"We?"

"Well, you. 'We' means we're tracking, on the same page. Me, Bolivar, Smith. My team on the ground in Puerto Rico."

Jake looked over McDonnell's shoulder at the two others in the small room. Hector Bolivar, an MIT graduate, sat hunched over a messy workstation with a dual-screen monitor setup in front of him. Denise Smith, retired Air Force pilot, sat across from him, her own workstation perfectly tidy and organized.

When McDonnell mentioned their names, Smith's head swiveled up and peered toward Jake, who was still standing in the entranceway of the room, then went immediately back down to her computer, obviously preoccupied with something far more important than Jake.

McDonnell's "command center," as he'd called it, was no more than a single-room office with four desks crammed inside. Two were face-to-face, where Smith and Bolivar sat, one was empty in the back corner, and the last desk was against the wall facing the door. That was the one McDonnell was heading toward now.

He collapsed into a worn office chair and smiled back up at Jake. "As I said, it's not much—but we all decided to spend our limited budget on a better remote team. No reason for fancy office space, since we're rarely entertaining visitors."

Jake took another glance around the room. His own apartment was sparsely decorated. After moving in shortly after Mel's death, he had left most of the walls bare and empty. If it were a "lame decorating" competition though, this office would put his apartment to shame. There was nothing on the walls but a few water-stain marks from ceiling to floor, a lone clock, and a tiny window behind the empty desk that only looked out toward an equally bare brick wall of the building next door.

Inside the office, McDonnell's two employees, Smith and Bolivar, could not have been more different. Bolivar was light-skinned, with messy blondish hair and huge Coke-can glasses. A freckled, pimpled, and pockmarked face told Jake that the guy had probably had a tough go at social life during grade school, but he had obviously landed on his feet.

Smith's ebony skin was smooth and perfect, and had McDonnell not told him, Jake would never have guessed that she had flown in some of the hairiest engagements in modern history—many of which weren't even on the books. She held her head high and steady as she worked, only her eyebrows moving as her eyes danced across the computer screen.

It was a motley crew, but Jake knew McDonnell had chosen the best—it was McDonnell's MO, and he had an entire military personnel catalog to choose from. These two were brilliant, and Jake didn't need to personally verify that.

He shook each of their hands—Smith's firm and steady and Bolivar's cold and clammy—and then he plopped down in front of McDonnell.

"So, I leave tomorrow. Puerto Rico, to meet with your remote crew?"

McDonnell nodded, looking down at the stack of papers on his desk.

"How'd you connect the dots between this group you're trying to track down in Puerto Rico and the bombing in Boston?" Jake asked.

McDonnell cleared his throat, but Bolivar spoke up. "Trace elements from the blast," he said, facing Jake from his position in the chair. "They match perfectly with the remnants of a couple of blasts down in Puerto Rico."

Jake frowned. "I'm not an explosives guy, but doesn't it seem like just about *any* bomb will leave remnants? How do you know they're from the same creators?"

"Actually, a good question," Bolivar said. "The answer is bismuth."

"The element?"

"Yep, one and the same. In this case, *bismuth trioxide*. It's the main ingredient in some fireworks—ever heard of a 'dragon's egg'?" Bolivar paused to wait for a response, but no one answered. "Anyway, it's a real nice sparking effect, and then it cracks really loud."

"So the bomb had *fireworks* in it?"

"Bombs," McDonnell said. "The bomb that detonated in Boston is identical to IEDs that have showed up in a couple of other countries around the world, but there are more than a handful that we've found detonated in one particular place."

"Let me guess," Jake said. "Puerto Rico."

"Exactly. There's also a lot of gang activity—organized crime that's intertwined with the pharmaceutical industry—going on right now, led by a large, organized ring that calls themselves Dominguez. Chemicals and drugs are their main exports."

"Whose? The pharmaceutical companies' or the gang's?"

"Yes."

"Right. So the legal stuff is coming from the businesses, and the illegal stuff is coming from the gang. And the gang is getting antsy, so they're trying to take more control by creating fear through these terror attacks."

Smith smiled without taking her eyes off her screen. "That's the operating hypothesis, yeah."

"Okay," Jake said. "That makes sense. So I need to get down there and meet this team of yours, see how I can help out."

McDonnell nodded. "I don't have a full dossier for you on the team, but there's at least a printout of the main figures. The only one you'll really need to know is—"

"Holland," Smith said, jumping in.

Jake looked over his shoulder at her, but she didn't avert her eyes from her screen.

"Jackson Holland. Pug-nosed, brawny, epitome of a soldier boy," Smith continued.

Jake nodded. "I see. I take it he's... imposing?"

At this, she turned, finally, and met Jake's eyes. "Imposing, no. Not to me. Noticeable? Sure."

McDonnell smiled and waited for Smith to turn back to her work. "They, uh, dated for a while, I believe."

"We went on *a date*," she said. "It wasn't *dating*."

Jake smiled along. "Got it. Okay, then, find the grunt who looks like one-date-only material."

At this, Bolivar chuckled, choking on a sip of coffee he had just brought into his mouth. Smith scowled.

McDonnell continued. "He's the leader of Alpha Team, but there's no Bravo Team just yet."

"What's their mission?"

"On the books? Aiding the Puerto Rican authorities as they try to find and bring down the Dominguez gang. Off the books? They're the only ones actually doing any policing. I'm doing my best here, and they're feeding me intel as they get it."

"You've got a squad of soldiers running intel?"

"I've got a team I trust watching the situation unfold."

Jake's chin raised and lowered. "Got it. These are your guys."

"These are my guys."

"So how do I fit in?"

"You don't work for Holland—you work for me. But you're *also* not in charge of him. You're officially a consultant."

"And unofficially?" Jake asked.

"You're a consultant."

"Got it."

"Parker, I need you down there for the reasons we spoke about yesterday, but the mission he's on is still proceeding as directed. There's been no reason to shift gears or delay, so I don't want Holland's guys to get spooked into thinking I'm doubting them. Your job is to help wherever needed, see if your detective's mind can uncover anything they might be missing, and keep things on track."

"I can do that." *I'll do anything it takes.* He knew it was a long shot, but if this mission might lead to finding someone responsible for Mel's death, he couldn't say no.

"I know you can. Things in Puerto Rico are heating up, but no one knows it yet. Holland's specific mission is to prevent another attack—another bomb—that we think will happen in four days. Margin of error is pretty small, give or take a few hours on each end, we're targeting 0930 as our zero hour."

Jake didn't try to hide the fact that he was impressed. "That seems specific. Why then?"

Bolivar nodded. "Right, well, we ran some algorithmic processes on the reverse correlation between—"

"Save it, nerd," Smith said, rolling her eyes. "He figured out that the bismuth is pretty traceable. Not all the way to its source, but at least in transit. They don't even try to hide the manifest. We can follow it all the way to where the bomb is prepared. Thing is, the chemicals are pretty unstable when the bomb is built, so it turns out they remove a chunk and ship it to wherever it needs to go, which ends up being blown up almost exactly four days later."

"Another calling card," Jake said.

She nodded. "They're not easy to catch, but this group doesn't seem to want to be too hard to *find*. They're setting all these dominos up and knocking them down in a perfect, controlled pattern. We just can't know the actual target, but we have our ideas."

"Oh?"

"Sure," McDonnell said. "I'll send that over in the brief as well. We know it'll be somewhere on-island, since the movement of the bismuth all but requires it. And we have reason to suspect it'll be an attack on a person, likely a US ambassador from the FDA hoping to meet with one of the big pharmaceuticals in Puerto Rico. It's the only real high-level target scheduled to arrive then."

"Interesting," Jake said. "Why an FDA target? That seems politically motivated."

"*Everything* happening there now is politically motivated," Smith said.

McDonnell continued. "You've heard of the slowly boiling frog?"

"Yeah," Jake answered. "Drop a frog into a pot of boiling water and it'll jump out. Drop a frog into cold water and slowly heat it up to boiling and the frog will be dead before it realizes what's happening."

"Precisely. We—the United States—are the boiling frog. Puerto Rico's the pot, and they've been heating it up slowly for the past decade or so. Things are rolling forward quicker and quicker each day, and it's only a matter of time before it's too late."

"What does it all have to do with terrorism? With the explosion?"

He noticed both Bolivar and Smith straighten a bit and stop typing, both interested to hear their boss's response.

"I'm not exactly sure yet," McDonnell said. "But, as I told you back at *Pete's*, it's related. The same players, the same routes, the same tricks each time. We're putting things together slowly, but I think you can speed that up a bit for us."

Jake nodded. "I can. You've got my word." He reached for the manila envelope on McDonnell's desk and picked it up. "I'll give these a read on the plane."

He stood up to leave, and McDonnell extended his hand. "You need to pack?"

Jake shook his head. "No, I'm ready to leave. I do need to give someone a call first, though."

CHAPTER 5

Jake walked out of the office and toward the stairs. The building was in New York, near West Point and *Pete's Hot Dog Stand where he'd met with McDonnell the day before*, but then again *everything* felt close to everything else in this area of the country. Jake hadn't moved terribly far from where he'd lived during his West Point days, but Hudson, Massachusetts, sometimes felt like a world away—a tiny suburb tucked against the outskirts of Boston.

Jake wanted to get a solid meal in him before the flight tomorrow morning, and since he'd now be spending the US government's money instead of his own, he exited the building and turned up the street toward an old, expensive Italian restaurant he remembered. He'd only been there once, with his parents after he'd graduated from West Point, and judging by the amount he'd seen his father drop on the bill, there was a reason they'd only offered to take him there that one time. But he remembered the food well enough, and if there was anything that could sate a man's hunger, it was a bowl full of noodles and a rich steak.

He turned up the block and headed in that direction, pulling his phone out of his pocket at the same time. He began typing a message, but decided against sending it and simply called instead.

The person on the other end picked up immediately.

"Jake?" the voice asked.

He laughed, feeling a warmth come over him. It was good to hear her voice. "Well yeah—who the hell else would it be?"

There was a slight pause, and the warmth suddenly turned into something more tempered. *"Sorry,"* she answered. *"Just been… busy here. Finals are coming up, and I've got an ever-growing stack of papers to grade. You'd think a famous epidemiologist would at least have a few TAs to pawn this stuff off to."*

"So helping a hot detective solve a case is all it takes to become a famous epidemiologist?" he asked.

"I'm not sure you're aware of who helped who," she responded.

"Whom, Eliza. I thought you were some fancy professor."

"Really? Seriously? Correcting grammar now?"

Jake laughed louder. It was good to hear her voice, especially since they hadn't seen each other in person for a few weeks. The time between their meetups had grown, and Jake felt it was only a matter of time before they would be struggling to keep the connection alive. Sometimes he felt they *were* already struggling to keep it alive.

"Hey," he said. "I, uh, just wanted to let you know I'd be off the radar for a bit."

"Oh yeah? And what exactly does 'off the radar' mean? You have another case?"

"Well… yeah. But it's for an old friend. Guy I went to school with."

"Right. I figured it would only be a matter of time before the world discovered that Jake Parker was back in business."

"I wouldn't go that far—it's probably only a week or so. But— Eliza—I want to see you. I'm not sure it'll work now, since I leave tomorrow morning, but…" *But, what, Parker?* he wondered. *You called to try to get together before tomorrow?*

"Jake, I'm in New York."

"I am too," he began.

"I'm in Syracuse," Eliza clarified. *"At school. My job, remember? I have deadlines, teams that need me, students that pay big bucks for my time. I can't just… leave."*

He sniffed. "Yeah. Yeah, I know. Sorry, it's just… It's just hard to…"

"Jake, it's fine," Eliza said. *"I get it. Believe it or not, you're not my first relationship, and you're not even my first long-distance one. They're hard. I mean, I wanted this to work, but…"*

"Yeah, it's just that I… I think it'll be good to clear my head for a bit. That's part of this trip, I think. It could help."

"Jake," Eliza said. *"You don't need to dance around it. Okay? It was hard, and that's just the way it is. I'm glad you'll be able to clear your head—you need it. But don't feel obligated to do anything, okay?"*

He nodded, then confirmed. "Yeah, definitely. I mean, I want to figure things out, see where we are and stuff. I'm just—I might not be ready for something… long-term."

"I understand that. Clear your head, Parker. I'm here, and I'll wait."

Jake closed his eyes as the whiff of fresh-cooked pasta hit his nostrils. He was close now, and he could almost taste the postgraduation meal once again. He hadn't realized how hungry he'd gotten, but then again he hadn't eaten anything after dinner last night, just a late-morning protein shake today.

"Okay, Eliza. I'll talk to you soon."

He hung up, thinking about her last words. *I'll wait.*

He knew those words were true—she wouldn't have spoken them if they weren't—but he also knew there was a depth to them she was trying to convey.

I'll wait.

But I won't wait forever.

CHAPTER 6

Cecil grabbed the cell phone from the desk and pulled it up to his ear, not bothering to look at the name. *Another call.* He didn't have time for this; it had only been a few minutes since his *last* phone call. He didn't take his eyes off the computer screen in front of him, either. There was work to be done, and he didn't want to be bothered yet again by petty mundane issues.

"Aló?"

"Aló, Cecil?" the voice on the other end responded. He slipped into the loose Puerto Rican Spanish Cecil had grown up with. *"This is how you speak to your elders in America?"*

Cecil straightened. He swallowed, feeling the blood cooling inside him. He may have just made a serious mistake. "I—I apologize, sir, I did not realize who was—"

The man laughed, but Cecil heard the venom behind the cold, dark chuckle. This man, like Cecil, enjoyed power. He enjoyed his position on the leadership panel of the crime organization—not in charge, but close enough to those who were to wield *real* power. The kind of power Cecil longed for. The kind he *deserved*.

"Cecil, Rodrigo tells me you have interest in the United States as more than a distribution network."

Not a question—a statement. A fact. It told Cecil that the man knew already what it was Cecil had taken on as his pet project; what he had spent so much of his free time working on.

"Yes, sir," Cecil responded. "I have been working hard on maintaining the integrity of our network. On the side, however, I have been exploring a potential option for US-based production of—"

"I will stop you there, Cecil," the man said. "Rodrigo gave me the details of your project, and what you hope to accomplish. I must admit it is quite expansive, and I find it impressive."

Cecil sat up straighter, tightening the phone in his grip.

"Yet there will be no expansion project in the United States. Our assets abroad have expressed interest in increasing our product's presence there, and with the heightened regulations coming from the US Congress each year, it seems as though our own interests there will diminish, not increase."

"Right, well, I believe this plan offers a solution to that. If you would simply inform the—"

"I will not be addressing the leadership about this issue," the man said. "Consider the conversation over."

Cecil didn't respond. He had nothing to say that would not come across as argumentative, and he didn't want to risk being considered insubordinate.

"Now—the reason I called—there has been unrest here."

"Is there not always unrest?" Cecil asked. In their line of work, "unrest" was a term they often used to describe the ongoing nature of the illicit drug industry—crime, theft, political maneuvering.

"Indeed. But it has begun to increase beyond expected levels. Word is, the United States has an investigatory team in place somewhere on the island, and they are beginning to pull at threads."

"I see."

"As such, I am requesting your presence here on behalf of the leadership, and asking for your reassignment."

Reassignment? Cecil was appalled. Never in his seventeen years had he been reassigned. Never had he had to stand in front of the leadership. Was he on trial? Had he done something wrong? Surely trying to expand the organization's operations was no grounds for reassignment.

No, it had to be something different. Something unrelated to his work here.

He gathered his thoughts, mustered some courage, and spoke again into the receiver. "May I ask what this reassignment is about?"

There was a pause. Brief. *"I assure you it is unrelated to your actions in the United States. Your work there is crucial, and you have performed admirably. As I mentioned before, your research and this project of yours is nothing short of impressive, even if it is misguided."*

"Then what is it?" He was still reeling a bit from his last call, but he had not intended to let his feelings color his tone.

"The matter we are concerned with is one that must be approached delicately. Something that must be handled with care, tact. For most of us that means we cannot be involved, at least not directly. And yet someone still has to do the work."

Cecil swallowed again. *Are they going to ask me to kill someone?*

"The reassignment is simple, I assure you. You will not like the work, but that is only because it will feel more like babysitting and punishment than it will productive work. But I cannot stress enough how important this task is."

Cecil frowned. *Babysitting? What on earth?* He could not imagine what scenario had taken place that now required him to fly to the country of his birth for a job this man believed would seem like *babysitting*.

But he didn't ask more questions. If the leadership required his presence, he would be there. He had already opened a tab on his computer and was preparing to search for flights out of Miami.

"Please do your best to arrive no later than tomorrow morning, Cecil," the man continued. *"This is a matter that must be dealt with soon. For us it is business, but for you it could become personal."*

At that, Cecil stopped typing and his frown deepened. Now he had more questions than answers, and he couldn't imagine what situation he was about to be called into.

But it didn't matter—he served the gang, and he was dedicated to its success. It was, after all, his own success.

And he would do anything to be successful.

CHAPTER 7

Jake's flight to Puerto Rico was long and uneventful. He read through the briefs given to him by McDonnell while airborne, learning a bit about the current situation in the island nation. He found that the main export of Puerto Rico had been pharmaceuticals for many years, leading to a rise in both profit and regulation, and an equal rise in illegal activities related to the drug trade. The company McDonnell's team was most interested in was called APHINT, or Allied Pharmaceuticals International, which was the main producer of bismuth on the island. McDonnell had set Jake up with a weeklong stay at a hotel in Fajardo, the same municipality shared by APHINT.

Nothing he'd read about APHINT gave him the impression that there was any foul play taking place, but since they were the ones most likely producing and selling the bismuth, he'd definitely take a look. At least it might be a step in the right direction. He planned to talk with Holland and his team as soon as possible, but he also needed to check in at the hotel McDonnell had booked for him and get some food in his belly.

He'd eaten enough last night at the Italian restaurant to stay full all through the morning, but it was getting to late afternoon by the time the plane landed. He'd flown from New York to Miami, then caught another nonstop flight to San Juan. When the plane had touched down on the runway, Jake's diving watch told him it was approaching 4 p.m. local time.

His stomach growled when he stood to collect his shoulder bag, and he knew he'd be stopping for dinner before meeting up with Holland. Jake traveled light, opting for modern, breathable wool clothing that kept him cool in hot weather and didn't smell after repeated wear, and he needed nothing but a slim laptop and a passport for this trip. He'd also left his SIG Sauer back at his apartment so he wouldn't have to deal with customs and TSA, but McDonnell had informed Holland as to his arrival and put in a request for a sidearm for protection.

He stepped off the plane and was met with an oppressive heat, full of humidity, with an alkaline, metallic taste that told him he was near water. There was a laid-back feel to the staff and locals in the airport, and he was greeted with smiles and waves as he exited and caught a cab.

The hotel McDonnell had chosen for Jake was near Holland's crew's own setup. Jake saw on a map that Holland's base of operations was currently a tiny two-bedroom home in a neighboring city, but there was no clear address. That area looked to be a solid fifteen-minute drive from Jake's hotel—not within walking distance, but certainly not far. It meant he'd have more time to grab a bite to eat and settle in at the hotel, since he wasn't scheduled to meet with Holland until later that evening.

Jake sent a text message to McDonnell letting him know he'd arrived, then another to Holland informing him of his plans. McDonnell had already emailed Jake's arrival schedule to Holland, as well as a neutral address for Jake to head to later that evening, so there was nothing left to plan. Holland would pick him up at the location and take him to the safe house himself, as per McDonnell's request. As such, he didn't receive a response from either man, but that was nothing strange—these men were military, professional order-takers and would only communicate a response when asked a direct question. He appreciated the blunt, direct approach—it got things done. Holland would be at the designated meeting spot.

As the taxi driver approached the hotel, Jake saw the grounds come into view, and he couldn't help but raise an eyebrow.

El Conquistador, a Waldorf-Astoria four-diamond property, built into the side of a cliff, sprawled outward from the road. The distant beach and shoreline were visible through the dense rainforest, just beyond the resort's village and main buildings. Jake's jaw dropped as the driver pulled the car into the unloading lot. *McDonnell really is pulling out all the stops,* he thought. He wondered whether or not there was a budget or if McDonnell had been given a blank check.

In his line of work, both in the military and then later at the Boston Police Department, accommodations such as this were never even a consideration. Any required overnight stays would be paid for by his office, but necessity and utility were the only factors. Jake couldn't help but think that his newfound role of consultant brought with it some decent perks. He didn't necessarily need the money—he'd received a substantial payout from the state after his wife's untimely death—but he knew money didn't last forever. Besides, he enjoyed working more than just sitting around and drinking beers at the bar he lived above.

The driver slowed to a halt in front of an elegant, well-appointed front entrance, where a bellhop approached and opened Jake's door. He got out and stretched, once again feeling the pangs of hunger setting in. He tipped the driver, followed the bellhop inside, and checked in, all while taking in the gorgeous rainforest design and decor on display. No plants were fake, and no detail had been left untouched. He approached the stairs at the far side of the lobby and took them two at a time to his floor, then unlocked the door to his room and stepped inside.

He had walked into an oasis. He was standing inside one of a curved line of rooms that had been built into the side of the sloping cliff, all peering down and out over a beautiful bay and swimming pool. A private island with a small water park lay just in sight beneath the horizon, and boats and beachgoers floated out on the water.

Jake tossed his bag on the bed and forced a smiled. It was a beautiful room, but it couldn't shift the heavy weight of Mel's absence, or that he was here to try to avenge it. The only thing at all wrong with the room besides the fact that he had no one to share it with was that it faced the wrong way. A quirk of his, Jake preferred booking hotel rooms that faced the busiest street. But when he'd pulled up the map of this place on his phone, he knew he'd have to sacrifice—the *El Conquistador*'s layout prevented any rooms from having a decent view of anything but sheer paradise.

Oh well, he thought. *I'll live.*

Jake knew he would be able to relax a bit, to enjoy himself, but he also wished Eliza could have been here with him. He considered that for a moment—the natural desire to share this place with her, yet in the same thought realizing that there was something not quite right about it. It almost felt wrong, sharing a place like this with someone he'd only recently met. They were close, but had they been growing closer to one another, or further apart?

And at the heart of it all, it felt wrong because it wasn't Eliza who he would have wanted to share this with—it was Mel.

Jake felt the exotic novelty of the place lose a bit of its luster. He turned and headed back toward the door. He was hungry, and needed to get a solid meal inside of him while he worked over his plan to meet Holland and the questions he wanted to ask. He grabbed the shoulder bag and slung it over his arm once more. It would be awkward at first to pull out a laptop and start typing away in the middle of the resort's flagship fine-dining restaurant, but who cared? He was a paying customer—and besides, no one would want to bother the lonely-looking laptop guy eating alone.

CHAPTER 8

As it turned out though, he *was* bothered by someone.

"You are not eating here."

Jake looked up from his laptop screen, frowning at the woman's voice. *What kind of waitress introduces herself like that?* The person who had spoken to him was standing just out of the light, her lithe frame all shadows and darkness.

And then, suddenly, she strode forward a few steps, landing only a couple of feet away from Jake's table. Her face and figure coming fully into view.

Jake had to catch his breath. This was no waitress or hostess—she wasn't dressed in the company-white faux tuxedos every other worker here appeared to be wearing. Instead, the woman in front of him wore a tight-fitting yellow skirt and a white buttoned shirt, with some sort of floral imprint embossed over its surface. Flip-flops, anklet, and a necklace with a small frog completed the attire. Her hair was as massive as her colorful array of clothing—long, slightly curled black hair hung past her shoulders, somehow trained to fall precisely around her face in a way that brought out her elegant features. And those features were as breathtaking as the rest of her. A petite, upturned nose, rosy cheeks, and dark skin complemented light-brown eyes that twinkled in the restaurant's atmosphere.

Jake cleared his throat, flashing his eyes down at his computer screen and then back up at her. "I'm sorry?"

"I said," the woman began, a small smile forming in the corner of her mouth, "that you are not *eating* here."

Jake's eyebrows rose. "Ah, right. And besides getting work done, just what is it I *am* doing here?"

Her smile grew. "What work are you doing?"

He frowned. "Well, I, uh—you know, it's just emails and stuff."

"Very good," she said. "And I am trying to warn you away from disappointment, is all." Her voice was smooth and calculated, perfect English but with a hint of a Puerto Rican accent. "There is no one else here, did you not notice that?"

Jake looked around. He *had* noticed it, but he hadn't thought much of it. The hotel itself seemed to be nearly empty, but he had only been looking for an empty booth and a bite to eat. He was far from picky.

He wasn't sure what to make of this woman. A beautiful, well-dressed woman, about his age, sidling up to him at a hotel restaurant? It wasn't an everyday occurrence for Jake. "May I ask who you are?" Jake asked.

She blushed, then pushed out her hand. "I apologize. I see now that this must be quite forward of me. I'm Veronica—Vero, actually."

"Hello, Vero," Jake said, grasping her hand. "Jake Parker. And yes, I *do* think this is quite forward." He chuckled. "And yet I'm not offended in any way, so please don't worry. But I *am* quite hungry. I have a meeting I need to get to soon, so—"

"It will not take that long," she said. "I believe you will be much happier at the restaurant across the street. *San Miguel's*. With me."

"With… you?"

She nodded. "I have been in this hotel for a week, and there have been three families staying here on vacation, all too busy to look around and enjoy their paradise. Two others on business, much too old for me."

Jake tried not to flinch at the implication.

"A handful of others, no one of note. And then me. Business, though I hesitate to call it that. More like 'lounging around and waiting for my company to call me back.' I have not had dinner with another human since Sunday, and I am dying for some interaction."

"I see," Jake said. He pushed his laptop closed and sighed, once again feeling the pangs of hunger in his stomach beginning to swell. "I would love to hear more, Vero, but—and I promise this is not to be rude—I am *starving*. I'd rather just order here."

She slid out of the way, but caught Jake's arm and began pulling him up. "No, you may not. Trust me, the service here is terrible. You would be lucky to get fed in two hours."

Jake allowed himself to stand, pushing his computer into his shoulder bag and slinging it up and over his arm. He wasn't excited about missing a sure meal, but he had to admit he was intrigued by this woman. "And you are comfortable dining with someone you have not even met?"

"We have met. You are Jake, I am Vero. You are working, I am bored. We are both hungry. Now, come on."

Jake shook his head as Vero swirled around and began walking out of the restaurant. Her long legs made short work of it, and Jake had to hustle to keep up.

What the hell is this about? he wondered. *What game is she playing?*

Vero didn't stop at the lobby, continuing out over the carpeted area and deftly navigating around the massive rose-petal-covered ceramic bowl sitting on a high table in the center of the atrium. She smiled and waved at the two bellhops standing sentinel near the front doors, and both men nodded once as she passed.

Jake noticed the man on the right following behind Vero as she left the building, but his head snapped back to attention as soon as Jake neared.

Outside, Vero, followed closely by Jake, turned to the right and walked slightly uphill to the street. She didn't slow down, crossing the road and ending up in a grove of palm trees, the sidewalk cutting through in a meandering route. On any other night, Jake would have slowed to appreciate the architecture and the landscape design of the place, but tonight he had only two things on his mind.

Who is this woman?

And, *if she keeps me from eating, I'm going to kill her.*

CHAPTER 9

The Cessna 172 XP landed on the water, just beyond the lighthouse at the edge of the harbor. Cecil looked out the window and saw the old landmark, quiet and dark, its light long since extinguished. When the gang had purchased the property, there had never been any intention of using the lighthouse, so they'd fired the groundskeeper and let the place fall into disrepair.

Now, the house at its base and part of the interior of the lighthouse tower itself was used as a storage and meeting place—a perfect refuge for members of the organization doing business around the nearby islands.

As the Cessna slid over the choppy waters toward the dock, Cecil looked out and longed for the promotion he knew he deserved. It would take years of hard work and no small amount of politicking, but there was a level of power he could reach that would allow *him* to make decisions like purchasing an entire lighthouse and surrounding land in the Guayanilla Bay.

He had the knowledge, the skill set. He could maneuver businesses and shell companies through structures that existed on paper only, and organize the gang's income and expenses well enough to keep the important bits out of the prying eyes of the Puerto Rican authorities. He could even massage the funds in the right way to ensure that some of them landed in the hands of those few authorities who needed to be persuaded the old way.

No, he didn't lack knowledge or training. He lacked experience. He had proven himself only enough to rise to his current level; the gang was not a democracy, it was a meritocracy. He would prove himself at each level, and at each level he would excel until he had the power he deserved. Then he would begin to change things. Not all at once, but slowly over time, so as not to upset the old leaders. He would move the organization into the modern era, bolster their income with diversified streams from more future-proof industries. Pharmaceuticals and its derivates was a fine business to be in, but the United States legal and governmental pressure was only increasing—at some point, the rest of the profit margins would be squeezed out of the conglomerates and there would be no more pennies to pick up off the factory floor.

The gang needed to be ready for that moment, and Cecil hoped he could make an impact before then.

The Cessna pulled up to the dock, and Cecil was ready to jump out. There was no one waiting for him, no members excited for his arrival. It was business—and he was far too unimportant to warrant a welcome party.

Disembarking, Cecil made his way up the dark, unlit path, wondering what his new mission would be. For the last two years, he had been based in the United States, improving the distribution network for the gang's drug traffickers. It wasn't unheard of for the leadership to move its administrative members around, but this particular move had been abrupt.

Something was happening, and Cecil feared it was a bigger deal than a simple reassignment. Best-case scenario was that someone had reported Cecil's talents and requested them here, which was flattering.

But it was also unnerving. While the summons meant they needed him, now, without delay, there was no way to know for sure *why* they needed him. Were they planning something they needed his help with, or was he in some sort of trouble?

He reached the back door of the lighthouse and only then noticed a few cars parked out the front of the property. Apparently he wasn't the only one here, though he couldn't imagine what they would be doing here at this hour. It had been many years since the lighthouse had been an actual *house*, so there were no beds, couches, or futons to sleep on. The place was no longer set up to receive overnight guests, and Cecil himself had planned on dumping his suitcase here and then finding a nearby hotel.

He heard voices inside. The gang was having a meeting, right now. He frowned as he twisted the door handle and felt the pop of the old, sea-weathered wood give way and pull open.

The voices grew louder, and he recognized one of them immediately.

Could I actually be at a meeting with the leaders?

He pulled the door open further and stepped over the threshold. The voices stopped, all eyes turning to him. One of the pairs of eyes belonged to the man who had called him to inform him of the reassignment. He was looking at Cecil, his eyes blank and empty.

Another man, this one sitting in the center of the room on a wooden box, was smiling. He spread his arms wide. "Cecil, welcome! I hope you had a good flight. We are glad you are here— the leaders and I were just discussing what we need from you."

Cecil tried to hide his shock. He had expected a note, a memo explaining his new job. Perhaps even a messenger—a low-level member to deliver the news to him face-to-face. But not this, to be attending a meeting with the actual *leadership* of his organization.

He saw the men seated around the room. No one else was smiling, but he was used to this. The leadership panel held the power within the organization, but there was only a single member who held the power over the *panel,* and that was the man who had addressed Cecil.

The others knew their place. They were here to listen, offer advice when requested, and otherwise stay silent. They would then disseminate the information as necessary down the ranks.

Cecil had never met the man addressing him. Now that he thought about it, he had never seen a picture of him, either. But he knew the voice from recordings, and he knew the leader by the power he held throughout the room. No one else had power like that. Cecil was entranced by it, dedicated to it. And if his new job would give him even a bit more of it, there was no other choice.

CHAPTER 10

The interior of *San Miguel's* wasn't dissimilar to that of the restaurant at the hotel, but it was a bit brighter and a bit larger.

Jake whistled as they approached the front doors of the building. An outdoor lobby had been constructed using concrete archways and an open-wall layout, and chandeliers hung from each arch, illuminating a thick wave of vines that curled around each concrete pillar. Tables and chairs that were decidedly *not* outdoor patio furniture dotted the tile floor, where a few groups of diners sat and waited for their seat inside the restaurant.

Jake glanced at a pair of empty leather chairs and began drifting toward it. His heart sank as his hunger increased yet again. *So close to food, yet so far.*

He was about to descend into the armchair when Vero swung around and grabbed his arm again.

"No," she said. "I have a reservation."

Jake frowned. "You made a reservation for yourself and *then* decided to pluck me out of my booth back at the hotel?"

She shook her head, and a sly grin crept over her face. "No," she said. "I made a reservation for two."

Jake wasn't sure how to respond, but there was no time for a response anyway. Vero pulled him through the heavy wooden doors and into the air-conditioned restaurant. More Puerto Rican artwork and Caribbean stylistic decor met them as they entered.

They barely slowed at the mâitre d' stand, and a young man grabbed two menus as they passed, then jogged out in front of

Vero to guide them to their seat. Almost as soon as they sat down, a basket of chips was plopped onto the table by another young man who had flown in from the opposite direction.

Something was muttered to Jake in Spanish, but he was too busy eyeing the basket. The chips were spaced around an avocado half, the seed removed and the cavity filled with olive oil. Next to the avocado was a shallow bowl of refried black beans, and sprinkled over the top of it all was a fine, crumbly white cheese.

"Oh, my God," Jake whispered, grabbing at the chips.

He caught Vero's raised eyebrow as he snapped off a piece of chip and shoved it into his mouth. He chewed, then felt the weight of all three pairs of eyes looking at him. He stopped, then looked up.

"Señor," the kid to his left said, gently pushing a small plate beneath him.

Jake pulled back, watching. The waiter pulled the avocado out of the center of the plate of chips and cut it in half, allowing the oil to ooze out onto the small plate, then he cubed the rest of the fruit and scraped it onto the plate. He pulled out a long, thin fork, then smashed the cubes until a guacamole was piled onto the plate, and he finished by sprinkling another dusting of cheese over the top of this dish. He then set the chips, beans, and avocado on the center of the table in a line, passing his open palm over the top of it in a flourish.

Jake nodded, his lips tight. "Impressive," he said.

The two young men laughed and Vero said something in Spanish to the man nearest her. He nodded, and both men disappeared.

"You are very hungry," Vero said slyly.

Jake just laughed, scraping more of the avocado paste onto his chip and shoving the entire delicious thing into his mouth as she continued.

"This would be a $7 appetizer at the hotel," she added. "Here, it is gratis."

"Free?" he asked. "Nice."

He ate three more chips, finally feeling the sharp pangs receding within him, then he once again focused on the *other* issue.

"So—Vero—please, explain to me why you have a standing reservation at a fancy restaurant, you live in a hotel, and you prey on unsuspecting male victims?"

She snorted, then held up a hand as she blushed again. "First, I do not have a 'standing reservation' here. I used to eat here a lot when I was younger, and the restaurant has only gotten better over the years. Second, I made a reservation for two earlier today because I *wanted* company, but if no one showed up they do not turn down a lady by herself."

"Makes sense," Jake said.

"And, third, I do not *live* in the resort. As I said, I have been staying there a week, while my company rebuilds the village."

"The village?"

"We call it that—it is a large plot of land they have used for housing projects for their employees. I am one of them. They are working to expand, and so my neighborhood is being offset for a month."

Jake nearly spat out his chip. "A *month*? What kind of company pays for its employees to stay at a resort for a *month*?"

"Well," she said. "When the company owns the resort, I guess it is not so difficult. Besides, most of the others in my neighborhood are now staying with family—we are all from Puerto Rico, so it is not so surprising. The company bought most of the rooms in the hotel, yet only a few of us are staying here, which is why it has been so empty."

Jake nodded. "Wow, that's… I don't know what to think of that. I doubt any company in America would go that far to take care of its employees."

"It is not so much 'taking care' of us as it is paying ahead of time for insurance against losing employees."

Jake frowned, almost unable to understand her meaning. He wasn't sure if she was translating in her mind before she spoke. "You mean it's *not* a great place to work? They need to buy your contentment?"

She shrugged as she picked apart a minuscule piece of chip and placed it lightly on her tongue. He sensed a slight hesitation before she answered, a bit of distaste in her eyes. Quickly, she pushed it away and continued. "For me, sure. It is a fine place to work. But I have a university degree, and experience. The others, perhaps not as much. It is our *life*, working. So putting us up here is not seen as a vacation for most."

Jake nodded again.

The waiter returned with a bottle of red wine. He pulled off the cork and handed it to Vero, who closed her eyes and sniffed, breathing deeply.

When she opened her eyes, she met Jake's gaze. "Do you enjoy wine?"

He thought for a moment. "I don't hate it, but I'm not really a wine guy."

"What sort of guy are you, then?"

"Well, I suppose I'm a just-about-anything-besides-wine guy?"

She paused, then a wide grin appeared. She handed the cork back to the waiter, who knelt down so she was speaking directly into his ear. He smiled, then nodded.

"He will return with my favorite drink," she said.

"Great," Jake said. "I cannot even imagine what *other* surprises you have cooked up."

She laughed, then her face steadied. "Jake Parker, I assure you this is not normal behavior for me. I have been stuck inside this hotel, alone, unable to work, for a week now. I simply *need* human interaction, and when I saw you come in, I was intrigued."

"Why?"

"Why not?" she said. "American, obviously. My age, so the conversation would be at least standardized toward something I can relate to."

"'Standardized toward something I can relate to?'" Jake asked, smiling. "What does that mean? You said you had a degree—was it in astrophysics?"

"Might as well be," she answered, looking up at the ceiling. "Chemistry, actually. And when I saw you in the restaurant in the hotel, you were working. That is not something you see much, in that resort. It is families and couples, on vacation, that is it."

"Why?"

"Have you researched this town?" she asked. "It is here for one reason, like many towns in Puerto Rico. It exists as a support structure for the company I work for."

"A pharmaceutical company?" Jake asked. He hadn't put it all together before she'd mentioned chemistry, but it made sense that there would be no other major businesses that called this place home. The resort, the small town around it, the land—it was all for one purpose: to serve the pharmaceutical company that had funded it.

She nodded. "Exactly. APHINT. Allied Pharmaceuticals International. We produce drugs and supplements of all kinds for the United States market, and the main compound we are known for is a treatment for Lewy body disease, a debilitating disorder like Parkinson's. I am a chief chemist for their research and development division in charge of all new products, and I am currently bored out of my mind. Which is why you are not eating, alone, at the hotel."

She winked at him, just as the waiter returned.

He was holding a tiny bottle of tequila.

CHAPTER 11

"Plausible deniability," the man said, his Spanish flowing out as if it were music. "You understand this concept?"

The leader of the Dominguez gang was directly in front of Cecil—*speaking* to him—and Cecil couldn't believe it. He listened with rapt attention.

The leader did not repeat the question, and Cecil suddenly realized he expected an answer. "Uh, um—yes. Yes, sir."

"Address me as Mr. Diego," the leader said.

Cecil was stunned. He knew this man's name. Everyone did. Hector Leon Allende de Diego. *The Lion*. It was a name uttered, yet rarely spoken. Cecil certainly never thought he'd be speaking it in the presence of the man to whom it belonged.

He nodded his head, quickly. The eyes of the other men in the small lighthouse living room were fixed on Cecil. None betrayed any emotion. "Yes, Mr. Diego," Cecil said. "I understand the concept of plausible deniability."

"Very good. I was told you are smart—intelligent, even. And I have seen reports of your business in the United States. Your work is impressive."

Cecil swallowed. "Thank you, Mr. Diego."

"Now, since you understand the idea of plausible deniability, and you understand that Dominguez needs you to perform a task, you must *also* understand that this task is one not to be taken lightly. It is a task that only the men in this room will know about."

"I am prepared for this task, Mr. Diego." And he was—even though he had no idea what it was, he was prepared for anything Dominguez might require.

Diego nodded once, plainly, still allowing no emotion to pass over his face. "I trust that you are," he said. "And I understand that you have been informed of the reassignment in order to accomplish this task."

Cecil confirmed.

"Very well," Diego said. "Your new reassignment is as follows: you will now be working a job in the mailroom of Fitzsimmons."

Cecil's heart nearly dropped out of his chest. This was certainly not the reassignment he had expected, and in no universe was it one he would hope for.

"You will receive and file mail, and you will be diligent," Diego continued. "There is an increasing number of correspondence between our allies and our enemies, and it is being funneled through legitimate channels in this mailroom."

Cecil listened, numb to the truth. He now understood what his boss had meant on the phone call. *It will feel more like babysitting and punishment than it will productive work.*

"A position there has already been arranged, and your work will begin tomorrow morning. Do the job as you are instructed, and call no unnecessary attention to yourself. The task should be completed within a week, and after that you will continue to work for six weeks, so as not to call undue attention to yourself."

"What is the task?" Cecil asked. "The job I am *really* supposed to do?"

"There is a US-based visitor coming to the island in a few days, from an office that works with the FDA. Do you know that organization?"

"The Food and Drug Administration," Cecil answered. "Of course."

The FDA was the unofficial watchdog of Puerto Rican manufacturing. With its hands in everything on the island, the US administration was ostensibly on-island solely to control the production and export of high-quality, safe products, but over the years it had been active, it had swelled in size and power, and now had a say in nearly every decision the local government made.

Most of the time, the FDA just wanted to "listen in" on political discussions or offer strongly worded advice, but lately the department had been interacting more closely with the heads of the major pharmaceuticals. Some claimed it was by design for efficiency, but others, like Cecil, saw it as an intrusion to the island's ability to support itself.

"There will be a representative coming in by boat by the end of the week," Diego said. "Your job is to find the correspondence confirming this appointment, then track the arrival to San Juan and let the Dominguez group there know which dock the representative will be arriving on."

Cecil listened, trying to put things together. He considered the words for a few extra seconds.

"Is there a problem?" Diego asked.

Cecil shook his head. "No, sir, of course not. I am happy to be in service to Dominguez, and I will perform this task admirably."

"And yet you seem hesitant. Is this reassignment not agreeable to you?"

Cecil couldn't help but frown. "I—I apologize, Mr. Diego. I am not ungrateful for the recognition that I have been doing good work. It's just—"

"It's just that you do not understand how this might benefit your advancement in this organization?"

A few of the men around the circular room shifted their eyes from Cecil to their leader.

"Yes, indeed," Cecil said. "That is exactly my concern."

Diego chewed the inside of his lip for a moment, and Cecil felt the fear returning. Had he spoken out of turn? Had he said something offensive? Perhaps even questioning this man was grounds for removal?

"Please be assured that we will take care of our own," Diego finally said. "Your performance will be closely watched. This is not a difficult task, but it requires care and attention and can easily become tedious. And yet it is a crucial job."

"I understand, Mr. Diego."

"And there is one more benefit—the main reason we have chosen you for this task."

Cecil's ears perked up. He would never have asked for compensation, but he was absolutely interested in the discussion.

"This task is uniquely suited to *you*, Cecil, because the future of the Dominguez organization is not in Puerto Rico."

"It is not?"

Diego shook his head. "It is not. The future of the Dominguez organization—a future I believe you will have a major part of—is in the United States."

Cecil wasn't sure how to respond.

"You have been laying the groundwork for expansion in addition to doing the work you have previously been assigned to. This is the type of person we need for Dominguez's future to be bright. There will come a day when this island is too small for us, and we must go where the money takes us. Right now, we can be content here, at home. But soon—very soon—Dominguez will need to broaden its horizons."

Cecil nodded, trying to contain his excitement.

"You have knowledge of our operations here," Diego said. "And you have intimate familiarity with the operations on the mainland. We will eventually need to expand, and only through working into the palm of the FDA's hand will we be able to accomplish that.

'Hiding in plain sight' has always been a major success factor for this organization."

"I understand," Cecil said.

"I know you do. We all do. And we also know that you have family on this island, so I hope you understand the full impact of failing a reassignment."

He did—there was no mistaking their intent. They were dangling a promotion in front of him, but the cost of failure was dire. He would succeed, or he would suffer.

His family would suffer.

CHAPTER 12

Jake was feeling the effects of the tequila, but he blinked a few times and stared straight ahead out the window. It wasn't bad enough to cause him to stumble around, but it did take his eyes an extra second to slide into place whenever he turned his head.

After dinner, he'd left Vero back at the restaurant, explaining that his meeting was across town, and even though the address of the rendezvous was only one postal code over from the one they were currently in, he wasn't exactly sure *where* that address was in relation to anything else. Vero hadn't seemed concerned, simply turning back to the dwindling bottle of tequila on the table as he'd left.

Jake couldn't help but feel intrigued by her—she was strangely abrupt and forward, as if she was running out of time and needed to be hasty. He had never met anyone like that. Mel had been the polar opposite, meek and hesitant and never interested in pulling strangers into their private lives.

In fact, during their marriage, Jake had been the outgoing one. He had approached Mel in the bookstore, noticing that she was browsing the *Current Events* section. He'd made some idiotic comment about something in the Middle East, intended to provoke a simple response that might allow him to then impress her with his military service, but he'd instead been met with a cool, calm response telling him she wasn't interested.

He'd had to work a bit harder to woo her into a conversation, but once she opened up to him, he found that she was passionately interested—and quite knowledgeable—in international affairs, since she'd spent most of her college career studying international politics. Jake hadn't intended to be sucked into a debate, but he'd also been wildly attracted to her. They'd spent an hour in the bookstore's coffee shop discussing foreign affairs and current events, and the rest was history.

That memory was soon replaced by his short relationship with Eliza. Her intelligence was unmatched, as deep as Mel's yet in a different space, and her intrigue was up there as well. Was he starting to develop a type?

He shook away the thoughts and felt a slight pang of headache forming. He hadn't had the intention of drinking before his meeting with Holland, but he knew that after a few minutes and a sip of water he should be thinking clearly once again.

The ride-share driver Jake had hired to deliver him to the scheduled rendezvous spot with Holland had picked him up at his hotel, mercifully given him a bottle of water, and now deposited him at the address, which was somewhere west of Las Croabas in a city called Fajardo. From what he could see, it was far more developed and urban then the oceanside resort he had been at with Veronica.

Jake was supposed to meet Jackson Holland at a location that seemed to be completely arbitrary—not the actual location of the safe house. For security reasons, they wouldn't want anyone knowing where, exactly, they were staying. So this destination was little more than a nondescript corner of a street with nothing important around—a few buildings behind him, a row of square-shaped houses to his left, across the street a corner store with bars over the windows and no lights on inside, and nearby and set back from the intersection an old, abandoned church.

He wasn't even sure if there was a place around here where Holland's team was meeting every day, so Jake began investigating the building behind him. Within a minute of being deposited on the city block, however, Jake saw headlights rising over the gentle slope, heading toward the intersection.

A sleek black sedan pulled up to the curb, its driver-side window rolling down as it came to a stop.

"Parker?" the man said from the front seat. He was pug-nosed, with a sour expression on his face that seemed to tell him that Jake had already somehow inconvenienced him. He looked like the sort of guy who would play a cop on TV, but even from the curb Jake could see wide, well-toned biceps. The guy probably had a bit more hands-on experience than a TV cop.

Jake nodded, then approached the vehicle. "Just got here. Good timing."

The man grunted something, then turned back to Jake. "Get in; we've got a lot to go over."

CHAPTER 13

Jake had seen a picture of McDonnell's team leader on the airplane, and though it was a much younger-looking and slightly thinner version of the Holland he was looking at now, Jake was sure this was his guy. He fit the description Smith gave perfectly.

Jake strode around the front of the vehicle and opened the passenger door. Before he had pulled it completely closed and buckled his seat belt, Holland gunned the engine and sped off down the road. Jake felt himself thrown back into the seat, but turned to look at his new acquaintance. "I'm assuming you're Holland," Jake asked.

"That a question or a statement of fact?"

Jake shrugged, then shook his head and looked out his window. He had spent plenty of time dealing with assholes like this over the course of his career—men who thought they were somehow above their peers; somehow above even their superiors. Jake may have appeared to be just a lowly cop from Boston to this guy, but he knew how to deal with it. Men like this responded to strength, to confidence. Besides, Jake understood that this guy hadn't asked McDonnell to send him here—Holland's attitude was related to the situation, not Jake personally. He also knew that McDonnell hadn't told Holland much about him, but Holland would have at least done a quick search on Jake's name, pulling up many articles about the publicized case relating to Mel's death.

Jake swiveled around in the seat and stared at the side of Holland's face. Holland brought the car up to speed on a dusty highway outside of town, but never turned his head.

Taking a breath, Jake jumped into it. "I'm going to tell you how it is, Holland," Jake said. "Take it or leave it, but it's a fact. I was asked to come here by the guy paying *both* of us. I didn't ask for it, you didn't ask for it. That means we're in the same boat. *My* job is to help you solve a case. *Your* job is to solve the case. You choose not to use my help, fine. I still get a *very* nice vacation for as long as it takes you and your team to get the job done. I have the same deliverable for McDonnell that you do: to stop the next attack. So I see no reason to insert myself into your business and change course."

Holland glanced sidelong at Jake, but didn't say anything.

"All that said," Jake continued, "I'm pretty damn good at what I do, and what I do is solve problems. It seems to me you've got one of those. I figure you'd like to get this job finished as well, and since McDonnell made it clear to me that you are still the one in charge of this investigation, a guy like *you* shouldn't feel threatened by a guy like *me*."

Jake knew the last sentence was potentially a triggering one. It was a thinly veiled threat in itself, but Jake assumed it would have the desired effect.

Holland's mouth never moved, but his eyes squinted slightly. His roundish face was solid as a rock, stoic and unchanging, but Jake still caught the slight change in expression. "What makes you think you know *anything* about guys like me?" Holland asked.

"Committed, driven, a little ticked off when someone meddles with my business; I'd say we actually *do* have a lot in common with each other."

"I've never been a cop, but I'm pretty sure working an international terrorism case overseas while undercover is not something the local police department had you 'boys in blue' doing very often," Holland said.

Jake shook his head. "No, it's definitely *not* something the department had me doing very often." He paused just long enough to watch Holland react with a small nod of his head. Jake could almost feel the man's satisfaction. "But I did plenty of that exact thing during my five years in the Army."

Holland turned his head ever so slightly, bringing his right eye in to view. "Army, huh?"

"Yeah. After West Point, counterintelligence, then moved into civilian law enforcement. Since you already know I was with the Boston PD, you probably at least know a bit about the time I spent there."

Holland shrugged, which was the most movement Jake had seen thus far from the man. "Catching bad guys on the streets of Boston ain't the same thing as tracking down a criminal organization in Puerto Rico."

"Actually," Jake said, "it's almost *exactly* the same thing. But I told you the deal already. You don't have to let me in, but you did just pick me up, and I'm assuming we're driving to your base of operations, not the airport. That means you've already decided to listen to McDonnell's advice, and it also means you've probably already decided to enlist my help—at least while it's convenient for you. I'm fine with that, as long as you do us both a favor and let me know when it's no longer convenient for you."

Holland sighed, then turned his eyes to Jake for a second before resuming his stoic watch out the windshield. "Nothing against you, buddy, it's just that I've been burned before by hotshots who think their shit don't stink."

"In that case, I'll be sure to mess up a few things while your boys are watching so no one thinks I'm a hotshot."

Finally, Holland laughed. He chuckled for a moment and then caught himself, riveting his eyes once again forward and toward the road. "All right, Parker, I'll give you that one. McDonnell told you correctly: I'm in charge; this is my case. That's not going to change, no matter what. My team has done good work here and we were getting close to wrapping it up, so I'd like to get this thing back on track as soon as possible and earn myself a few days on the beach."

"You were close until what?"

Holland frowned.

"You said you were close to wrapping this case up. The attack three days from now, right? What happened? Did you have a lead go sour?"

Holland shook his head. "Something like that."

That was it. No more explanation, no more detail. They'd lost an informant. Someone helping them had disappeared or was no longer cooperating.

Jake thought for a moment. "Who was the informant?"

"Doesn't matter, they're no longer in the picture. But we still have an asset. I think we've got all we can out of him, so we're probably going to let him go before anyone starts noticing. He's leaving for vacation tomorrow anyway."

"I'm assuming it's a long shot, but is there any chance I can read over the transcripts of your communications with them?" Jake asked.

"I'll do you one better," Holland said. "He's waiting for us back at the house right now. You can meet him face-to-face."

CHAPTER 14

Jackson Holland didn't dislike Jake Parker. He didn't even know the man. But he had been trained by life and experience that things were easier if one didn't get emotionally attached. It worked in relationships, in professional partnerships, and in life in general.

He didn't dislike the guy, but that didn't necessarily mean he *liked* him either. Parker was simply a new variable, untested and therefore unable to be trusted. It was nothing against Parker; Holland was sure the man was a capable detective, and he had held his own in the car. Few others could pull that off without flinching.

But just because the guy was solid and seemed to have a good head on his shoulders, and just because McDonnell had told them they would be working together, it didn't mean Holland was looking forward to it. A new variable, no matter how interesting and potentially beneficial, was still a new variable. It added unknowns to the equation, and there were already more unknowns than Holland was comfortable with.

So far, the team had tracked down dozens of leads, each pointing to a common outcome: somehow, the local gang called Dominguez was behind the terrorist attacks. The problem was that they couldn't get any *further* than that. They couldn't get past the veil of the outer ring of gang members. Sure, he and his teammate Thompson had brought a few low-level thugs to jail for drug-related crimes, but none of them had spoken about the leadership or plans of the gang. Holland suspected that they either didn't know, didn't want to spill the beans, or both. The threat from Dominguez itself would be far worse than any threat the local police could offer.

And he knew that the local police were in Dominguez's pocket as well. He had investigated a few of them, looked into their connections and after-hours dealings, and found most of them had poorly cooked alibis. It was one of the shaky leads he had tasked his team with, but it was due diligence. He would continue watching, waiting.

If Parker could help with any part of that, he needed to get him up to speed as soon as possible.

Holland pulled the black Chrysler sedan into the small, one-car garage beneath the rectangular home where the team had set up in Fajardo. Like all the other houses on this tiny street, the homes sat atop their garages, and many of the exterior walls were shared with the houses next door. The top levels jutted out a few feet as well, forming a natural overhang above the narrow sidewalks.

The street itself curved upward and around a bend, and during the day, Holland's team could hear children playing ball and riding bicycles up and down. Men and women mingled on their stoops, some drifting around to the few shops and stores sprinkled between the garages.

In all, it was a decent Puerto Rican neighborhood—nothing fancy, certainly not a slum. Somewhere in-between, in the forgotten realm of island-style middle-class that seemed to grow wider each year. Holland had observed it for some time now, as a distant outsider. He probably made more money than the households on this street combined, but he knew it wasn't a fair fight. He had no family to send the money to, and here in Puerto Rico, on the clock day in and day out, for fifty weeks a year, there wasn't much he could do to spend any of it. All of it added up to a ridiculously sized retirement account that, because of the pension he'd soon start receiving, he'd never need.

As Jake pushed the car door open, Holland reached beneath the seat and retrieved the jet-black Beretta. It was a 92D, the enhanced and slightly shortened model of the 92 used by the US military since the 80s. The 92D was a double-action model with no safety, fitted for 9x19mm NATO rounds. It was a personal favorite of Holland's, and he carried it with him at all times, usually hidden beneath a holster and shirt or beneath the seat of his car. He hadn't had any reason to use it yet, but that was because most of his job was spent observing and tracking, not facing down active enemy threats.

For that, he was grateful. He'd served three terms overseas and seen plenty of combat in a previous life, so the relatively slower pace and the odd weekend morning spent on a white-sand beach was a far better alternative.

He pulled the pistol into his belt and saw that Jake was watching him. "You'll get yours inside," Holland said. "Beretta, just like this one. Standard-issue 92. Hope that's okay."

Jake shrugged, but Holland couldn't tell in the dim light of the garage's interior whether he was satisfied with that response or not. He didn't care—if this guy wanted something different, he'd have to find it himself.

He led Jake to the door and knocked four times, a slight pause after the third hit. He pulled the handle, then stepped into the house. There, the similarities between a traditional house and this place ended. The interior space had been all but gutted, only the carpeting on the floor remaining in place. Instead of living-room furniture stood four folding tables, one along each wall, with computer stations and monitors on each and office chairs in front of them. A fifth table sat in the center of the room, on which sat a printer and fax machine combo, a pile of computer paper, and a stack of Diet Coke cans, unopened. To the left, the carpet gave way to old, scratched linoleum, and a tiny kitchenette and dining-room space stood mostly empty. Two folding chairs sat against the wall to Holland's right.

"Hey, boss," a voice called out. A man appeared in a hallway straight ahead, on the other side of the room.

"Delmonico," Holland said. "This is Parker. Just grabbed him from the drop spot."

Delmonico, a sandy-haired linebacker of a man with a beet-red face, nodded. No smile offered.

"Where's Jacobsen?" Holland asked. He stepped farther into the room to allow for Jake to enter, who took a few steps into the kitchen area.

Delmonico threw a thumb over his shoulder. "Back in the bedroom with El Gordo, looking into the last explosion. Trying to figure out if there's a pattern. Hey, where you staying by the way?"

Jake told him, and Delmonico shook his head and snickered.

"Don't worry about it," Holland said. "McDonnell's got a completely separate budget for what he calls 'consulting work.'" He grunted something else toward Delmonico and turned to Jake. "Feel free to sit. Thompson and Krueger are out getting groceries. Should be back by 2200. You're probably tired, but I figured you'd want to get started ASAP."

Delmonico threw a thumb over his shoulder. "Oh, your piece is in that box. Still wrapped up nice, too. You'll need to be careful with it—no open carry here."

"Noted," Jake said. He addressed Holland. "Actually, I need to rent a car. I'd feel better just picking it up tomorrow—only thing left on the agenda tonight is sleep, so I can come back this way first thing after I get a vehicle. You said we could get started ASAP, though. What's up?"

"Informant I was telling you about. Goes by 'El Gordo' on the street. Full name 'Jaime Escalante Garcia.' Works for APHINT, which is one of the pharmaceutical giants on the island, and close to being the biggest. He's the brother-in-law of Delmonico, which is why he'll talk to us. But it's a delicate situation either way."

"How so?" Parker asked.

"Well, for one, we get the sense he doesn't want to be cooperating with us. We're soldiers, professional police officers, essentially. We're not detectives. So we're really here to try our best to keep the peace. What we hear about, we try to stop. Our mission is essentially to wait around and clean up the mess when an attack happens. We try to figure out if one's coming, but we're sort of relying on McDonnell and his nerds for that—not much else we can do on the ground except look for small-time crime."

"Has it worked?" Jake asked. "I mean, you're still here."

"Right," Holland said. "We've been able to prevent a couple of small smash-and-grabs, one bombing a month ago, and we were on the tail of one of the gang's leaders last week but lost him. We have some intelligence, but it's not good enough, and we're not really equipped to be able to *use* it."

Holland hoped he didn't have to spell it out for this guy: *We're not good enough to be able to use it.* He wasn't a detective; this kid was. Holland hoped he could pull his weight and help put his team on the right track. He had no specific problem with adding a trained detective to their mission, but he also did not want to admit just how desperate he was getting. McDonnell was getting antsy, and Holland couldn't blame him.

He continued. "We know our informant is involved with the gang that's been screwing with stuff around here, but he won't give us good leads on anyone in any position of power. Just small tips here and there, nothing substantial. Led to a few arrests, but he's mostly just dropping hints to try to keep us happy—and, I'm sure—to keep himself out of trouble."

Holland didn't feel the need to explain further. Parker's background implied he was familiar with this song and dance.

The informant wanted to make good and help, for fear of retribu-
tion. In this case, it was less because of the goodwill he had with
his brother-in-law and more to do with the fact that his job at
APHINT could be easily jeopardized by Holland's crew.

At the same time, Holland knew the man was involved
somehow with the gang—he either ran drugs for them or knew
those who did, and he knew El Gordo wouldn't be so careless as
to drop any information that might get him killed.

"Got it," Parker said. "So we're trying to get an extraction from
him. But of what?"

Holland almost smiled. *This will be smoother than I thought.*
Parker had already made the connection—an informant was
brought in not just to give tidbits here and there, but actionable
intel leading to a specific question. It was a tactic used only when
things were beginning to get heated. *And things have started to
get heated.*

"You know we suspect that there's an attack coming in three
days," Holland said. "A big one. El Gordo has all but confirmed
that, but he doesn't know the details. We picked up a teenager
and his older brother a few days ago based on a hunch: couple
of street urchins we've seen before with some of the other gang
members in a neighborhood not too far from here. We let them
go, but they were arrested a day later for shoplifting. While we
had them, though, the younger one also admitted to hearing
about 'an attack.'"

"*The* attack?"

"Yeah, probably. His information was vague, just pieces he'd
overheard, but we're pretty sure the target is Fitzsimmons. It's
another huge pharmaceutical—the biggest in the country, actually—and it's already been the target of a few of these attacks.
Bombs usually, in cars most of the time. Some in offices, one
in a home. We're hearing that this one in three days is probably

going to be a game-changer, something that will really shift the balance of power."

"I see. So we need to figure out where, exactly, this bomb will be set up."

Holland nodded and watched Parker. His face was difficult to read, but Holland could tell the man was thinking.

Maybe this guy will be useful, after all.

CHAPTER 15

Bombs.

Jake hated the word. The word had been the cause of nightmares ever since Mel had died in the terror attack. As Holland spoke, Jake caught himself drifting off, to a place he hadn't been in a while. A place Mel still existed, in a deep part of his brain he kept locked away, for fear the memories would leak out and disappear forever.

"Parker, you okay?" Holland asked.

Jake blinked a few times. "Uh, yeah. Sorry about that. Just tired."

Holland grunted, but Jake couldn't understand if he'd said anything or it was just a verbal tic.

"Why Fitzsimmons?" Jake asked.

Holland shrugged. "Hell if I know. They're the biggest out there, and all signs point to one of their competitors being in bed with the gang, trying to cause enough grief for Fitzsimmons that they'll back out of the area or something."

Jake nodded as he took this in. It seemed unlikely to him that an entire corporation would simply back out because of terror attacks, but then again, while this place was technically protected by the United States, it was clear everywhere he'd been already that it felt like a different nation.

It was quite possible that the United States government hadn't done enough to quell the terror attacks, and that Fitzsimmons was getting upset that the supposedly United States-owned territory was not being protected well enough. Either way, Jake and Holland's team needed to figure out what the attack in three days was going to be, and where.

"Can I talk to El Gordo?" Jake asked.

"Be my guest," Holland said. "He's not our prisoner, so don't make it an interrogation."

"Noted," Jake replied.

He followed Holland and the huge slab of butter named Delmonico toward the back bedroom. Like the living room, there was nothing about the space that said "bedroom." Instead, two more tables had been erected and were placed along one wall, and four suitcases sat on them, each open, three of them piled high with clothes. One of the suitcases was a stark contrast: clothes that were immaculately folded and placed carefully within the suitcase. He didn't have to ask which one was Holland's.

Five chairs were placed around a circular table, this one made of wood, on which sat a small open case with poker chips and cards inside. A bottle of cheap local rum stood next to the case.

There were two men seated behind the table. One was white, American, with brown, short-cropped hair and deep, sunken eyes. A dark-skinned, rail-thin man sat near him in another chair, also facing the doorway, and raised an eyebrow when Jake entered.

So this is the relaxation room, Jake thought. He wondered when was the last time the poker set had been used.

"One more bedroom behind you, to the left," Holland said, leading the way. "Cots in there for all of us. Sometimes we shake things up and sleep in the living-room area."

Jake wasn't sure if it was meant to be a joke, but there was no laughter from any of the men in the room.

"Hey," Jake said as he entered. "Jake Parker. Just got in." He extended his hand to both men. Neither man smiled. "You must be Jacobsen and Mr. Garcia?"

"Call me El Gordo," the man said. His accent was thick, but his English was clear and precise.

"Right. Doesn't that mean 'fat' in Spanish?"

Half of Garcia's mouth turned upward. "Old joke," he said. He set his arms on the table in front of him. He was wearing a long-sleeved shirt with the sleeves rolled up past his elbows. The shirt was tightly fitted, with pearl-snap buttons over a dark maroon print. As he turned his arm upward, Jake caught sight of a slightly faded tattoo on the inside of his wrist. About four inches square, it depicted a curvy, four-limbed creature, its eyes two dots hovering near its head. Jake raised his chin and was about to ask.

"Coqui frog," El Gordo said, noticing Jake's gaze. "Symbol of Puerto Rico. There are millions of them hopping around the island, but far fewer now than there were before. Some are endangered."

"Why is it a symbol?" Jake asked.

He noticed that El Gordo and Jacobsen shared a quick glance before El Gordo responded. "It used to be a symbol for us. 'Small island, small frog, big voice.'"

Jake nodded. "Not any longer though? Why not?"

El Gordo sighed. "*La piña está agria*. It is still a symbol for the Puerto Rican people, but the Dominguez organization has been growing for two decades, recruiting anyone who will prove their support for their country. And they have chosen the coqui as their symbol as well. It is beginning to take over as a *Dominguez* symbol."

"Seems convenient."

"They wish to be seen as Puerto Rico's liberators," El Gordo said. "But instead they say 'we will be heard.' They have been working to involve their leaders in local politics, with the hope of one day becoming sovereign once again."

"And I guess they've also been blowing things up on the side?" Jake asked. "Is that what this attack is about three days from now? Do you know where it will be?" Jake had decided on the direct approach; he assumed Holland and his men had tried diplomacy, knew they had tried coaxing bits of related information out of their informant over time.

But time was a commodity they were running out of.

El Gordo paused, then looked at Holland, whose face had returned to its normal stoic expression. "You are new to the island, Mr. Parker," El Gordo said. "If I knew that, I would tell you. I assure you. But I do not."

"Is there anything you can tell us?" Jake asked. He felt as though he were slipping into interrogator mode, but he didn't want to let an opportunity go to waste.

El Gordo didn't respond at first. Then, he stood up, shook hands with Jacobsen, and started toward the door. "I must be going now," he said. "I will be gone for a week—on vacation with my family at Dorado Beach. Let me know after that if you need something else."

Jake looked at Holland, who stepped out of the way as he passed. When El Gordo had left the small house and the door shut, Holland met Jake's gaze. "We knew he would be unreachable. He's an informant, so we can't detain him. It'll put too much attention on us, and it would likely get him killed."

"So we just let him walk away?"

"He's told us what he knows. There's nothing—"

"If you'd let me *actually* talk to him, we—"

Holland held up a hand. "Trust me, we've done it. We know his movements, his interactions, hell—we know which hotel he's going to be staying at for the next week. It's a company retreat sort of thing; he's going a few days early to get some time away from everything. He's as clean as it gets, Parker."

"Clean informants aren't usually very helpful," Jake said.

Holland sighed. "Okay, I mean he's not *actively* part of Dominguez. He's got connections with them, still, which is why we think he'll be useful. He knows some, but not enough. As I said, El Gordo is Delmonico's brother-in-law. Delmonico knocked up the guy's sister way back when and they've been living here ever since. El Gordo got married a few years ago, shed his pre-marriage relationships with the gang. But before that, he was more involved with Dominguez. Knew their drop points, habits, some possible targets, that sort of thing."

Jake nodded. "So you trust this guy?"

"Enough, I guess. He gave us the lead about the attack. Knew some folks from way back when and he mentioned he thinks Dominguez is moving on something in a few days. Probably another bomb. That's it."

"But we should at least follow him."

"It's a waste of time, Parker," Jacobsen said. "He's *an* informant, not *the* informant. He's run his course. Helpful, but he's not going to miraculously drop a valuable nugget on us now, after weeks of helping. If *he* knew more, *we'd* know it. He's used up."

Jake wanted to argue, wanted to explain that there was usually something more, just beneath the surface. Something he could extract with enough time. Something that might push this thing along. But he had gotten here too late. Holland and his crew felt that they had gotten everything they could out of the guy, felt that they would be just chasing their tails if they kept El Gordo around.

He shook his head. He was just the consultant, and this was Holland's game.

"Okay, fine," he said. "So where do we go from here?"

Holland looked at Jacobsen and Delmonico, who were both smiling. "Well," Holland said. "That's why you're here, right?"

Jake wanted to laugh. He had been brought in to solve a case he had learned about just over a day ago. It was silly to think he would be able to offer any support whatsoever, but there might be something…

"Okay," he said. "I know what I want to do."

"Shoot," Holland said.

"Those two kids you had arrested? The teenager and brother? I want to talk to them."

CHAPTER 16

It had taken Jake some verbal maneuvering, but he had eventually gotten Holland to spill the beans on the two young men who had been arrested. As it turned out, Holland's team had only passed them along to the local authorities, and from there it seemed the kids had "fallen into the system," a cryptic way of admitting Holland had no idea whether they would be locked up, detained, or back on the street.

Holland advised against trying to find them. Any information they had, he likely already knew, and by prying open dead cases, it would only serve as a reminder that the gang was still under scrutiny. Holland urged Jake to let it go, that there was nothing useful that would come of it. Instead, he wanted Jake to help research Fitzsimmons and their ongoing warfare with seemingly every other pharmaceutical company on the island. He wanted to find out as much as possible about the gang's involvement with the company, if there was any.

But after leaving the safe house, Jake had no interest in doing research. That could happen at any point later tonight, back at the hotel. Right now, he felt out of the loop. Just because Holland didn't think the two young gang members were a useful lead any longer didn't meant Jake agreed.

Holland, while trustworthy, was a soldier. Jake, however, was a detective, and he had been brought onto the case right in the middle—there was no by-the-book documentation he could refer back to; Holland's team was not operating as a police unit, but as a squad in enemy territory—kicking rocks and seeing what predators flew out. The two young gang members hadn't led toward anything immediately useful, so they had moved on.

But Jake knew there was more to the story. The kids were part of the Dominguez organization, which meant a trained investigator like him might be able to get more names, more facts, more clues.

He caught a ride-share and gave the driver an address. When he arrived, he was happy to note that the place was open for another half-hour. It was getting late, and Jake already felt the sleepiness hitting him, but he wanted to get a head start on this portion of the case, especially if Holland wasn't interested in digging up old leads.

He paid the driver, got out, and walked to the front door of the building. The vinyl lettering on the glass door verified he was in the right place: *FAJARDO POLICE DEPARTMENT.*

Jake walked in and was met by a tiny antechamber, like something he'd seen at banks, where the ATM was installed. Unlike most banks, though, it seemed as though this place hadn't been swept in years. The doors leading into the inner room were wood, heavy, thick things that looked older than the building itself.

He let the outer door close behind him before pulling the inner door open. Bright yellow light spilled out from inside, and Jake blinked to let his eyes adjust. He stepped inside, finding himself inside a rectangular gated area, about waist-high. The place was a single large room with a few doors sprinkled around the exterior, much less crowded than his old Boston precinct offices, and while nothing else in the room was familiar, this gated section seemed to be a staple in police offices worldwide.

Three police officers looked over at him, two seated behind desks and one standing near a table with a cup of coffee in his hand, preparing to fill it. Clearly this was the officer who'd drawn the short straw and was going to be working the night shift.

"Hey," Jake said. "Sorry, I didn't even think about it, but I don't speak Spanish."

Jake looked around the room, waiting for some recognition of what he'd just said.

The man holding the coffee mug finally gave it. "I speak English," he said. "How can we help you?"

Jake was relieved. He made a mental note to check in with McDonnell about finding a translator while he was here. He wasn't sure if Holland and his team spoke fluent Spanish, but Jake had only taken a few years of it back in high school and all he could remember of it now were the words he'd never use in real life. "Thank you," he said. "I'm a—I *was*—a cop. Police officer, from Boston."

The man's eyes widened. "I know Boston!" he said. "Love Boston."

"Right, great. Well, uh, this is going to sound weird, but I was wondering if you could help me find something."

He wasn't sure of the rhetoric for interdepartmental policing policies and information sharing among Puerto Rican departments, but he was almost positive he would need to do some convincing—and paperwork—if these guys wanted things to be "official."

He hoped it wouldn't come to that.

The man walked over, slowly. He was round, shorter than Jake by about a foot. Jake saw that the badge on his shirt pocket said "Quintanilla," and he stuck out his hand as he approached. "Luis Quintanilla," the man said. "Come in."

After they shook hands, he lifted the gate latch and Jake followed him back to an empty desk in the opposite corner of the room from the other two officers.

Neither of the other two cops so much as looked up as Jake passed.

They're definitely at the end of their shift, he thought. *Don't want to get involved and have to stay late.*

Quintanilla seemed nice, and Jake's plan shouldn't get him in trouble, so he launched into it. "Nice to meet you, Officer

Quintanilla. Jake Parker. I'm working on tracking down some kids—teenagers, I believe—that were arrested a few days ago. Not sure which precinct it was, but I'm assuming you have a shared database around the island."

"Yes, yes of course," Quintanilla said. "Do you know their names?"

"Ah…" Jake paused. "I don't, actually."

He was woefully unprepared for this, but what could he expect? If he'd asked Holland for the kids' names, Holland would have known immediately that Jake was planning to disobey him and start snooping around. Jake had no problem trusting his gut about what to investigate, but this early in the process, he didn't want to ruin whatever credibility he might have with Holland. Besides, if this little errand turned up nothing useful, Jake wouldn't even have to mention it to Holland tomorrow when he checked back in.

"I doubt they came through here," Jake said. "But it would have been in this area, at least. Seems like a sleepy town, so I bet you'd know who I'm talking about."

The man arched an eyebrow.

"A younger boy, probably fourteen or fifteen, with an older brother. Maybe nineteen, twenty, I'd guess?"

"Is there anything in particular about them you know?"

"Brought in for shoplifting," Jake said. "Would have been only a few days ago, I think, so they might even still be—"

"I can't help you," Quintanilla said. Jake watched his eyes flick to his right, toward his fellow officers.

"You can't?"

He shook his head. "No, I am sorry." He began to stand up. "Thank you for coming by, and can I recommend any restaurants? If you are not from around here, there are world-class places to eat just down the—"

Jake held up his palm. "No, thank you." He smiled. "But I can't help but ask again—" Jake lowered his chin and dropped his voice. "Are you *sure* there's nothing you can tell me? I'm just a concerned citizen interested in—"

"You said you were a cop."

"I said I *used to be* a cop."

"So why is a *used to be a cop* looking for two gangsters?"

"I never said they were gangsters."

Quintanilla's face cracked, a thin spark of a grin appearing and then disappearing immediately after. "Okay, Mr. Parker."

"Call me Jake."

"Okay, Jake," Quintanilla said. "Call me Luis." Jake noticed that the officer's voice began to speed up as it rose in volume a bit. "I do not think I can help you, but there is a corner store two blocks down on the left side of the road. They may have what you need."

Jake frowned.

"It is only a minute walk from here. Should still be open."

Jake nodded slowly. After a long pause, he extended his hand. "Got it. Thanks, Luis. Much appreciated."

Jake turned and strolled through the office just as one of the other officers looked up. They matched eyes for a moment, and Jake saw the cold, calculating expression on the man's face, sizing him up.

He nodded once at the man, who returned the gesture and then turned back to his colleague.

As Jake lifted the latch and prepared to exit, he turned back to Luis, who was once again standing at the tiny coffee station. He smiled, swallowed, and then waved at Jake with his free hand.

CHAPTER 17

The corner shop was just barely open, two minutes before 10 p.m. Jake could see someone behind the counter inside, bustling around and obviously working quickly to close up and get out of the store. As he approached, the man looked up, noticed Jake, and his shoulders fell.

Jake was about to pull the handle open and apologize, telling the man he just needed to ask him a quick question, when he heard a whistle from behind him.

He whirled around and frowned into the darkness. A small, dark shape bustled toward him, crossing the street just as it came beneath a streetlight.

It was Luis. He lifted an arm in greeting, and Jake dropped his hand from the store's handle and stepped back to the curb.

"Mr. Parker," Luis said, huffing a bit and hiking his belt back up over his gut. "I am sorry for the confusion."

"What's up?" Jake asked.

Luis looked left and right, and then his eyes flew upward to meet Jake's. "I could not be truthful inside the office," he said. "The other officers I was with—one of them has many family members in the Dominguez group."

"The gang."

Luis nodded. "I do not believe *he* is a member, but I do think he is loyal to their concerns."

"I see," Jake said. "In that case, I appreciate you not ratting me out."

He stuck a hand out. Luis seemed confused at first, then he shook Jake's hand. "Of course. You said you were looking into the arrests of two young men. Thought they were involved with Dominguez?"

Jake nodded. *Good guess.*

"I have been interested in finding anyone working for the Dominguez for years, Mr. Parker. My wife's brother was killed by one of their members, about ten years ago. A ruthless, unnecessary murder. Since then, I have become a police officer, and though I must keep my head low—the Dominguez are everywhere these days—I want nothing more than to root them out and put them all behind bars. But I cannot simply open an investigation when some man comes in off the street and asks for sensitive information."

Jake considered this for a moment. In the dim yellowish glow of the streetlights, the dark shadows on Luis' face made him difficult to read. But there was no malice in his voice. No reason for this man to lie to him.

"I'm no longer a cop," Jake said. "I resigned a few years back. But I am legally in your country, and I can—"

Luis waved him off and chuckled. "I am a US citizen," he said. "Though not yet Americano. I vote for it whenever it comes up, and one day I hope my daughters will be able to set foot on US soil and be seen as an equal citizen. And that will not happen until we can prove, as a nation, that there is no problem with terrorism or drugs."

Jake didn't respond.

"What that means, Mr. Parker, is that you and I are on the same side. I have no reason not to trust you, and I assure you I have no reason not to be trusted. I have shaken your hand, that is that."

Jake smiled. "That is that, I guess. So what are you out here for? Do you know something of the boys that were arrested?"

He nodded slowly. "Yes. The two young Dominguez members were arrested in Ponce, on the south side of the island. Only a few days ago. I heard about it because they grew up here, and we knew their names."

"What happened to them?" Jake asked. "Are they still in Ponce?"

Luis shook his head. "I am afraid not. These things... they typically all end the same way. Young men, considered by half the police to be no better than rats on the street, and by the other half no longer loyal to the Dominguez, they end up no longer in the system. If they spoke to someone about the gang... someone Dominguez does not want them speaking to, then they are definitely no longer in the system."

"No longer in the system?" Jake asked.

"Sí, yes. No longer in the system." He shrugged as though it were no big deal.

"You mean... they were released?"

Luis' eyes widened slightly as he explained. "Perhaps, but most likely no. There are not enough jail cells on the island to hold all of the petty thieves and minor criminals. Most, sure, they will be released. But if you have the coqui..." He pronounced the word just as Holland's informant El Gordo had, with two syllables. *Co-kee.*

"The frog tattoo?"

"Yes, the symbol of Dominguez. If you have it, and you are brought to the police, you are removed from the system."

Jake scoffed. "I don't understand. How can you 'remove' someone? And what system? Are you saying they are no longer on the books? So the police can turn a blind eye to the corruption the Dominguez are involved with?"

Luis sniffed, and then stepped forward while turning his chin up to address Jake in a whisper, his hot coffee breath lingering just in front of Jake's nose. "That is true, yes. But that is not *just* what happens."

"They're... killed?"

Luis paused a moment, then he stepped back and checked his watch. "I must be going, Mr. Parker. I wish to help you, however you may need it. But I cannot jeopardize my station."

"I understand," Jake said. "Thank you. Can you at least point me in the right direction? Someone who can find these kids?"

Luis seemed as though he weren't going to answer at first. Finally, after a long pause, he nodded. "There is someone. Another young man here in town who may know for sure. But, please, he cannot know that I sent you."

"You have my word," Jake said.

"He is my wife's cousin—he knew her brother, and I believe they were involved in the Dominguez gang together for a few years."

"Are you afraid he'll tell the higher-ups?"

Luis shook his head. "He is family. Family is first in Puerto Rico. But I do not want to risk it."

Jake took out his phone and pulled up an app to take notes. "I'm a professional, Luis. Trust me. Give me the information. I'll store it here—it's secured, and not uploaded to any cloud service."

Luis gave him the name and an address where Jake could find him. Then, he looked back up at Jake and waited for him to finish typing. "We can meet tomorrow, after I finish work?"

"Why? There's more?"

"No more," Luis said, "but I need to be sure you are not putting me or my family in danger."

"Sure," Jake said. "When are you on duty?"

"I am finished tomorrow evening."

Luis seemed saddened by this, but Jake didn't press him on it.

Jake shifted, feeling a slight breeze in the humid air begin to chill him. He wanted to get back to the hotel, to crawl into bed and sleep for half the day. But he knew his instincts had been right. Holland hadn't lied to him, but he definitely got the feeling he had withheld information. Information about the two arrests, about the breadth and influence of Dominguez, and about how delicate this situation *really* was.

Puerto Rico was a bright and beautiful place, but Jake feared it was also concealing a very dark and sinister game. And he felt as though he had inadvertently become a player in that game.

CHAPTER 18

Cecil Romero rubbed the coqui frog on his left wrist, working one miniature ache at a time. He had never thought moving individual envelopes into small mailboxes would cause so much pain, but then again he had never done it for nearly seven hours straight.

He was standing just outside the building of his new job—the massive gray monolith of Fitzsimmons' headquarters. There were three others just like it set in a semicircle around this one, but this building was considered the "main" facility on campus. It housed many of the management offices, and the campus-wide mail distribution center took up the entire basement floor.

Trucks would back up to the mailroom at lunchtime every day, when a handful of mailroom employees would pile the truck beds high with bags of mail-filled boxes, each organized and catalogued for the proper destination on campus. The trucks would then head to other buildings on this campus or elsewhere on the island, and by evening every employee in the mail system would have received any and all mail designated for them.

It was a fast, efficient system, and while Cecil hated that he played the part of a powerless cog in the massive wheel, he couldn't help but feel impressed by its function.

His job was to retrieve the mail from the main drop after the postal trucks carried it in early in the morning and dumped it down the three long conveyor belts. He stood at position nine—ninth from the end and second from the front of the drop station—and he had been trained to read each piece of mail that reached his station, categorize it—packages or envelopes—and then, when the box was full, head to the mailbox station along the wall and distribute each piece to the proper box.

It was miserable, mindless grunt work. Cecil hated every minute of it, from the ten minutes of training he'd received to the end of his first full day.

However, he'd had a brief respite during the scheduled lunch break. The large man who worked next to him, with a tattoo covering half his face, had approached Cecil and motioned for him to follow. They'd found a spot near the back of the room, in a tucked-away corner shared by a mop and dry bucket. There they'd eaten their packed lunches, and the man had explained how things worked.

"Half of us are Dominguez," he'd said, showing Cecil the frog on his wrist. "The other half don't care."

Cecil had taken a bite of his sandwich and tried to look interested.

"What are you looking for here?" the man had then asked.

Cecil had tried to feign surprise, but the man saw right through it.

"You are here for a reason, correct?"

"Yes."

"So what is it you are looking for?"

Cecil had weighed his options. It was clear this man—also a Dominguez brother, though Cecil couldn't be sure where exactly his loyalties lay—knew how things worked. He'd explained that he had been a mailroom employee for Fitzsimmons for ten years, and no one started on position nine. Usually the newcomers picked off the last remaining pieces of mail from the end of the line—positions one and two—after the experienced employees processed everything they could. So he had known immediately that Cecil was more than just an employee, and Cecil had decided to trust him.

"I am waiting on a letter about an FDA visit," Cecil had said. He didn't want to give away more information.

"I see," the man had said. "That will come to our belt."

"How do you know?"

"Do you see how they are organized? The largest packages for belt one. The smallest for belt three, where they are put into the carts. All the paper mail and any packages clearly labeled that will fit in the mailboxes go to belt two. Our belt."

Cecil had nodded. "So I will not miss the letter?"

The man had shaken his head. "Of course not. You will know." He had then explained to Cecil how to "process" the mail like the letter he was waiting on. How to apply just the right amount of heat to the underside of the envelope, so the insides could be extracted and then reinserted and sealed without any evidence of tampering.

Cecil had thanked the man, gone about his day, and now found himself standing in front of the building, awaiting the company bus to take him to the cheap motel he would be staying in. While Dominguez could certainly afford to put him up in nicer accommodations, he was now officially on the payroll of Fitzsimmons—and they would only begin offering him housing after six months of employ.

Until then, it was low-class living for him.

CHAPTER 19

Jake had arranged to meet with Officer Luis Quintanilla in the evening, after Jake's work with Holland—whatever that may be—was finished and Luis was off duty.

He also had a laundry list of items to knock off. First on the list was finding a rental, which had proven to be as simple as asking for help from the concierge at the hotel. He was on his way to pick up the car now.

After, he intended to meet with Holland and get the pistol that was waiting for him, as well as try to persuade the older man to spill the beans on anything they might have uncovered about this Dominguez group. Jake knew the man wasn't a detective, so he probably couldn't put the numerous threads together in a way that allowed them to take immediate action. And that's why Holland's team had been mostly docile—they wanted *action*, to take down an obvious threat in the most abrupt and permanent way, yet they couldn't do that without a clear and obvious threat staring them directly in the face.

While Jake understood the stance, he also understood that Dominguez would never allow for such an obvious, overt confrontation. Whatever was brewing between the pharmaceutical companies and the Dominguez gang, whatever Holland's team was trying to get involved with, it was playing out like a slowly unraveling spool of thread. Slow, menacing, and constant. Unnoticeable at first, unless you knew where to look.

So the last item on his agenda, if there was time for it, was to meet once again with Vero. He couldn't look her up—he had never gotten her last name—but if she was as forward with him as she had been last night, he figured he would have no problem tracking her down. Jake was well aware of the possibility that physical attraction might be playing against his better judgment, but there was a business and professional reason he wanted to speak with her: she had told him she worked for APHINT, the same pharmaceutical company that Holland had mentioned was neck-and-neck with the largest corporation on the island, Fitzsimmons.

But why had she been so up front with Jake? What was her *true* motive? How had she known Jake was here in Puerto Rico to snoop around and dig up intel on both companies?

Or was Jake just jumping to conclusions? There was no way she could know that's what he was doing, because *he* hadn't fully known it, and as far as he knew, he had given her no indication as to why he was here. The truth was that he was here only to try to help prevent the next Dominguez attack; he knew that Dominguez' business had something to do with that of the pharmaceuticals, but there was no reason to suspect Vero was anything but what she claimed to be. Had her presence in the hotel restaurant last night been nothing but a coincidence? Was she—as she had explained—simply interested in human interaction?

Five minutes after entering the car rental company's office, he was out on the street with a set of keys. The SUV was parked in a lot next door, and Jake walked up to the dark-blue Mercedes and clicked the fob.

As he got inside the car and started the engine, he took his phone out and found his location on the map. He recognized the main highway the ride-share driver had taken to get here, and a few of the larger side streets. As he analyzed his location on the phone, he noticed that there was another road name he recognized.

It was the name of the street Officer Luis had given him. The street where Jake could find the gang member who might know more about the young men who had been arrested.

He glanced at his watch—the old diver watch still affixed to his wrist, where it lived every hour of his waking day. Jake had plenty of time before he was going to head toward Holland's safe house, and visiting the kid first would save him even more time since he was already close. He synced the rental SUV's Bluetooth input with his phone and sent the address to the Mercedes' onboard navigation system. This was luxurious and cutting-edge technology for him, as he normally drove an old Corolla that barely had power windows. Within seconds, a computerized female voice was telling him to exit the parking lot and return to the highway.

After five minutes of driving, Jake realized he was being routed into one of the poorer neighborhoods in this area. The houses were low, the rusted sheet-metal roofs all slanting slowly toward the dirt-covered streets. He pulled off the highway and onto a narrow street that seemed no wider than an alley. A chicken and a massive rooster squawked and ran away as he passed, and he saw a few more fowl along the side of the road, pecking at invisible pieces of food, scratching at the hard, sun-packed road.

A few children ran through the streets as well, causing Jake to slow the vehicle's progress. There was barely enough room for a second lane, so he wondered if the large car would be able to turn around if he got stuck back here. He wasn't sure what the etiquette was for getting lost in an unknown neighborhood, but he hoped the locals were nicer than the homes they lived in.

At the end of this block, the road turned sharply to the right and widened as it began sloping downhill. He couldn't see the coast, but his sense of direction knew he was heading toward the beach. The houses were stacked now, some three-high on both sides of the street, and a few of the bottom-level dwellings were occupied by storeowners, their wares hanging from racks and over windowsills.

Finally, his destination appeared. A group of men were standing in a circle on the opposite side of the road. All were tattooed up and down their arms, and a few even had markings on the backs of their necks. Jake wasn't about to jump to the conclusion that they were gangsters, but he decided to keep them in his sights as he approached the rendezvous point.

As he put the car in park, he stared out the windshield and caught sight of the men across the street, staring back at him.

Here goes nothing, he thought.

CHAPTER 20

Jake had been in plenty of small, run-down neighborhoods. Outsiders were frowned upon, and he might as well have had a neon sign on his head that said "I'm not from around here." He knew the group of men across the street were sizing him up, trying to see what this newcomer was doing in a place that was clearly not used to commercial business.

Jake locked the Mercedes, knowing it was a worthless safety feature, and looked for the address he was after. It was a simple home, nothing but a front door and a single barred window.

He knocked. The men across the street had their eyes on him, but none had moved toward him. He pieced together a plan anyway, mostly out of habit. If they started toward him, or started yelling, he would be able to get back to the Mercedes before anyone got across the street—he hoped.

He hadn't stopped by Holland's yet, so he had no weapon to protect himself—not that he'd want to wave a gun around in a place like this. Chances were good he wouldn't be the only one armed, and if that was the case, showing a firearm would be one of the *worst* things he could do.

Knocking again, Jake finally heard shuffling from somewhere inside the house. Another five seconds passed. The men's eyes were still on him. There was a voice at the door, but it sounded to Jake like no more than a grunt.

"Hello?" he asked.

Another grunt, then some shuffling.

"Hey, sorry—I don't speak Spanish well. Do you speak English? I need to ask you—"

"*A mí, plín.*"

He'd heard the phrase a few times already on the island, and it was delivered with enough context to get the point across. *I don't care.* He took a breath. "Okay, sorry. I—I'm an American. I'm lost, just passing through. I thought maybe—"

The door clicked and fell open a crack. There was nothing but darkness within, until a small face appeared. It was haggard, weathered, and leathery, as if it had been left on a beach for a year.

"Hey," Jake said. He held his palms up so the person could see he was unarmed. "I just—I wanted to ask you something. Are you this person?" Jake held up his phone and showed the man the name and address on his phone.

"*Tu madre,*" the man said. Another local slang, this one of the not-so-friendly variety. His voice was young, but there was a dryness to it that almost made Jake's throat hurt.

"Sorry," Jake said. "I'm just trying to figure out—"

The kid's face fell forward, abruptly, as he glanced out to the street, then across. *At the men standing in a circle.* He pulled his head back, breathing in sharply.

Jake also saw the kid's dark-skinned, leathery arm. A small coquí tattoo stretched for a few inches just under his wrist.

"You know them?" Jake asked, throwing a thumb up and over his shoulder. He made a point not to look back. "Dominguez?"

The kid suddenly threw his head and stared bullets into Jake's face. He nodded, slowly. Blinked a few times, then pulled his head back into the house.

Jake's suspicions had been confirmed. The men *were* gang members, but they didn't care about Jake or his rented Mercedes. They were keeping an eye on the neighborhood. On one of their dealers. The kid had probably answered the door because he thought one of the older gang members was on the other side of it. That told Jake that he was going to need to change his strategy a bit. He wasn't armed, and he wasn't interested in setting off a turf war or getting into a scramble with these guys. He had nothing tangible to use in his favor, so he had to come up with something *intangible*. Something he knew every wet-behind-the-ears young drug dealer was afraid of.

"What... what you want?" the young man said. His English was clipped, broken. Jake guessed he'd had a few years of it in school, but he couldn't be older than eighteen.

Jake sighed, trying his best to look relaxed. He refused to glance over his shoulder, hoping his ears would pick up the slack and alert him to any oncoming gang members. He needed to come across as confident, calm, cool. Like nothing could ever bother him. He was no longer a tourist. "Do you know who I am?" Jake asked. He spoke the words deliberately, slowly.

The kid shook his head.

"Do you know... FBI?" Again, Jake articulated each word carefully, putting the necessary weight behind each letter of the acronym.

And then he saw it. It was subtle, but it was there. The kid's eyes widened ever so slightly, his nostrils flared. He was suddenly terrified. This was no longer an interaction with an undercover police officer—whom the kid most likely assumed Jake to be.

He had turned it into an interaction with an entity Jake knew the kid would inherently be fearful of.

Around here, a kid like this might play games with the cops.

But that same kid knew better than to play games with the FBI.

CHAPTER 21

Perfect. Every unscrupulous person Jake had ever interacted with seemed apathetic toward law enforcement, until it was brought to their attention that the *federal* agents had gotten involved.

"I am not here to bring you in," Jake continued. "I don't want any trouble, either. Just have to ask a question."

"What?" Jake had seen the shift in the kid's demeanor even before he'd spoken again. The fidgety, annoyed youth had shifted into a nervous, anxious adult.

"Did you make some Dominguez gang members disappear? A few days ago? Young men, brothers?" He hoped the keywords—gang, disappear, brothers—would get the point across.

The young man sneered and shook his head.

"Fine," Jake said. "Do you know anyone who *did* make them disappear?"

Again, Jake was met with a quick shake of the head.

Jake clicked his tongue on the top of his mouth and sighed. He wanted to seem disappointed, let down. "Okay, that's fine," he said. He still had his phone in his hand, and he pulled up to his face, the kid watching him the entire time, and then held it up to his ear. Even though there was no one on the other end, he spoke into it. "Suspect is refusing cooperation. I can bring him in, if you—"

"Not me," the kid said, nearly spitting out the words. "Not me. Rafael. Three days… eh, *Miércoles*, uh…"

"Wednesday?" Jake asked, pulling the phone from his ear.

"Sí, sí," the kid said. "Yes, *Miércoles*. I not know them."

"That's fine," Jake said. "I don't need names. Where are they?"

The kid shrugged. Jake didn't press it.

"You saw them?"

The kid shook his head. "No."

"But Rafael did?"

After a pause, the young gang member nodded profusely.

Jake brought the phone back. "He's being cooperative now, yes. Yes, sir. Rafael. That name mean anything?" He waited for five painful seconds. "Yes, sir. Got it. Thank you, sir."

The kid seemed torn between slamming the door on Jake's face and throwing it open and making a run for it. Jake was somewhat impressed he hadn't tried either, but he had a feeling the gang members across the street had something to do with that.

Jake had had a few encounters with low-level organized crime in the past. Most of what he'd seen were wannabe gangsters trying to make a name for themselves—uneducated dropouts who had nothing better to do than terrorize the local neighborhood.

A few times, he'd been on a case trying to track down one or more individuals who operated at a slightly higher level. Criminals who were into money laundering, sex trafficking, even legitimate enterprises like real estate and business lending.

But he'd never heard of a gang that was so large and dispersed that it was both a gang *and* a crime ring. The Dominguez group, as McDonnell had pointed out, wasn't just one thing. It was a conglomerate. Multiple *groups* of gangs—each vying for power and attention and control.

And Jake knew now that even though many wore the sign of the coqui frog on their wrist, it didn't mean they had each others' best interests in mind. It didn't mean they were on the same page about day-to-day operations.

Jake wondered what had happened between the group outside and this younger drug dealer. What sort of falling out had taken place? Or was about to take place?

He sniffed as he hung up the phone. "Anything else?" Jake asked. "You know the two guys who were taken? The ones who disappeared?"

"*Tres*," the kid said.

"What's that?"

"*Tres*. Three."

Jake looked at the young man, trying to understand him.

"Sí, three. El Yunque, like the others."

Just then, Jake felt movement in his peripheral vision and noticed that someone was walking in his direction. He didn't recognize the man, but he thought he had seen him in the group from across the street. He'd gotten what he needed from this guy, and when he met up with Luis later, he could compare notes.

"*Gracias, amigo*," Jake said.

The kid simply stared up at him.

Jake pulled away from the door. The gang members across the street began walking toward him.

Jake quickened his pace, staying in front of the man who was now ascending the sidewalk toward where Jake was standing seconds ago. The kid closed the door just as he passed.

Behind him, Jake heard the footsteps beating on the dirt road. They were running now. Jake picked up speed and clicked the key fob in his pocket, just as the first of the men reached his side of the street.

"Señor," one of them called out, followed by a string of words he couldn't understand. There was a lilt at the end, a question. Jake wasn't interested in answering.

He reached the SUV door and pulled it open.

Two of the men were on him now, but he was already getting into the car and starting the engine. He locked the doors with one hand, moving the key with the other. They banged against the windows with their fists, their angry voices rising in volume. He slammed his foot on the gas pedal as soon as the engine turned over.

Shit. The parking brake was on, and the car went nowhere, digging into the street as the RPM dial flew upward.

A shadow from the rearview mirror caught his attention. A small, thin line, moving quickly, and then—

Bam! Something smashed the back windshield, hard, cracking it. Jake saw the baseball bat rising up once again, preparing for another swing.

He needed to disappear, now.

He pushed down on the parking brake and simultaneously floored it, sending dirt and dust up into the faces of the men standing behind the SUV. He saw the bat-waver coughing, choking on the rocks and debris as Jake flew down the hill toward the city that lay below, on the coast.

He'd made it—for now. Any one of the gang members would have been able to see his license plate, and it was quite possible one of them had. Jake needed to figure out what his next move was before they started asking questions of their own.

Before the plan, however, Jake wanted to be armed. He needed to get to Holland and his gun.

CHAPTER 22

"Holland," the man's voice called out. "We're not tracking El Gordo, are we?"

Holland's ears perked up at the question from Delmonico. He was seated, eating a bowl of cereal. It was almost noon, but one of the perks of being a career bachelor was that he could get away with eating cereal at any hour of the day.

Delmonico was stretched out between two chairs, playing a game on his phone.

"No, why?" Holland asked through the side of his mouth, between crunches.

"Just thinking, that's all."

"Stop thinking, Delmonico," Holland said. "That's my job, not yours."

Holland heard a chuckle as Jacobsen strolled into the kitchen area. "That what you do all day, Holland?" he asked. "Think? I thought it was eat, sleep, shit, make us pick up your laundry."

"Making you assholes do stuff for me helps me think," he replied. He sucked in a dribble of milk that was trying to escape down his chin.

"Someone's coming in," another voice, Thompson's, called out from the back bedroom. Thompson was currently on the group's main computer and must have gotten an alert from one of the security cameras. "Looks like a navy SUV. Mercedes."

Holland had chosen this location for their living quarters and safe house not just because it was off the beaten path, away from most of the drug areas and pharmaceutical employees, but because it was, technically, a low-rent area. The vehicles that traversed these blocks were usually beat-up old trucks, vans, or decades-old sedans, full of workers heading to or from a job site. The older inhabitants of the neighborhood simply walked everywhere, and the younger kids caught the bus or rode bikes to the nearest school. That meant that a nice, new-looking Mercedes SUV would certainly be cause for investigation, or at least an extra cursory glance.

"He's parking on the street," Thompson called out. "Looks like that Parker guy you met yesterday."

"Buzz him in," Holland said, dabbing a napkin over his chin and mouth while carrying his bowl to the sink. "And you're on KP duty today, Thompson."

Thompson made an exaggerated groan from the other room. "I don't even use the dishes here."

Delmonico grinned and looked up from his phone. "That's 'cause all you and Jacobsen ever eat is takeout shit. No wonder you're fat."

The three team members busied themselves with chores, phone games, and casually standing around as Parker reached the front door. Holland was there to greet him.

"Parker," he said as the man walked through the door.

"Holland. Good to see you."

"You look like shit. What's up?"

Parker glanced around the room, no doubt an old detective habit. Trying to see if anything felt out of place, missing or otherwise.

"*I* look like shit?" he asked, grinning. "You should see this place with fresh eyes. I thought yesterday was a fluke, but you guys actually live like this?"

Holland wanted to laugh, but he also didn't want to let his men see him with his guard down. "It's mostly Delmonico," he said. "Guy lives like a teenager."

"He *is* a teenager," Jacobsen hollered from the kitchen.

"I'm twenty-three," he answered.

"Come on in," Holland said, offering Jake a folding chair. "Come by for the gun?"

Jake nodded. "That and an update. Wanted to see if there was anything you needed help with, at least in the immediate future."

Holland chewed his lip for a moment, then shook his head. "Not sure there is, actually. El Gordo's on vacation, but there's really no sense plying him for more. He wasn't really in with anyone at Fitzsimmons, just a low-level accounts guy."

"What other leads do we have on this attack?" Jake asked.

"Nothing, really. When we found out about the attack, the other informants we were trying to work got spooked and disappeared. But listen—these attacks *always* turn up something. People talk, others gossip, eventually word gets out. We've gotten pretty good at tracking those voices back to their origin point now. And the chatter always increases right before the event. I'm hoping that in a couple of days we'll have some solid leads to track down. It sucks that El Gordo was the only reliable informant we had, but my guys are looking into a few other options. Thompson was the one who found the link to APHINT."

"The bismuth trioxide?"

Holland nodded. "Yeah, it's pretty much only manufactured by APHINT, so it's terribly difficult to track the exchange of it, since they've got their shipping manifests and inventory lists locked down tight. But it always pops up somewhere, and we can always determine its manufacturer then. Not much use for it as a trade export, so it was interesting to see it appearing in the explosives residue. Like a calling card."

"Why are they calling attention to themselves?"

"Well, it's terrorism, right? That's sort of the point. The Dominguez group wants some attention, and by linking the explosions they're behind, they can make sure anyone paying attention knows it was them."

"I don't get it," Jake said. "Why can't we just barge into wherever Dominguez' main office is? Whoever's running it—just show up and start arresting people?"

Jacobsen walked over and joined the conversation. "For starters, there *is* no 'main office.' It's organized crime, but it's not the Mafia. It's not like some crime family, all under one roof and running one large organization, easy to see and relatively easy to topple. We get bad intel, show up somewhere we're not supposed to be, and then Dominguez knows that we're looking for them and most likely where to find us too."

"*Someone* has to know who's running the show."

"Someone does," Holland said. "But it's not us. That's why you're here. If you know where to find them, tell me. We'll show up with the doorkickers and gunslingers."

"Right," Jake said. "I can work on that, sure. Tell me more about the companies. APHINT, Fitzsimmons. You said they were in a sort of stalemate?"

Holland moved his head from side to side. "Well, they're competitive with one another, but really the stalemate is with the United States government."

"How so?"

"The companies answer to the US government, by law," Jacobsen said. "But these terrorist attacks are becoming more and more frequent, and *all* the pharmaceuticals want them to stop."

"Because they're the targets?"

"Usually, yeah. And it's in the government's best interest to stop the attacks, but nothing's really been done."

"You're here," Jake said.

Jacobsen snorted. "Right. We're here. All five of us—six, including you. And McDonnell's got, what? Three more guys back in DC?"

"It's an intelligence-gathering assignment, Jacobsen," Holland said.

"Bullshit," the man responded. "If that was true, they never wouldn't sent us. They'd have sent in some black suits, high-tech agents."

"Still, we're just trying to figure it all out, provide some on-the-ground intel, pass it up the chain, that sort of thing."

"I got all that from McDonnell," Jake said. "And it makes sense. What I can't figure out though is why the US government isn't doing more to stop it. Why send only you guys if they *know* there's a problem down here, and they now know it's as big as a countrywide gang? No offense, but six guys against the Dominguez group? How's that supposed to work out?"

"Well, when McDonnell was given the assignment, we didn't know who Dominguez were. If anything, we just thought they were the grunts carrying out the orders of the *real* group behind everything, so we were sent out to check it out, poke around, and send reports. A small-time gang, trying to make a name for themselves by helping out the big terrorists. Then, we were told to do our best to prevent the attacks from even happening in the first place, and… well, here we are."

"And Fitzsimmons and the others are probably trying to throw their own resources at it as well," Jake added.

"No doubt," Holland said. "Charles Lafleur, the CEO of Fitzsimmons, has been working on the local politicians here, begging them for more support in Congress. He basically wants a standing army at the docks and around the island, to assert control and let him and the other pharmaceutical exporters operate in peace."

"The US can't afford that."

"They can, but they won't. It's just not *that* big a problem—not enough to establish that kind of permanent presence here. They see pharma's problems as isolated, industry-related nonsense. 'You make enough money to fix it yourself' sort of thing."

"But that will change if there's a bigger attack coming," Jake said. "Right?"

"Maybe," Holland said. "But that's not the point. The point is for there not to *be* another attack."

Delmonico, who had left the room a moment ago, returned and walked up to Jake and handed him the Beretta 92. "You don't need a lesson or anything like that, do you?"

Jake's head fell sideways and he simply stared at the younger man.

"Don't be an asshole, Delmonico," Holland said. He turned back to Jake. "What's on the agenda today?" he asked.

"Research," Jake asked. "I want to know every pharmaceutical company on the island, and everything they're involved with. Shipping dates, ports, all that. I'm assuming there will be overlap with your own information, but I want to start with a fresh set of eyes. I could use some help with any known associates—anyone on both payrolls, for example."

"I'll send what I've got, but it's not much. Anyone working for Dominguez keeps their name far away from pharma ledgers. That doesn't mean there aren't scores of people double-dipping, though, just that the gang's pretty careful."

"Understood," Jake said, tucking the pistol into his waistband. It was strange at first, putting a weapon back into his belt. And then a second passed and it seemed as natural as ever. He was a detective, and there was no question in his mind he was prepared for the job. "I'll head back to the hotel where I'll set up shop for the day. Send what you have, and I'll reach out if I need anything else."

They shook hands, and Holland watched the tall detective leave the house and return to his rental car.

Let's hope you're good at your job, Parker, he thought. *We could use the help.*

CHAPTER 23

The back windshield of Jake's SUV had been battered, but on closer inspection it was just a small spiderweb where the bat had connected. Holland's men hadn't seen it or they would have asked about it.

He pulled out his phone as he got settled in the car and pressed call on the number he'd saved, allowing the phone to route it through the Mercedes' speaker system.

"McDonnell," the voice on the other end said after two rings.

"Hey, buddy, it's Parker."

"How's the weather down there?"

"Sticky. Hey, I wanted to ask a favor?"

"Something Holland's guys can't do?" McDonnell asked.

"More like something I don't *want* them to do," Jake answered. "The gang—Dominguez—is carrying out the terrorist attacks, but they themselves aren't the actual terrorists, in my opinion. It's whoever's *hiring* them to do it. I don't think Dominguez has a good motive for these attacks, so they're obviously working for someone else. Either way, Dominguez is a big organization, and they've got threads everywhere on the island. I don't want to bring Holland's team any more scrutiny than necessary."

"Understood," McDonnell said. *"What can I do?"*

"I want to check out some local arrest records. Can you get those?"

There was a pause, then a shuffling sound and a click. When McDonnell's voice piped back through the car's stereo system it was boomier. *"Just put you on speaker. I've got Bolivar here too. I don't think this is much more complicated than looking something up in the phone book, but if it is, Bolivar will be able to do it."*

"Hey, Parker," Bolivar said.

Jake acknowledged the man's presence and pushed on. "I don't have names, unfortunately, but it's a relatively small island and I know the area the kids were picked up in. Fajardo, not far from the resort you have me staying in. Two males, one only a teenager, another one around early twenties. Nabbed on charges of petty theft."

Jake waited as McDonnell or Bolivar typed something.

"By the way," Jake continued, "the *resort* is a *bit* more than I was expecting. Especially since Holland's guys are holed up in a two-bedroom slum flat."

McDonnell laughed. *"Well, let's just say I felt like treating you a bit. You're doing us a huge favor. And I hear you're pretty much living in a slum flat in Hudson, anyway. You deserve a bit of an upgrade."*

"Well, I appreciate it, McDonnell," Jake said. "Anyway, what do you think? Are these kids findable?"

"Anyone's findable," Bolivar said. *"If they're in the system and there aren't a thousand others just like them, I'll pull them up. Might have to give you a list of multiple matches."*

"That's fine," said Jake. "I'm still working on buttering up Holland enough to let me into his inner circle. I've got plenty of other threads to pull to keep me busy."

"Sounds good," McDonnell said. *"We'll get on it—expect to hear from us within the hour."*

Jake confirmed, then hung up the call. He navigated toward the outdoor market he had seen advertised in the resort, finding that it was only ten minutes away. He wasn't interested in shopping, but he did want to pick up some essentials for his room: a better brand of coffee than what the hotel provided, a small bottle of whiskey or Puerto Rican rum, and a swimsuit. Jake hadn't planned on hitting the beach—it was a work trip, after all—but there was a nice hotel pool that would be perfect for some laps as an early-morning workout—assuming he could accomplish the task at hand, first.

Jake reached the marketplace and found a parking spot along the road. He got out and was just about to head toward the rows of small shops and large umbrellas when his phone rang.

It was McDonnell. "Hey," he said, answering the call. "That was fast."

"Bolivar's good, what can I say?"

"He already found something?"

"We think so. Easy enough to get access to the arrests database, but it was more difficult to wade through the petty crime records to find a match. Thankfully, again, Bolivar is good."

Jake heard the phone move through space. *"Hey Parker—Bolivar here—just set up a few GREP commands on the server, which pulled records for everything dated—"*

McDonnell interrupted the man, and Jake stifled a laugh. *"He doesn't care how you did it, Bolivar,"* McDonnell said, away from the mouthpiece. *"Anyway, Jake. I think we found your guys. They're the only ones who match all the criteria you gave with a low margin of error, but they were picked up with a* third *suspect as well."*

Jake gripped the phone tighter, recalling the kid he spoke to earlier. *Tres.* Not two, three. "Who's the third suspect?"

"We have no idea. Not even a name on this one, but he was brought in with the other two—a Miguel Reyes and his older brother Juan Reyes, Jr. all three on petty theft."

"Any other details?"

"Taken to the Caguas region, town of Juncos. I can probably get you the location where they were picked up, but it'll take some time."

"No, don't worry about it," Jake said. "Where are they now?"

There was a pause. *"That's just it, Parker,"* McDonnell said. *"Bolivar has the entire database table, and it's pretty much been* washed. *There's just the names, ages, time and date of arrest, a brief note that only lists petty theft as the charge, and then another marking. An asterisk, next to their names."*

"Doesn't say they transferred out?"

"Nothing. For all intents and purposes, they're still in the Caguas jail. Waiting on bail, I guess."

I doubt that, Jake thought. *Dominguez has most likely already gotten to them.* "Okay, great," he said. "Thanks a million. I'm going to reach out to a new friend I made here and see if we can't get some more information."

"You think it's a solid lead?" McDonnell asked.

"It's an interesting one."

"Right, sounds good," McDonnell said. *"Holland's on board by the way, he'll just take a minute to fully warm up to the idea of having a consultant along for the ride. Either way, he's not holding anything back from you—just trying to see how you two can play well together."*

"Well, if he drags his heels any longer, whatever event they're worried about in a couple of days is going to go off without a hitch for the bad guys."

"I know, and I'll talk to him if I need to. I think you just need to keep working the investigation from the point of view you're best at: the one no one else sees. If you're just following up on the same stuff Holland's already covered, you're a waste of resources."

Jake nodded. It made sense. "Got it. Thanks, McDonnell. I'll let you know how things progress."

"We're here if you need us."

The phone connection clicked off and Jake put it into his pocket, then headed toward the market.

CHAPTER 24

After visiting the marketplace and grabbing a handful of items for the hotel room, Jake had returned to the hotel to start doing research on the pharmaceutical firms on the island. With around 50 FDA-approved corporations and all the support infrastructure involved with them, pharmaceuticals were far and away Puerto Rico's number one export. Many of the conglomerates operated from more than one site on the island, and Fitzsimmons—the largest of them all—and APHINT even had a plant in the same region Jake's hotel was in. It made sense; part of the reason he had run into Vero was that she'd explained that her company was refinishing the barracks-like neighborhood in which many of its support staff lived.

The people who worked for the largest of the companies, like Vero, often chose to live in the fully furnished offerings built and owned by their employers. He'd read that the deal often extended to these workers was a decent one: free rent, some staples provided, in exchange for only a slightly reduced salary. While their take-home pay would be less, they would not have to use a sizable chunk of it to pay their rent or mortgage, nor would they have a utilities bill.

The company, for their part, could save money on the salaries, and since their offices and industrial complexes required the power intake of a small city, they found it easier to essentially operate as one.

Jake was fascinated by this concept, but he wasn't interested in moving to Puerto Rico and getting a job at a pharmaceutical company. He had a job to do. And this job, unlike all the others, was personal. With any luck, by the end of it, he could have more information about the person who was responsible for Mel's death.

By late-afternoon, he was hungry, and he wanted to see if there was anything new Luis Quintanilla might be able to find about the two—now three—arrests he had asked about yesterday.

Jake munched on a protein bar and some beef jerky as he drove in the direction of Luis Quintanilla's department office once again. He knew Luis was scheduled to work until that afternoon, but he wasn't sure what time. He wanted to be there when the man came off the clock.

He arrived at the station just as Luis got off his final shift, at 6 p.m. on the nose. Luis hadn't expected Jake to be waiting there in the street, judging by the look on his face, but he motioned for Jake to follow him around the side of the building.

Jake slowly pulled the Mercedes into the lot, where Officer Quintanilla's squad car was parked. Instead of asking Jake to get out of his own vehicle, Luis surprised him by pulling the passenger door open and getting in next to him.

"Mr. Parker," Luis said.

"Hey, Luis." Jake smiled. "I'm assuming you want me to buy you dinner?"

Luis sniffed as he buckled his seatbelt. "My wife is out of town. I am a shitty cook, and I know you have a meal budget."

Jake cocked an eyebrow.

"You are an American consultant, no?"

Jake laughed. "Fine. Yes, I've got a meal budget."

Luis nodded. "*Also*, I believe I have some information. Potentially a location."

"Spill it."

"First, food."

Jake tried not to appear frustrated. He had no problem buying dinner, but he wanted to know what this man knew. Instead, he turned to Luis and met his eyes. "I'll make you a deal: I buy, but it's takeout. We eat in the car, and you tell me what this location is and what it's all about."

Luis paused for a moment and Jake feared he was going to try to negotiate. Instead, his grin widened and he pointed to the left side of the parking lot. "Leave through that exit. There is a tapas restaurant that has to-go. Have you had *tostones?*"

Jake shook his head as he put the car into drive and made for the exit.

"You will not be sorry. They are like the Puerto Rican French fry."

"I'm a fan of French fries," Jake said.

He allowed Luis to navigate him to the restaurant, where they sat in a short line around the building and ordered their food. In short order, Jake found a Styrofoam container on his lap that smelled amazing, and inside it a mound of food—something called *pernil*, set atop a precarious mound of rice—that looked even more appetizing. He pulled into a parking spot, hoping to eat a few bites and get Luis to tell him what he knew.

"How about that location?" he asked, as soon as he switched off the engine. "What did you find?"

Luis swallowed his own bite and looked out the front windshield. "Mr. Parker," he started.

"Jake, please," Jake said.

"Yes, of course. Mr. Jake, I was able to get the arrest records and find the two men's names. As I told you, they have been removed from the system—there is nothing but their names, a quick notation, and not much else."

Jake knew this of course, but he nodded along.

"But I found something interesting. Instead of two young men, there were *three.*"

Jake looked over at Luis, again feigning ignorance. "Three?"

"Sí. I believe they are all somehow related to Dominguez, but it is impossible to tell just from the records. The third man was arrested for the same charges—it seems he simply had the same notations next to his name in the database."

"So we're not any further along than yesterday?" Jake asked, through another bite of roasted pork. It tasted like lightly smoked pulled pork, but it was served in its pre-pulled format.

"Well, I was alone most of the day. There was little to do, so I decided to check the recordings for the arrest."

Of course, Jake thought. *How did I forget about that?*

In the United States, when he'd served as a police officer and detective, most of the officers wore body cameras that recorded their every move. In recent years—after he'd left the force—many departments had mandated that these cameras be constantly recording, each video file uploaded to a central database. Even if someone wanted the evidence to go missing, they would have to work through a maze of digital encryption—it was not as simple these days as walking into a computer room and finding a tape labeled with the date of the activity.

Luis continued. "I found it. The video is difficult to see—it was dark—but there is a license plate, clearly in view. All three were in the vehicle together."

At this, Jake couldn't hide his interest. There was nothing to fake: this was all new information to him.

"I was able to view the plate well enough to run a trace on it, and I found out that it is owned by a gentleman who also owns a tract of land just outside El Yunque."

"El Yunque?" Jake asked. He recalled the kid's statement from earlier, after he had pressed him a bit.

Three. El Yunque, like the others.

Luis nodded his head profusely. "Sí, sí. It is our national forest, on the northeast corner of the island. The land this person owns is well-known by my department as *Campo de Almas*."

Jake frowned.

"The *Field of Souls*, Mr. Jake. It is Dominguez territory."

Jake felt his blood run cold. He swallowed, but there was no food in his mouth. He felt the tingling in his fingertips, on the back of his neck. The feeling he knew well—a case thread was revealing itself, and all he had to do was tug it just a bit…

"So we're heading toward El Yunque, Luis?" Jake asked, eyeing the officer in his peripheral vision.

"Sí, yes. Mr. Jake, I believe the answers you are looking for may be found in Campo de Almas."

CHAPTER 25

El Yunque National Forest sat near the northern tip of Puerto Rico on the Eastern side of the island.

The land Jake and Luis were aiming toward was just between the outskirts of the town Jake was staying in and the national forest.

They drove through the town of Ramos and parked at a neighborhood park around a mile from the entrance to Campo de Almas. Together, the pair made their way to the dirt road that snaked uphill toward a lush rainforest valley.

The sky was beginning to darken, long streaks of orange interspersed with purple and a hazy blue where the sunlight still fought for control. It would be only an hour before the densely forested area they were heading into was completely dark, and Jake hoped there was at least a bit of moonlight to guide the way.

The humidity in this area of the island—only twenty miles west of the resort—was unbelievably high as they took the uphill path, and the afternoon heat hadn't yet started to dissipate. Jake wiped at his brow just as Luis pointed.

"That hill marks the edge of the Campo de Almas."

"You've been here before?" Jake asked.

He shook his head. "No, but everyone knows of it. There is dense rainforest everywhere that makes it impossible to see through, and some people have been caught inside, wandering around for days until the heat or starvation gets them."

Jake frowned. "Is that another myth?"

Luis shrugged. "I do not know anyone who comes here on purpose," he said. "Even I am a police officer, and I am afraid to come here."

"It's private property," Jake said. "Why would anyone come here?"

"It is beautiful land," Luis answered. "And the nature here is attractive. Because it is on the edge of the forest, many tourists believe it is simply part of El Yunque."

Jake thought of the hard lump of metal shoved beneath his belt. "Are you armed, Luis?"

Luis glanced at him from the corner of his eye. "Sí, of course." He didn't ask Jake the same question, and Jake didn't offer an answer. *Better for him to assume he's the one protecting both of us,* he thought.

They walked side by side up the hill and onto the edge of the ridge that formed the bowl. Jake could see the lip of the bowl curving around on his right and left, though the right side seemed to flatten out a bit before it completely disappeared in the thick flora, about a hundred feet away.

"Who owns the land?" Jake asked, his voice a mere whisper. "You said he was a 'gentleman,' but also related to the Dominguez?"

"Sí, yes. He is a local businessman, but it is well-known that he is part of the Dominguez. I am not sure exactly what his role is, but with an estate such as this, he is probably not a part-time drug dealer."

Jake looked around at the land. It was beautiful, but mostly unusable in the shape it was in. Leaves, grasses, ferns, and thousands of other species of bush and tree surrounded him, covering the forest floor in a tight web of green and brown. The dirt path itself was merely two flattened, pressed lines of growth that were barely marking the way ahead.

For an "estate," Jake hadn't seen anything yet worthy of the title.

"Is there any security?" Jake asked.

Luis shook his head. "No, not out here. There are likely cameras close to the house, and guards may be patrolling, but it would not be necessary to have them walking around out here. We are not going toward the house, anyway."

"We're not?"

"There is a shack on this land, Mr. Jake. It is large—visible from the satellite images—and the road looks well used. I think that is where we are most likely to find the young men."

Jake nodded, a lump forming in his throat. Luis hadn't said that they would find the *bodies* of the young men there, so Jake had to be optimistic that they might still be alive. He hadn't known the kids, but he hoped they would find them, and, if possible, rescue them from the clutches of Dominguez.

If the man who owned this land had somehow offered a space to the Dominguez gang to act as some sort of makeshift prison compound for the people they wanted "out of the system," then that person would be every bit as guilty as the ones who were actually committing the crimes.

And if the kids *had* been taken here, why? What was it about them that had raised a red flag? Why did the Dominguez want them silenced? Especially if the young men were part of the gang?

"Luis," Jake whispered. "Why are you helping me? If you've never been here before, why are you coming now?"

Luis stopped walking and looked at Jake. "Mr. Jake, I am a good police officer. There are those who are corrupt, and I suppose we are all corrupted in our own ways. But I have lived in Puerto Rico my entire life, and I have seen it in its good times, as well as its bad. Now, at this time, it is bad. I want to fix it, and I believe you are hoping to fix it as well."

"But you don't even know who I—"

"You are Jake Parker. That is just a name, but I always try to find out more about the person I am working with. As I said, I am a good police officer. Your name was easy to find. You were Boston PD, and Army before that."

Jake looked toward a mounded spot of earth in the distance, nodding. "So you found out a bit of my history?"

"Of course. And it is good history, Mr. Jake. It makes you who you are, and who you are is a good man. You want what I want, even though you are not from here. We both want to find answers, and we both want to make this place a little better."

Jake thought about this for a second, and then nodded once again. "Okay, I buy that. You have my word that I've got your back. I *do* want answers, and I *do* want to leave this place a little better than when I found it, however I can."

Luis stuck his hand out and they shook. "Then we are agreed, Mr. Jake. I have your back, you have mine."

Jake smiled, they continued walking, and the dying light poking through the rainforest canopy began casting long shadows in every direction. He felt a slight cooling breeze push against his damp T-shirt. He also noticed something else quite peculiar. In every other place he'd been on the island, outside of the city, he'd been able to easily hear the sounds of nature. Coqui frogs croaking their incessant melody, crickets and insects screaming at one another as they buzzed around looking for food, and plenty of birds. Here, however, there was no noise but the trees and wind. No frogs, no bugs, no birds.

The Campo de Almas seemed to be devoid of life.

CHAPTER 26

Cecil Romero held the phone up to his ear, waiting for the connection. He paced silently back and forth in front of the Fitzsimmons building, his second day on the job completed. He was tired, sore, and ready to give up mailroom work forever.

He'd been told his reassignment would run for another six weeks so as not to attract unwarranted attention to himself. It seemed like overkill to him, but Cecil was not about to defy the orders of Mr. Diego or Dominguez. He would keep his head down, act as though he enjoyed the mailroom job, and wait for his next reassignment.

But it appeared as though his task here was nearly complete. Just as Mr. Diego had predicted, a letter came through the mailroom early that morning. As the Dominguez man who worked next to him had instructed, the letter was passed directly into Cecil's hands. He'd nearly missed it as it passed by him on the rollers, but he'd grabbed it at the last moment and tossed it into his bin for "sorting."

When there was a break, Cecil had brought the letter to the corner area out of sight from the security cameras, prepared and eager to see what the letter held. He'd opened the letter carefully, just as he had been taught, and pulled out the goods inside.

The phone at his ear connected. *"Mr. Romero?"*

"Sí," he responded.

"You have the information?"

"I do," he replied in Spanish. "Are you ready?"

The voice on the other end confirmed, and Cecil heard a crackling as the phone moved. Probably grabbing a pen and something to write with.

"Okay," Cecil continued. "The FDA representative will be here in two days, aboard the US Coast Guard vessel docking in Fitzsimmons' entry point at 10:45 a.m."

"Which dock is that?"

"The letter does not say."

"Noted. Go on."

"The representative is listed as a 'systems and deployment security analyst,' but there is no name."

"That is fine," the person said. *"They often do not know who is available before the ship leaves the harbor."*

"Wouldn't a plane be faster?" Cecil asked.

"Yes, but there is far less regulation and red tape required this way, and it gives them a way to verify the pharmaceutical companies' shipping methods firsthand."

"I see. Anything else you need?"

"No. Thank you for your service to Dominguez."

And the voice hung up.

Cecil looked down at the phone after the call disconnected, wondering what it all meant. Surely the FDA person was important, or Dominguez would not be so interested in their arrival. Perhaps they were marked for a hit?

He had heard of those things, and he knew that there were others—guided by more violent delights than he—in Dominguez who thrived on that sort of thing. Lately, the gang had been operating in a much less subtle way, causing explosions and deaths and kidnappings that were only vaguely denied.

He wondered if Dominguez wanted to kill this representative from the FDA for some reason—if that would advance their goals somehow? But then, if they were interested in taking out this specific person, why did it not matter that they still did not have the person's name? If the FDA was sending a junior-level analyst instead of a high-ranking official, would that matter? Would the Dominguez plan be scrapped?

These were all questions he didn't have answers to, and they were all questions he would likely *never* know the answers to. He had been given a task, a reassignment, and he had completed the most important part of it. Now it was time to wait. To lay low, to pretend like he was just another cog in the wheel, sorting mail and placing it into bins for delivery throughout the company, because it was his job.

He pushed away the feelings of failure. This wasn't failure, nor was it a step backward. He wanted more power, and he felt as though he may have been on the cusp of that back in the States. Now, he was flinging mail around a mailroom and would be doing exactly that for the next six weeks.

It was mind-numbingly boring work, but perhaps that was part of the reason they had chosen him? Perhaps Mr. Diego didn't want just an intelligent, driven, entrepreneurial candidate for this reassignment—perhaps he wanted someone who could prove their loyalty by bringing themselves down to the lowest levels. Someone who could perform admirably, even in the dregs of a thankless, invisible position.

He would do that job, and he would do it correctly.

But he was also curious, and now that the wheel in which he was just a cog seemed to be moving, picking up speed, he was growing more and more interested in Dominguez's play. He didn't know who had been on the opposite end of the phone today, but it didn't matter. He knew someone important was going to be arriving on his island tomorrow morning, and what time they would arrive. He also knew generally where they would be, and he wanted to be there to see things with his own eyes, whatever it may be.

As it happened, he was starting third shift tomorrow—beginning after lunch, and working through part of the night. That meant he was off until 1 p.m.

Plenty of time to get to San Juan and back.

Finally content, Cecil stowed the phone and waited for the next driver in the line. He needed to get some food in him, and then some rest.

Tomorrow might turn out to be an exciting day.

CHAPTER 27

Jake and Luis reached the mounded area of forest floor Jake had seen from afar. From its perch, they could see smaller mounds around the area, lifting the otherwise flattened valley floor in a pockmarked, bubbled way.

Luis pointed to the southeast. "Over there is the estate. You cannot see from here, but there are multiple buildings I saw on the satellite. One large house, another smaller one, and what appears to be a cabana or pool house."

"So stay away from there," Jake muttered. He had no interest in a thirty-on-two standoff, and even if the odds weren't that bad, he didn't want to be caught by any heavily armed security.

"We should move this way," Luis said, taking a step off the mound, toward a break between a copse of trees. "I believe the building we are looking for is marked on the map. It is from the old days, during the Spanish settlements. Stone, originally."

"Right," Jake said. He wiped his brow and followed behind Luis as he headed downward. Jake's second step caught beneath a softened section of moist dirt, and he nearly tripped.

He cursed under his breath, then looked down.

The land where his foot had been a moment ago had caved in a bit, turning inward and forming a shallow hole.

He stopped, turning around and crouching down.

Luis looked over his shoulder. "What is it?" he asked.

"I don't know," Jake responded, keeping his voice low. He wasn't sure why his subconscious had pulled his attention downward, but he knew from experience not to question it. "The ground here has given way a little."

"Probably a small sinkhole beneath the mound," Luis said. "They are common on the island."

Jake was only half-listening, moving the dirt around with his hands, digging into the earth. "No," he said. "It's not a sinkhole, but almost like a layer of dirt—" He stopped, feeling tightness in his chest. He pulled a dirt-covered hand back, smelling the loamy soil and…

Luis suddenly stumbled backward, and Jake rocked on his heels, only staying upright thanks to the hand still inside the hole. A wave of nauseating fumes hit him in the face, as though someone had slapped him with it.

"My God," Jake whispered. "What the *hell* is that smell?"

He used his free hand to pull his shirt up over his nose, still working on something from under the dirt. Finally, recovering a bit from the smell, he yanked his other hand back.

With it came a shoe.

Jake was now holding a medium-sized tennis shoe, dirty and soiled but otherwise in good condition. He wanted to drop it, to throw it even. To turn around and run, to get away as fast as his legs could carry him.

No. He took a breath, held it. *I've got a job to do.*

He held up the shoe, examining it. He recognized the brand.

Luis had his phone out, the flashlight on and pointed down toward the shoe. Together, they peered at it until Jake had the courage to face his new partner.

"Luis, I think we need to look inside the hole."

Luis only nodded, once. He swallowed, then took a breath through his mouth and held it, all while pushing the flashlight's beam closer to the edge of the small hole. He held the light as steady as possible while Jake allowed himself to sink farther to the dirt, now on his hands and knees. He didn't want to do it, but he needed to know.

Jake cocked his head sideways and peered down into the opening.

What he saw nearly caused him to look away.

"What is it?" Luis asked.

Jake didn't answer—he didn't have to. Luis Quintanilla was a police officer, active duty. He had seen this sort of thing before, and likely much worse.

It was a leg—a human leg, poking out from beneath the mound of dirt. The foot, now naked, was still surrounded by the loose dirt Jake had freed while trying to get at the shoe. While he had been working, he hadn't wanted to admit what he feared: that he was pulling at a human corpse.

He stood up. "I can't see anything else. Just a leg."

Luis nodded.

"That's the cause of the smell, as well. My guess is there's a whole body down there."

Again, Luis nodded.

"And this is not just a natural formation, Luis." Jake kept his voice steady. "We were standing on a gravesite."

Luis bit his lip, then looked away, his brow furrowing. "Not just one."

The sentence was quiet, but Jake heard it clearly. This mound was far larger than a single body. The shoe and leg he'd inadvertently uncovered was likely not the only shoe and leg beneath this pile of dirt. And Luis had implied what Jake knew to be true: that the other mounds, the smaller bubbles over the landscape, as far as he could see in this direction, were one and the same. They were burial sites.

All full of the bodies of murdered Dominguez victims. And, with a sinking heart, Jake realized the boys they were looking for were amongst them.

He was about to comment that they needed to leave, to get out of here and figure out how to find help they could trust, but before he could speak, he heard a voice.

He looked at Luis.

Another voice—this one a shout, from the direction of the estate.

Luis' eyes widened. He turned to Jake and spoke.

"Mr. Jake, they are coming."

CHAPTER 28

The noise grew to a cacophonous roar as more shouts joined the mix. Above the voices, Jake heard the sound of a revving engine. It sounded like a four-wheeler, one of the small two-man recreational all-terrain vehicles.

"Who's coming?" Jake asked, addressing Luis. "Dominguez?"

Luis nodded rapidly, simultaneously pulling out his pistol from behind his belt, and Jake recognized it immediately as the common police-issued Smith & Wesson M&P. "Come on," Luis said. "Just by being here you are an enemy of Dominguez. And they will hunt us, especially since we are sneaking around on their land."

Jake inadvertently followed suit, lifting up the back of his shirt and grabbing the Beretta he'd tucked there. Luis looked at him, then down at his weapon, then back up to meet Jake's eyes. Neither man spoke. Jake didn't feel that it was an appropriate time to explain himself, but he also knew that Luis hadn't specifically asked him earlier if he was armed. By now, hopefully, the officer trusted him enough to want his support.

"What's the plan?" Jake asked. "I'm assuming we can't just start shooting these guys, but there's no way I'm going to let them capture us, either."

Luis didn't answer at first, instead moving sideways to hide behind a small copse of trees near a few of the burial mounds.

Jake felt disgust as he saw the mounds outlined in the moonlight, knowing that beneath the dirt there were dozens—potentially hundreds—of dead bodies. The remains of human beings.

But he couldn't dwell on the thought of it right now. The weight of sadness he had felt moments before had almost completely been replaced by the adrenaline-fueled fear of knowing his life was in danger.

He took a few steps toward Luis, bunching his free hand into a fist and squeezing—an old trick to help calm his nerves. *Think, Jake*, he thought. *You've been trained for this.*

But trained or not, it had been years since he had been on active duty, and the only excitement he'd seen in the last few months had been a scuffle with two bodyguards who had wanted to make sure he didn't leave a building alive. Shots had been fired, but he'd held his own. He had made it out unscathed, but he had also made a mental note to not make that type of excitement a habit.

And yet, somehow, he now found himself in the thick of a Puerto Rican rainforest, gearing up for an altercation with men who were most likely equally armed. And this fight was not going to be as fairly balanced—instead of the two-on-one situation a few months ago, they were dealing with an unknown number of assailants, and he wasn't sure how well Luis would handle himself.

"I'm going to move to those mounds to our right," Jake said to Luis. "If I can get behind some trees and still have a clear shot, it might give us a way to flank them if they all come from the road."

Luis nodded silently, still watching the two lines of bent grass that formed the road.

The whine of the engine was joined by another from a different direction. Jake turned to his right and noticed that there was at least one more ATV coming from that side of the valley. He suddenly realized that they were going to be far outmatched, even undercover and using the dark to their advantage—and they certainly weren't going to be able to outrun the ATVs.

He ran back over to Luis' spot. "This isn't going to work, Luis." Jake felt his heart rate accelerating, but he was keeping his breathing in check. He wasn't sure how much of this sort of thing Luis had experienced in his time as a police officer, but Jake didn't want to find out the hard way if this was his first firefight. "There are too many of them. I heard another ATV coming from the southwest. We need to get back to the car. If we can stay behind the trees—"

Before he could finish the sentence, the whizz of a bullet came zipping past his head, making a smacking sound as it impacted through leaves and branches.

"Shit," he said. Jake fell to his knees next to the roots of the trees. "Someone's already here," Jake said. "You start heading back toward the car and I'll cover us."

Luis was shaking his head. "No, Mr. Jake. Let me stay here and—"

"I'm not asking, Luis. You know as well as I do these guys aren't messing around. Start moving toward the car. I'm going to swing around and see if they are all on the road or some are in the trees."

Finally, Luis complied. He stood up, his back to the tree, his gun in both hands, holding it pointed outward and upward. He risked a look over his shoulder, around the side of the stand of trees, just as another bullet whizzed by.

This one smacked into the trunk of a tree just behind Jake. Luis yanked his head back.

Jake eyed the officer. "It doesn't sound like they've got much more than pistols either, so as long as they're coming one at a time, I think I can take at least a few of them out. But we still need to move back. I'm not interested in an all-out battle royal with these guys."

Luis agreed, then crouched and ran back toward the tree the last round had landed in, ducking and crawling behind it before popping his head out once more.

Jake silently counted to three, then dove to his left and side-stepped, his front facing the road, his feet shoulder-width apart.

A dark figure was making its way up the path, and Jake could clearly see the outline of a large pistol in the man's hands. Jake lifted his own weapon and waited for another second. So far, it didn't appear that the man had seen him, as he was moving one step at a time down the path but looking in the wrong direction.

It wasn't Jake's favorite thing to do to shoot at dark silhouettes, but shots had already been fired and he could see the man's weapon held aloft. This was a combatant, plain and simple.

Here goes nothing, Jake thought. He brought the pistol up as the scream of ATV engines grew louder.

From his left, somewhere in the forest, he heard the shouts of two more men working their way to the road.

He lined up the shot, steadied his aim, and pulled the trigger.

CHAPTER 29

Crack!

A deafening explosion from directly behind him caused Jake's ears to ring. The silhouette in front of him on the path froze in place, then slid sideways and fell to the ground, shifting and trying to crawl to cover. Another shot rang out from Luis' pistol and the man stopped moving completely.

He couldn't see the others, so Jake took the opportunity to duck down and double back around Luis' position, trying to pace his way back to the parking lot at the end of the road, near the playground. It would take a while moving this slowly, but they needed to make sure they were retreating while covering their steps. The gang members to their left were now at the edge of the forest where it met the road, and Jake could see the first man's silhouette, blanketed by moonlight. They were both wearing T-shirts, shorts and boots. Both were carrying pistols.

And, it appeared, both had seen Luis and were homing in on his location.

"Luis!" Jake shouted, trying to get the man's attention. "There, to your left!"

But Jake knew Luis hadn't seen them. He brought his own pistol up and began to swing it around toward the two newcomers. The sound of the ATVs grew louder, and he saw the shadow of one barreling over the flattened grass path.

He lined up the shot once again, but his aim was off. His first two rounds sailed through the air and ended up flying harmlessly right between both of the men, landing somewhere in the forest behind them. One of the men shifted and recognized the new attacker, but the other man had already fired toward Luis.

Jake heard the impact as it landed in Luis's side. He wondered if the officer had been wearing a vest, but the next sound gave him his answer.

Luis let out a yelp of pain and stumbled backwards, right into the line of fire. The second man's volley was three quick shots.

Two of them hit Luis in his chest, killing him instantly.

No. Jake hadn't intended for this to happen. He had wanted to do this alone. He'd needed Luis' help earlier, but he wished the man would have stayed in the car. He never wanted anyone, especially someone like Luis—an innocent man—in the line of fire.

Wide-eyed, Jake stumbled backwards once again and sought cover behind another tree. He still had the second man in his sights, and he pulled the trigger three times in rapid succession. The man fell, his cohort surprised by the sudden counterattack. His hesitation gave Jake just enough time to line up another round.

He was about to fire when a new sound entered the mix: the unmistakable rhythmic pounding of a submachine gun. The branches and leaves above his head were immediately disintegrated, pieces of green flesh falling around him. Jake crouched lower and saw the first ATV rounding the curve and bearing down on his location, about a hundred yards away.

Time to go, Jake thought. He wanted to check Luis for any signs of life, but he knew there was absolutely nothing he would be able to do for the man. He couldn't afford the extra weight, and he was positive the man was already dead.

Jake turned, hoping the ATV driver hadn't seen him yet, and ran. He had twenty yards before reaching the top of the road, where he would be in the open and most vulnerable. He closed the distance in five seconds, crouching at the very top as another volley from the submachine gun pockmarked the dirt around him. One round glanced off the side of his shorts.

Jake lost all sense of composure, his arms flailing wildly and his legs pumping faster than they had ever gone as he made for the parking lot at the end of the road. His heart was pounding as he heard the engines of both ATVs throttled to the max and knew it was going to be a close call. When he realized the ATVs were just about cresting the hill behind him, he knew it was going to be *too* close. They would overtake him with fifty yards remaining. He would be gunned down without a chance to defend himself.

And that wasn't an option. Instead, Jake opted for a different tactic. He suddenly dove sideways, darting into the forest and trying to get as low as possible. He was immediately tangled in the vines and roots, the thick, large leaves easily covering his prone shape on the forest floor. Jake shifted around and faced the road, coming to a stop just as the first ATV crested and began its descent from the top of the hill.

It picked up speed as it flew down the hill, and the second ATV was only about twenty feet behind it. Both vehicles blasted past his position, heading toward the end of the path.

Jake knew he couldn't stay out here all night—the men would eventually get flashlights and begin scouring the forest. He also knew that they had somehow been alerted to his and Luis' position earlier, and he wondered if there were security cameras mounted and hidden in the trees to guard this area from intruders.

The second of the pair who had shot down Luis appeared at the top of the rise, jogging behind the ATVs. Jake perked his ears up and focused on the man's progress, his body coiled in preparation. Just as he passed Jake's position, Jake shot upward from the earth and aimed for the man's back.

He didn't have time to get around to the man's front or side— the shot would alert the others to his position, anyway. He had never liked the idea of shooting someone in the back, but this wasn't a fair fight. It never had been, and he had the dead body of a police officer—and hundreds of other innocent victims lying beneath the dirt nearby—to prove it.

The three rounds landed, forming a triangle on the man's upper torso, and he stumbled forward and landed face-down on the path.

Jake was about to continue toward the parking lot, hoping that the men in the ATVs had veered off, following one of the side trails, and wouldn't notice the Mercedes parked a mile away from the entrance to the property. Before he took two steps, he stopped.

Might as well make it difficult for them, he thought. He leaned down and grabbed the dead gang member's legs and dragged him off the path and as far into the forest as he could manage. There, he made sure the body was completely covered by leaves and branches, then he checked there were no visible signs of blood or scuffling between the corpse and where it had landed on the path.

Satisfied with his handiwork, Jake started jogging to the end of the road. The ATV engines were still driving around in the distance, but it sounded as though they had left the property and taken a sharp right, heading east back up the road.

It took Jake another ten minutes to reach the car, and he allowed himself three seconds of relief when he got inside and turned on the engine.

He kept the headlights off and slowly navigated around the parking lot, finally finding the second exit that led west, away from the ATVs.

On an open road, the smaller vehicles would have no chance of catching up with him, but out here on these side roads and in the narrow roads of the neighborhoods, Jake wouldn't be able to get enough speed to get distance between him and his pursuers.

He snaked around the neighborhood, keeping the lights off, until he found a larger street that looked like it might head toward a highway. Once he was on that road, he turned on the GPS and the headlights.

And only then did he allow himself to finally breathe normally.

CHAPTER 30

Jake got out of the shower and toweled off, his hair requiring a bit more effort. It had grown longer over the past few months, since he had no day job and no boss or coworkers to measure up against. Military haircuts had been easy and quick, but then trying to shave his head on his own had become difficult. Lately he had taken to letting his hair grow out for about three months between cuts, the curly tips of his brownish blonde hair nearly touching the tops of his ears—a fact that would drive his father nuts.

Jake examined his hair once again and almost wished it were longer. Something about this petty, secretive way of lashing out against his old man gave him a bit of joy. His father was a cold, hardened Marine colonel who had effectively shut down after his wife—Jake's mother—passed away when Jake was twelve.

They had never resolved their differences, and Jake mostly blamed himself for it. It was far too late to make amends; his father would never change.

He finished drying his tousled hair and body and strode through the hotel room to his suitcase to pluck out some fresh clothes—another pair of shorts and boxer briefs and another T-shirt.

The sight of Luis falling seemed to be all he could think about. He had to understand what the burial site they had found meant. Luis had paid for the knowledge, and Jake had to figure out how it fitted in to the puzzle. If the boys had been murdered, why?

Jake was massaging his temples when he heard a rap on the door. He frowned, then walked over to it and peered through the hole. He had left the pistol locked inside his Mercedes in the hotel's parking garage, wanting it safely hidden and ready to go in the car in case he needed to get somewhere quickly, so he had nothing to arm himself with.

As it turned out, alarm was unnecessary. The person standing on the other side of the door was hotel staff, dressed in the garb of the bellhop crew—white long-sleeved tuxedo shirt and khaki pants. The man also wore a massive smile as Jake pulled the door open.

"Holá. I apologize for the intrusion, sir. You have a message."

"A message?" Jake asked.

"Sí, Señor." The man thrust his hand out and gave Jake a small piece of paper, on which was scribbled a single sentence.

Meet me at the restaurant.

Beneath the sentence the note was signed with a V.

Vero.

The woman had requested Jacob's presence at the restaurant once again. While he appreciated the sentiment and was even a bit flattered at the realization that she might have a thing for him, he also knew that he didn't have time to be traipsing around the island with a woman on his arm. He was here on business, and he had already excused himself out of a couple of hours of work in order to dine with the beautiful Puerto Rican yesterday.

And he was still reeling from Luis Quintanilla's death, and what he had seen out in the rainforest.

The bellhop's smiled faltered as he stood in the doorway, waiting. "Is there anything you would like me to do, sir?" the man asked. "A response to leave at the front desk, perhaps?"

Jake shook his head. "No, thank you. This will be all."

The man nodded and then walked down the hallway toward the elevator.

Jake returned to his room and let the door close behind him, wondering what the right move would be. Last night, Vero had commandeered him to the restaurant, where they had enjoyed a delicious meal and drinks together. It was possible that was all she wanted now—to enjoy an evening with someone her age whom she thought might be single, just for the fun of it.

But there was something else, something nagging at him: why would she tell him to meet her there *now*? Why wouldn't she give him a time? If she had just wanted a date, wouldn't she have phrased the invitation differently? And, why hadn't she just waited to find him in the lobby? Why the covert note?

It was all a bit strange, and Jake had seen enough strange things in the past twenty-four hours to wonder if there was, in fact, something more to this request than the note let on.

He took a deep breath, pressing his T-shirt down over his chest to smooth out the wrinkles that had formed in the suitcase, and then gave himself a cursory glance in the mirror.

I guess it's a date then, he thought. *Let's hope there's not more to it than that, Vero.*

Jake walked over to the restaurant on foot, just like they had done together the previous night. He found Vero at the same table they'd sat at before, a bottle of tequila, unopened, sitting next to her on the edge of the table.

She looked stunning. A floral dress with massive hibiscus flowers decorated her body, pinks and yellows and blues and greens all swirling together in a mess of a design that only someone like her could make sense of.

She was looking down at the table when he walked in, but her eyes rose to fall on Jake as he stepped closer to the table. She smiled, but it was not as wide and carefree as it had been when he'd first met her.

"Jake," she said. "I am glad you got my message, and I am glad you are here."

CHAPTER 31

Jake swung into the booth and then sat down, eyeing the unopened bottle of tequila and then trying to read Vero's face. "Is everything all right? Your note seemed... abrupt."

She hesitated, swallowed and then picked up the bottle of tequila. "I ordered nachos. I hope you like nachos. Would you like a drink?" she asked.

Jake shook his head. "Sorry, got a lot on my mind. I'm not sure it's a good idea tonight. Nachos are fine, though. Thank you."

She didn't respond to this other than nodding quickly and placing the tequila on the far edge of the table, a clear sign to the waitstaff that they were not going to be indulging tonight.

And a clear sign to Jake that something was amiss.

"Vero, I don't really know you very well. So if there's something you need, I'm not sure I'm—"

"You are American," she said.

Jake's mouth moved, but no words came out.

"You are with the Americans?"

Jake's eyes swirled around, widening and narrowing as he tried to understand her meaning. "Yes, I *am* American, but I don't know who it is you think I am with."

"I have heard that there are Americans here, investigating my company."

It was stated as a fact, not a question. Jake wasn't sure what to do with the information other than see if he could get more of it. "Vero, I don't know what you're talking about. Your company—

Allied Pharmaceuticals International—APHINT, right? Why are they being investigated? And why do you think I am the one investigating them?"

Vero paused, clicking her fingernails on the top of the table as she examined them. She spoke down toward the table. "I am sorry, I do not mean to sound accusatory. It's just that…"

Jake suddenly felt the urge to reach out and grab her hand, to try to console her and tell her it was going to be okay.

Don't be insane, he thought. *You don't know this woman. You have no reason to act any differently toward her than any other acquaintance.*

He cleared his throat. "Vero, look at me. You can trust me. My name's Jake Parker, and that's it. I am *not* here investigating your company, or any other company."

It was the truth, albeit just a small portion of it. He was technically *not* investigating her company or any other pharmaceutical company, at least not directly. His mission parameters were slightly different. He didn't know this woman, and therefore had no reason to feel the need to explain all of that to her right now.

She nodded, then looked up at him. Her face was mostly unreadable, save for a small crease of concern around her eyes. He wasn't sure if she would trust his answer, but it didn't matter—he wasn't about to offer more than was absolutely necessary.

"Okay, yes," she said. "You are who you say you are, Jake Parker. May I be honest with you, Jake?"

"Please."

"While I am who I say I am as well—a chemist from APHINT—I have been wanting to talk to someone I can trust."

"And you trust me?"

"You are the only person I have seen who is not a tourist and is not from the island. I don't trust you. But I have no reason not to trust you."

"But less than a minute ago you thought I was part of a group of Americans who were sent here to investigate your company?"

She nodded. "If you are not part of that group, then I will merely be telling you a story to get it off my chest. If it *is* true, and you are in fact here for that purpose, then it is even more crucial you know."

Jake suddenly took a breath through his nose and held it for a few seconds. *This night is getting more and more complicated,* he thought. "Okay, I'll bite. I like good stories."

Vero turned her hands up and set them on the table as she began. "As I said, I am a chemist. My job is to research amalgams and potential combinations of chemicals for our development departments. I am very good at my job, so there are not a lot of things that happen there that are lost on me."

"Go on," Jake said.

"As such, I have noticed over the past few years that APHINT has been ramping up production on a new drug that has not been marketed anywhere, nor has it been discussed by management in any capacity."

"Is that normal?"

She nodded. "Sometimes, yes. It is normal for our company to develop products in secret as much as possible, only reviewing our research when we have something that's as good as ready for market. It is a competitive strategy, and you can imagine that competitive advantages are nearly a requirement for companies such as ours. But this new drug is different from others."

"In what way?"

"Well, production volumes for this drug have surpassed any other of its kind, and we have yet to even finish laboratory testing on it. This, Jake, is *abnormal*. Usually we produce the product and run it through vigorous testing, and then seek FDA approval while we begin preparing our marketing and sales plans."

Jake nodded along. "And APHINT hasn't done that yet? You haven't begun preparing the marketing for this drug?"

"We haven't done *any* of the normal lifecycle events: FDA approval, marketing and sales figures and projections, nothing. We simply created the chemical compounds, turned it into a testable product, and suddenly it was in production."

Jake chewed his lip. "That does seem strange. Any idea as to why? Could this be just a way of staying ahead of the competition?"

"It could be, but it's suspicious for this type of drug. It is a medication that already exists in the market in some capacity, and we are trying to create something that is more acquirable, easier to administer, and cheaper to produce. In fact, it is intended to be a drug that replaces our main line of products—the medication that fights against Lewy body disease. Cheaper for the patient, but also cheaper for us."

"I see. And," he added, "probably makes your company a bit more money?"

She looked at him. "A *lot* of money."

CHAPTER 32

Jake sat across the table from Vero as she explained her reasoning.

"When we produce a new drug, most often it is something that is created to be in direct competition with another pharmaceutical company, especially one in Puerto Rico. This is why there are name-brand drugs that have many knockoff drugs following along made up of the same active ingredients.

"My job in the lab, often, is to reverse-engineer a competitor's name-brand drug in order to come up with our own version of the same thing. This is a standard, typical practice, and it breeds and thrives on healthy competition. It also allows us to keep the United States' pharmaceutical industry supplied with profitable drugs that are not outrageously expensive to the end user."

"I feel like there are plenty of diabetics who might disagree with that assessment," Jake said.

"Of course," Vero replied. "Pharmaceutical companies are not perfect—far from it. When there is a profit to be made, they will chase it. But, generally, these businesses operate in tandem with one another while they are in competition. One produces a drug that, in its own microcosmic world, is a 'miracle drug' for its users. They can artificially inflate the price as high as it needs to go to make as much profit as possible until another company comes along and produces the same thing with a different name, and the prices of both come toward an equilibrium. Add a third and fourth competitor and the price comes down again."

"And your job is to reverse-engineer these drugs so that your company can produce cheaper versions of them?"

Vero nodded. "Yes, but there is also an element of exploration and discovery in my job. My lab at APHINT is not just in charge of reverse-engineering our competitors' products, but in combining them and studying new strains of chemicals—either laboratory-produced or found in the wild—in order to make new products altogether."

"And your company has been doing this with the drug you said they are producing en masse?"

"Yes. Again, this is a common practice. We want to ensure secrecy before our launch, but even still, the industry is very tightly regulated and we have to submit everything we are doing, at just about every step along the process, to the FDA for their final approval. Usually we begin this process when we have a viable prototype. A drug that works in laboratory testing, or in isolated cases. At that point, the FDA will sanction further research and allow us to continue along the normal testing chain. Eventually, we seek final approval and begin producing the drug for public consumption and sale."

"You begin producing drugs for sale before they have been FDA approved?"

Vero moved her head up and down rapidly. "Before *final* approval. Yes, of course. It is the primary way we stay competitive. FDA approval can take ages, sometimes up to a decade, or more. We cannot afford to wait that long, so we begin selling the drugs to manufacturing companies and anyone in the supply chain the FDA acknowledges as someone who is not a 'final consumer.' Remember, their ultimate job is safety—to protect the United States public from illegal or harmful chemicals and foods. Until they deem our product worthy of their stamp of approval, we are just selling products to companies, and it will never be sold to the final consumer until they approve it. That is not illegal."

"I understand," Jake said. "So the problem with your drug now is that you have been manufacturing *far* more of it than you would a typical drug before final approval?"

"Yes, but it has also been the way things have been kept secret that is different. This time, there is no mention of it in company correspondence, internal papers, nothing. Our research and development team has prevented any of us from speaking of it outside of our laboratories, and the marketing team isn't even aware it exists."

Jake's eyes widened. "Wow, that does seem a bit cloak-and-dagger, doesn't it?"

"The idea is to help prevent Lewy body disease over time. It is sort of like an oncological chemotherapy treatment for the brain, but isolated to a very small region and with a treatment that is internal rather than external."

"And is this some sort of groundbreaking discovery?"

She shook her head. "No, I wouldn't think it would be. Other companies have medications that help with this sort of thing—namely Fitzsimmons—and many cancer patients are given drugs just like this based on other chemicals. Our cocktail of chemicals, if you will, is unique, but the effects and ultimate goal of the drug is nothing new."

Jake shifted in his seat, trying to make sense of what she was saying. He didn't quite understand the repercussions of this—and, in all honesty, he couldn't. He wasn't versed at all in the operations of the pharmaceutical industry to know if this were a typical research and development work flow cycle or something abnormal, so he had to take her word for it. The fact that they had this particular drug under wraps only told Jake that they thought it was going to be a goldmine for the company. In his mind, there was nothing wrong with that—the sooner they got it to market without competitive delay, the sooner people could be helped.

"Okay," Jake said. "So you have been testing this drug in the laboratory, working toward the goal of releasing it to the public.

Sure, it's been kept under lock and key since you first produced it, but that doesn't sound to me like something out of the ordinary. If all the tests have been successful, and you are merely waiting on FDA approval, then—"

"No," Vero said. "That's what I haven't mentioned yet. The testing—based on the laboratory results we have been getting—is not at all what we expected, and not at all what we have wanted."

"Can you be more specific? What has been happening with the tests?"

Vero glanced around at the other patrons in the restaurant. She lowered her voice, then flashed her eyes upward to Jake once again as she continued. "The tests we have done seem to indicate that the drug is not helping with Lewy body disease in any way."

"Really?" Jake asked, frowning. "So the drug is meant for something else besides LBD?"

She shook her head. "No, Jake. I mean the drug doesn't help with LBD *at all*. It seems to *cause* it."

CHAPTER 33

The waiter returned with a plate piled high with Tex-Mex-style nachos. He filled their waters and removed the bottle of tequila from the edge of the table.

They gorged on the food for a moment, until Jake took a sip of water and spoke again. He kept his voice down. "So your company has been producing one of the most popular drugs on the market that helps combat Lewy body disease and now they're *also* producing a drug that *causes* it?"

Again, Vero looked back and forth over the people in the restaurant. Jake was sitting in the booth facing the back wall—not his preferred spot, but Vero hadn't given him a choice. As such, he couldn't see if there was anyone looking back at them. He assumed they were safe, as Vero began her explanation a moment later.

"Yes. Well, the whole story is that someone at Fitzsimmons created a brand-new designer chemical that does a better job at treating LBD than our original medication does. We acquired a sample of this chemical, reverse-engineered it, and we are now trying to improve upon it to create a cheaper, more effective medication."

"What does the original medication do?"

"It helps prevent against abnormal deposits of the protein alpha-synuclein in the brain, but there are some other benefits that make it specifically useful for Lewy body disease, like the inclusion of an antipsychotic, which is something most neurological patients with this disease have severe sensitivity to."

"And what does this new chemical do?"

"We call it 'Chemical X.' There is no actual name yet. It acts as a parasite would, one that slowly siphons off alpha-synuclein and causes it to build up, to be removed from the system by the body. There is more to it, but that is the basic premise."

"I see. That's… problematic."

Jake took a massive bite of a nacho, chewed, and watched Vero do the same.

After a sip of water, she asked, "So you understand my concern?"

He nodded. "I think I do. APHINT is producing the market-leading medication for Lewy body disease. But they're not content with the profits from just one side of it. They decided to double-dip and produce a drug that *also*—secretly—*causes* the issue people think it's trying to solve."

"Exactly."

"And that can't be legal in any country."

"Not only is it illegal, Jake, it is a federal criminal offense. And it isn't just the FDA in this case. The SEC could investigate, as well as the FBI if it comes to that. And there are dozens of state agencies that would love to pick over the remains."

"So," Jake said, "you're dealing with a pretty serious offense. *If* what you're telling me is true. I've got a few questions." She looked at him oddly, and he realized he had inadvertently slipped into his detective stylings. He quickly shook his head. "Sorry," he said. "I'm interested in this, from a purely entrepreneurial perspective."

"You are an entrepreneur?"

He shrugged. "No. I mean, not really. I'm self-employed, I guess, but I just meant I'm interested for the sheer entertainment value of it all. It seems hard to believe that a company that size—big enough to own the resort across the street—would be careless enough to think they could get away with this."

Vero raised an eyebrow and peered at him over the edge of her drink glass.

He snickered. "You mean they *have* gotten away with this sort of thing before?"

She nodded. "Not APHINT. But there are others. The FDA, like any good American organization, is bloated and corrupt. It's not bad, but it is far from perfect. They can be fooled, and those who can't, can be bought."

"You think your company is doing that?"

"Jake, I have been assigned to stay at the resort while they 'remodel' our living quarters on campus." She made finger quotations in the air when she said the word "remodel." "I do not believe for a minute that they are actually doing that out of the kindness of their heart."

"So it's sleight of hand. They want you to hang out in a resort, relax a bit, get your eyes off whatever they're cooking up in your lab."

"Sleight of hand is a good term," she said. She looked off into the distance for a moment, then back at Jake. "You still have not told me why you are here, Jake Parker."

Jake swallowed. "I'm self-employed, remember? It's a mini-vacation. I'm scouting for a future office—"

"You are law enforcement?"

"What? How—?" Jake was baffled that she'd suddenly jumped to that conclusion. What had he done to give anything like that away?

She smiled. "Jake, I like you. I think you are cute, and I hope we can be friends. But I am telling you all of this in case things do not go well. In case something happens to me, I—"

Jake shifted in his seat and straightened his back. He leaned forward. "Is something going to happen, Vero? Is something going on?"

Her smile grew. "See, I knew you were law enforcement. A cop, maybe? Something undercover?"

Jake narrowed his eyes. "What's this about, Vero? What's going on?"

She laughed, then took a sip of water before responding. "Please, calm down. I am mostly playing with you, because—as I said—I think you are cute." She winked at him, but Jake didn't budge. "What I told you about my company is true. All of it. They put me here because they hope that if I know something, I will let it disappear quietly. I am not in danger, and there is no reason to be worried about me."

"But?"

"*But*," she continued. "I knew you looked different from the rest of the tourists and locals around here. And it is not just the color of your skin. You are serious, Jake Parker. And you look it. When you arrived earlier, I saw the hole in the back windshield of your Mercedes."

Jake's mouth dropped open a bit, but he didn't bother to close it.

"You did not mention it at all, which tells me that you are hiding something exciting—but that seems unlikely, seeing as how you are here with me now—*or* you do not even care about it, which tells me this is not something new to you."

Jake shook his head in disbelief. He thought *he* was the detective, and this woman had just run circles around him. "Vero, I must say, you are—"

"Correct?"

He sighed, then nodded. "Yes. Sort of. I *was* a cop. Boston PD, actually. I was a detective. But I retired after—"

"After your wife was killed by an explosion at a café."

Again, Jake was flabbergasted. He sat there dumbfounded for a few seconds until Vero burst out laughing.

"'Jake Parker.' I thought it would be a common name, and a Google search would lead me nowhere. But wouldn't you know, you are the top result—*multiple* results, actually, and they even have your picture on the page." She winked again. "You are more handsome now, Señor Parker."

Jake let out a breath. "So… you knew I was a detective, and you were just playing with me this whole time. Great."

"Do not be upset with me," Vero said. "I was just having a little fun. Look, Jake, I told you all about my little problem. You are a detective, here for some reason that I am not allowed to know. Fine. But I figured if I at least gave you some information about my company, you might be able to… I don't know. I don't know how these things work."

"You want me to start investigating APHINT? Open a case against your *employer*? Vero, I'm not a detective anymore. I'm not even a citizen here. Or I am. I don't even know how *that* works."

She laughed again, then reached out and took Jake's hand. "Jake, I am not asking you to do anything. I just needed to tell someone, and I thought you would be a good person. I am sorry if I have been too forward."

"No," he said. "No, I'm sorry. I just—it's been a weird few days." He wanted to add *it's been a weird few years.* "I do need to get back to my room, though. I need to finish up some work."

"Some *entrepreneurial* things?"

He smiled. "Yes, exactly."

They finished the last of the nachos, Jake paid the tab, and they stood up from the table.

As he turned to leave, Vero pulled him back and slipped something into his hand. She leaned toward him and kissed him on the cheek. "I will see you soon, Jake Parker," she said.

As he left the restaurant, Jake looked down at the piece of paper.

It was a phone number, with her name next to it.

CHAPTER 34

"Holland, just got an update from Krueger and Thompson."

Holland opened his eyes and stared straight up at the ceiling. The same ceiling he'd been staring at for weeks now. Listening to the same voices he'd been listening to for far too long. Both the ones in this tiny house and the one inside his own head.

Careful, Holland, he thought. *Get too used to this and you'll go crazy.*

"What's the report?" he asked. He'd sat down in the house's only comfortable chair—an old, worn armchair in the corner of the living-room area—and tried to take a nap. He'd found that the only guaranteed way to move a mission along was to try to take some time for himself.

And as he'd expected, it worked. No more than five minutes had passed before Delmonico stumbled out of the back room, where he'd been on his computer waiting on an update from the other soldiers on his team.

"They say there was a firefight, not far from here."

Holland frowned, then yawned. It was getting late—in his normal life, he'd be in bed by now—but his team—all younger men than him, except for Jacobsen—usually stayed up for hours past midnight. Jacobsen, for his part, was already asleep on a cot in the bedroom.

"A firefight," Holland muttered.

"Yeah. El Yunque area. They say it's probably land owned by Dominguez."

"What land *isn't* owned by Dominguez?"

"Fair point," Delmonico said. "But this place is some sort of stronghold. An old estate, lived in by a rich guy and his family, but with other buildings that are probably sort of like barracks and mess halls for a Dominguez army."

"Just what we need," Holland retorted. "A Dominguez army."

"Reports are that at least a dozen shots were fired, from different weapons. Couple of submachine guns, mostly small arms otherwise. No way to know how many dead or injured since it was on private property, but the police who called it in also mentioned something about an officer from a nearby station not showing up at home earlier tonight after his shift."

"A nearby station?"

"Yeah, the one right up the road, actually."

"Hmm."

"What?" Delmonico asked.

"Seems odd."

"Why's that?"

Holland sighed. "When did this happen?"

"The shots were reported about an hour ago, so I'd guess one-and-a-half to two hours ago?"

Holland nodded, then stood up. "We need to check in with our consultant, Delmonico."

"That Parker guy? Why?"

"He's involved. Somehow."

"But you told him to start looking into Fitzsimmons, right? That our investigation is linked to whatever's going on between them and Dominguez?"

"I gave him vague orders about it. More importantly, I explicitly told him what *not* to do. I told Parker not to investigate those arrests he was obsessed with. Those two kids, remember?"

"Yeah, the Dominguez drug grunts. I'm not seeing how they're connected?"

"Parker did, though. He dug around and found out what happens to Dominguez gangsters the gang doesn't want around anymore. How they fall off the grid. He's a cop, remember? So he would have been able to walk into a department branch and smooth-talk his way into getting information about them."

"And you think he was out there, in El Yunque?"

"I think he was involved. Not sure how, but that cop who died out there? Probably working off a tip from our very own Mr. Parker."

"I see. So he disobeyed an order. We need to bring him in."

Holland shook his head. "No, I'm not in a place to order him around. It's my investigation, but he's a third-party consultant. Technically, he can do whatever he wants. If it interferes with *our* mission, we can tattle and get McDonnell involved, but otherwise we'll need to just talk some sense into his thick detective skull."

Delmonico nodded. "Okay, right. I'll mention it to Thompson and Krueger when they get back. You going to at least talk to McDonnell?"

"No. He picked Parker for this gig, so we know where his loyalties lie."

"Whose? McDonnell's or Parker's?"

Holland paused.

Delmonico smiled. "Okay, I get it. We're playing dumb when it comes to Parker, but the assumption is that he's embedded. Deeper in this than what McDonnell's letting on?"

"That's my reasoning. How else would Parker get himself tangled up in this so quickly? He's a good detective, but I have a feeling he's got a different angle to it only him and McDonnell know about."

"So what's the play?" Delmonico asked.

"We watch him. Not full-on surveillance, mind you—we've still got the mission, and there's only five of us. But we can peel off in shifts and just keep tabs on him. Maybe get a trace on his cell phone or something, is that possible?"

Delmonico shrugged. "I bet Thompson could figure something out."

"Okay, we'll start there. That fancy-ass Mercedes he's rolling around in probably has onboard GPS, too. See if there's a way we can access that data."

"Right."

"We're not taking him down, so there's no reason for babysitting. But I want to know where he goes, what he's doing, and most importantly, who he's talking to. If he's targeting some Dominguez higher-ups, it could make trouble for our own mission. Ditto with Fitzsimmons. Any of those guys might get spooked and make hell for all of us if they think there's a covert American investigation going on."

"Even though there *is* one."

Holland scoffed. "Yeah, but we're on *their* side, remember? Fitzsimmons might be getting attacked in a day or two, and we're supposed to stop it. If they think we're here for any other reason, they might inadvertently speed up the timeline."

"Sounds good."

Holland nodded. "I'm going to get some shut-eye. Tomorrow starts early: 0600. I want to get on the road, all of us except for Thompson, see what else this island's hiding. We'll head up to San Juan first. And if Thompson can get us some recon on Parker's movements, even better. We'll already be gassed-up and ready to track him."

Delmonico confirmed and started toward the hallway.

Holland closed his eyes and was asleep before the man left the room.

CHAPTER 35

Back at the resort, Jake had stripped down to his boxer briefs and a fresh T-shirt he had deemed his "sleeping" shirt. He had processed Vero's confession about Allied Pharmaceuticals International, the company she worked for, and he had decided it was a thread worth chasing.

The fact that a Puerto Rican might be engaging in some rather unscrupulous research tactics was par for the course for competitive businesses. But he had been sent here explicitly to investigate any suspicious activity between Dominguez, Fitzsimmons, APHINT, and whatever hell they were causing locally, especially the terrorist attacks that had grown in volume lately.

If APHINT was indirectly related to that investigation, great. Looking into their financials and quarterly reports might turn up something useful, but that was information Jake wasn't sure how to find.

No, he needed someone else to help. It wasn't worth his time to try to find something he had never been trained to find—a link between the financials and research conducted by APHINT and possible subterfuge, and the illicit activity of Dominguez. He didn't have the requisite resources to carry out an investigation of that nature.

But Holland *might* have those resources. His men were soldiers, sure, but they were also well trained and intelligent, and—most importantly—they were connected. Puerto Rico wasn't just a remote, exotic location for an operation for some of his men. It was a backyard.

He remembered that one of Holland's men, Krueger, was the brother-in-law of the latest informant they had been working. The man had ties to this place, and there was no doubt in Jake's mind that Holland was using those assets to their advantage.

But he wasn't sure how accommodating Holland would be to Jake's little side project. Using one or two of his men to investigate Vero's fear that APHINT was playing dirty wasn't enough of a case.

So he couldn't call Holland—at least not yet. He wasn't sure if the man trusted him, but the deciding factor was that Jake might be shooting himself in the foot if he played his cards this early in the game. If he revealed to Holland that he had been meeting with Vero—that he had learned something about one of the major pharma players on the island and how they might be related—then the dominoes might start to fall. Holland would ask questions about his schedule, about any other interactions, and Jake might also let slip his activities with the kid from Dominguez and the thugs who'd smashed his windshield, and that he'd been interacting with Officer Luis Quintanilla.

His mind drifted toward the officer who'd lost his life near El Yunque, in Campo de Almas. A man who had trusted Jake, who had given him the lead and helped him gain access to Dominguez-controlled territory and paid the ultimate price for it.

No, he couldn't bring this to Holland—not yet. Instead, he needed to send this directly up the chain and see if there was anything to it before playing his hand.

And he knew McDonnell *did* have the resources he'd require. McDonnell had more than enough brainpower and tech savvy to find out every possible thing he needed as it related to APHINT, Fitzsimmons, and the other pharmaceuticals.

He picked up the phone, dialed, and it was answered in a few seconds.

"McDonnell."

"Hey," Jake said.

"Good to hear from you. It's late—I'm not at the office anymore. Everything okay?"

Once again, Luis Quintanilla's face flashed before his eyes, but Jake shook the image away. "Yeah. Uh, fine here. Hey, sorry, I didn't think about the time. Just trying to piece something together and thought I'd give you a call first."

There was a pause. *"First? You didn't want to take it to Holland?"*

Jake matched the pause and gave it a few extra seconds. What he didn't say was more impactful than anything he could have said.

McDonnell, thankfully, understood. *"Got it. He's trustworthy—you have my word. But I get it; you're a good detective and your gut's telling you something different. Fine."* There was a crackle as McDonnell played with the phone on the other end. *"So, what's up?"*

Jake didn't waste any time. "There's something I'd like you to look into for me, if you can spare the manpower. Shouldn't take a lot of effort either."

McDonnell laughed. *"Don't make the same mistake I always make and assume that just because my guys are good and we're idiots, that this stuff is easy."*

"Fine—that's fair. But really, I just need some basic numbers, I think. There's a—I met someone here, and I think her story checks out. I'll type it up and send it over, but I want some verification."

"Okay," McDonnell said. *"I'll be on it first thing tomorrow. I'll look for your message. You're thinking this relates to the terrorism somehow?"*

"I do. I'm not sure how, though. If it turns up nothing, fine. If it does, great. I'll be able to use it. But it's not high-priority at this point, which is part of the reason I'm asking you instead of trying to convince Holland's team to reallocate."

"Okay, sounds good. If this needs anything more than research, I'll be able to coordinate from here."

Jake sighed, suddenly feeling relieved. "Thanks, McDonnell."

He hung up and then turned to the mirror and examined himself for the second time that night, but for the first time in a long time, he actually paid attention. He saw a man who had seemingly aged years in the span of months. A man who could no longer, by anyone—superior or otherwise—be described as a "kid." He wondered when it had happened. When the world had passed him by and he'd become his father, when he'd become "old." People at the pub on the bottom floor of the building he lived in joked about his "old man" Corolla, as if it were some old-school ride and not just an efficient, affordable vehicle. He wondered when he'd stopped thinking of himself as youthful, eager, and driven and instead started thinking of himself as experienced, capable, and bold. Barely forty, he wasn't old by the world's standards, but he wasn't young, either. He was reaching the early years of middle age, but the career he'd had in both the military and then in law enforcement seemed to tack on a decade or two.

Jake ran a hand through his hair, noticing for the first time the specks of gray that were beginning to speckle around the longer streaks of light brown. When his hair was shorter, it was almost impossible to spot. But now it was impossible to miss.

What was he doing here? Nothing in Puerto Rico would bring Mel back. McDonnell was a friend, but was the man using him? Was he using Jake's proclivity to solve a case, at all costs, against him?

He wanted to find the man who had killed Mel—the reason the terrorists had attacked that particular café on that particular day. He wanted answers. He wanted to understand their motives. And yet he knew full well it wouldn't change the past. It wouldn't bring her back. It wouldn't help him forget.

But he was drawn to it. He *needed* it. Had McDonnell known that somehow?

He suddenly realized why he'd come. It wasn't about the mission—though that was a case he wanted to solve. It wasn't about doing McDonnell a favor, either.

No, he was here for a different reason: he wanted to find closure. He had the mission—prevent the next attack—and he would accomplish that.

But to do that, he needed to find his ghost.

CHAPTER 36

The next morning came quickly. Jake rose with the sunlight streaking in through the tall curtains. He rolled over, groaned, then jumped out of bed. He'd long suffered from the same dilemma every military night owl experienced: no matter how late one could stay up, the next morning's drill began early.

He'd kept his military routine even after joining the police department, where it served him well. Now, even though he had no such duties and responsibilities and no day job, he could never get himself to sleep past dawn. And today he had the extra motivation of having a plan: he wanted to get to the port in San Juan and see how the pharmaceutical industry on the island actually did their business. By seeing things firsthand, Jake's gut could tell him in which direction to head next.

Adding to the motivation was the fact that he wasn't going to be alone. He'd decided last night that visiting Fitzsimmons and APHINT and the other companies that used the port in San Juan would be easier if he had a guide.

He'd gotten back to his hotel room and pulled the paper from his pocket and called the number on it. Ten minutes later, he'd had a date.

That date would be waiting for him down in the lobby in less than an hour, and he intended to make the appointment, no matter the stress and strain on his body begging for an extra hour of sleep.

Besides his appointment, he had also called the rental company last night to complain that someone had smashed a hole in his rear window—technically not a lie—and they had asked for his address and told him that they would be sending someone out to retrieve his vehicle. However, a replacement was not readily available, so he would be without a rental car today. That meant he needed to get the gun and personal belongings out of the car and call for a ride.

He showered, shaved, and threw on a clean shirt and shorts, then headed down the elevator and across the resort's lobby, just as Vero walked through the front door.

Jake couldn't help but notice that not just the two doormen but each of the male hotel staff in sight caught a quick—or lingering—glance at the stunning Puerto Rican woman. She strode through the doors as if she owned the place, smiling and waving at the staffers as she passed.

He waved as well, meeting her by the massive pot of multicolored hibiscus. "I thought you were staying here?" he asked.

"I am," she responded. "But I was up early. Thought I would get a quick walk in before we left."

"Right," Jake said, shaking his head. A "quick walk" apparently ended with her looking as though she'd just walked out of a salon—manicured and pedicured, hair in immaculate shape, and makeup and eyeliner performing their duties admirably without being overwhelming. "Well, you look fantastic."

She seemed to blush—a facial feature that was adorably endearing to him, and one he hadn't thought her capable of. "Thank you. I just went to the restaurant and grabbed a coffee."

"You seem to like the restaurant a lot," he said. "Is there no other good place to eat around here?"

"Plenty of places," she answered. "My cousin Vincent owns that one, though."

Jake nodded. "That's why you're getting free dinners and drinks all the time, and why the waitstaff is wrapped around your finger. I thought it was your good looks."

She scowled, then jabbed him in the side. "It *is* my looks, of course. I'll have you know, *everyone's* cousins here in Puerto Rico."

"I see."

"Okay, Jake Parker. Let's head to San Juan. I hear you need a tour guide."

"I'd like to see this famous port section."

"There is not much to see. Just old cargo containers and rusted ships."

"I saw there's a market across the street on the western side of the bay. I like those open-air markets. Could make a nice walk."

"And this has nothing to do with the fact that the market is directly next to where the APHINT ships dock?" she asked.

He shrugged. "Who knows? Maybe it will help answer some questions for you. I'm just here to help."

Jake knew it sounded disingenuous, but he also knew she'd play along. He hadn't told her the full truth about why he was here in Puerto Rico, but he was pretty sure she trusted him. He wanted to find answers, and he had a feeling she was onto him.

The Uber driver arrived in the resort's drop-off station and opened the door for Vero. Jake piled in through the opposite door, and within a minute they were sailing down the highway toward the nation's capital city.

Their ride was smooth and flew by quickly. Jake asked some questions about growing up here, and Vero answered with flowery, descriptive responses that painted a picture of quaint, charismatic island life punctuated by a recent swath of criminal activity.

"It has gotten harder to live here," she said, her voice dropping as the driver pulled off the highway and onto a smaller road. "Not impossible, but different than it used to be."

"Dominguez?" he asked.

She turned in the seat. "You know about the gang?"

He nodded. "It's not hard to hear about it. Even US-based news sites talk about the rise in gang-related activity in Puerto Rico, and how organized crime is in bed with the pharmaceuticals."

"You believe that?"

"What? That they're working together?" he asked. "Sure. I mean, why wouldn't they? They're all just trying to make a buck, and it's hard to ignore the two biggest industries around. Why not partner up with each other and see how to get as much as possible out of the deal?"

"Two?"

Jake smiled. "Yeah. Drugs, and illegal drugs."

CHAPTER 37

The stretch of road that paralleled the shoreline was flanked on one side by low, flat buildings with massive ocean liners docked behind them, and on the other side by hundreds of small shops and stores that kept the port infrastructure supplied. The small island just off the north coast of San Juan shielded the bay to its south, providing piers for both commercial and passenger ships, including cruise liners.

In a sense, it was beautiful. But something plagued Jake's mind, enough for the beauty of it all to be covered in a pall of darkness. He knew something here was off—something was awry. He couldn't see it overtly, but the answer, he felt, was down here somewhere.

He assumed that the Dominguez gang had been behind the attacks on Fitzsimmons, some of which had taken place in this very port. They had been behind the attack in Boston that had killed his wife—they had targeted someone, for some reason, and his wife had been in the wrong place at the wrong time. But he didn't get the feeling that they were working alone. Dominguez was working *for* or *with* another entity. Some group that wanted something slightly different than what Dominguez wanted. He wasn't sure what it was, but he felt close to an answer.

Or, at least, close to a *clue* that might lead to the answer.

Vero had also revealed that her company, APHINT, was engaging in some rather unscrupulous activities, and had alluded to the idea that perhaps their motives weren't sound. Could they be the ones working with Dominguez?

Two of the cruise ships sat idle to the northwest, and Jake could make out their shining white hulls docked just under the horizon. None of the other ships he could see seemed to have the Fitzsimmons logo on them. He wanted to see those ships, to get a feel for them. Previous attacks had targeted Fitzsimmons property and ships, so it was a good bet they'd be a target in the future as well.

They had crossed over a bridge to get onto the island, and immediately below the bridge sat dozens of yachts. The driver pointed them out, as well as the two piers next to them, mentioning that these were the main commercial docks for the island. He pulled off the highway and steered toward the market just to the north on the right side of the road, within eyesight of the two piers, both currently empty.

"Those are all million-dollar yachts," the driver said. "Maybe one will be mine one day."

"I guess we'll have to leave a better tip," Jake joked.

The driver winked at him in the rearview mirror as he continued. "Those piers—4A, 4B, and 5 and 6 down the road a bit—are mostly used by the pharmaceutical companies."

"What about APHINT?" Vero asked. "Do they have a designated pier?"

The driver nodded and pointed at the two piers closest to the yachts. "4A and B are usually Fitzsimmons, but 5 and 6 on both sides are typically APHINT, since they do more shipping. But it depends on the day, and who's manufacturing. Lot of pharmaceuticals on the island."

"Where are the Fitzsimmons ships?" Jake asked.

"Not here," the driver said. "Who knows? Delivering their goods around the world."

"When do they return?"

The driver's eyes flicked sideways, then back up at Jake in the mirror. He hesitated. "Eh, I do not know that. Their schedules are probably posted somewhere, though. Why?"

Jake shook his head. "Just curious."

The driver found a parallel parking spot near the entrance to the open-air market and pulled in. Vero got out as Jake paid the man and thanked him, then told him they'd be getting a ride back later that afternoon if he was still around.

Vero was walking toward the market's entrance, and Jake joined her. She weaved her arm through Jake's and started pulling him along, but he allowed it. It felt good to have someone giving him attention, even though his thoughts were drifting back toward Eliza.

He and Eliza had dated for a few weeks, but it had felt forced, strained. Their attraction to one another was apparent, but it seemed their shared trauma only made things awkward when they tried to make their relationship something more. He felt as though they should always be talking about their case and the crisis with Immigration and Customs Enforcement they'd helped avert, but whenever either of them brought it up, the conversation seemed to fade. He hadn't been lying when he'd told Eliza on the phone that he would take advantage of his time here to clear his head. He wanted things to work out with Eliza if it was meant to be, but he wasn't going to force it. She'd seemed to agree with that sentiment.

Vero was obviously attracted to Jake as well, and now it seemed she might be more interested than just having someone to talk to while she waited for her company to let her go home. He couldn't help but think he'd just started his first official date with the woman.

It wasn't a bad thing, just a confusing thing. Jake had never worried much about dating—he'd been focused on hockey all through school, so much so that any girl he could get to bat an eye in his direction quickly lost interest when they realized he wasn't about to budge on his commitment to sports and his athletic development.

In college, he'd thrown himself into his studies on and off the ice, and after his injury he'd decided to change direction a bit and double down on his intellectual pursuits. If there had been anyone interested in a relationship then, he'd missed the signs.

It was only after his return from his first overseas engagement with the Army that he'd met Mel, and things had progressed quickly after that. They'd gotten married, and from then on "dating" meant a once-a-week dinner with the woman he loved.

He was well aware of his naivety when it came to matters of the heart, and he wondered if he'd sent some inadvertent message to Vero letting her know that he was on the market and interested. If so, he'd have to consider whether or not that was actually true. Where did he stand with Eliza? How should he mention her to Vero? Should he even bring it up?

They entered the marketplace and Jake was suddenly bombarded with the smell of fresh fish. It wasn't an unpleasant odor, but it was striking, especially as his nose hadn't expected it. Whatever feelings of giddiness or childish butterflies he'd felt toward Vero momentarily disappeared.

They walked together, arm-in-arm, toward the line of fishmongers, each shouting their daily specials, with hourly workers and dockhands behind them tossing massive sea creatures back and forth until they landed on ice.

Two fatigue-clad US military personnel drifted by, deep in conversation, and Jake noticed a few more Navy men and women shopping the marketplace as well. Behind them, another group of young sailors walked hurriedly toward the exit.

He hadn't noticed them all at first, but it seemed odd there would be so many all in one place. He'd read in McDonnell's brief that US military personnel on-island were sparse, but he hadn't expected them to be mostly gathered in one place.

"Why all the US military?" he asked. "I know there's a base here, but are they doing a training or something?"

Vero frowned, then looked around. "Oh, it is normal. At least now. About three years ago the local government petitioned for a heavier presence of US Navy. They stop in port here always, but they asked for the ships to stay longer, or at least to keep more Navy staff at the docks."

"Why is that?"

"The thought was that having more official US presence would cut down on the crime."

"Like the terrorist attacks?"

She nodded. "Yes, explosions. Some deaths, too. Targets seem to be officials working for the big pharmaceutical companies, and it is said that gangs are involved. Hired by the terrorists to plant their bombs and destroy ships. The companies are scared, and the US obviously wants to keep its supply chain intact, and it certainly does not want to have Puerto Rico fall because of terrorism. So they have begun sending more soldiers and sailors here, to help keep the peace."

"Has it worked?"

She smiled. "Exactly as you would think. There is still crime, perhaps more than ever. But it has now moved away from the docks and into the smaller towns mostly. Dominguez has snaked its way through the entire island, so the crime is less obvious, but still present. However, it is nice to feel safer at the markets and other places like this."

Jake nodded, thinking about his time on the Dominguez-owned property near El Yunque. He knew firsthand the imposing, ever-present threat of danger in Puerto Rico due to the gang's activities. On one hand, he even understood the reason they had grown powerful, and the reason for the temptation of the local government to reach out for help from the US. The gang was working toward more power, and that would inevitably lead to more money. It was an age-old desire, and Jake had dealt with it at every level during his short career as a detective.

But a question still nagged at him. One he had found himself needing to answer in order to move forward with his case for McDonnell.

What, exactly, was Dominguez up to? And why?

CHAPTER 38

Three stalls down from the entrance, deep within the open-air market amidst the many tables and ice chests, Jake stopped. He and Vero had been arm-in-arm since arriving, laughing and talking as they passed fish, oysters, shrimp, and countless other seafood delicacies.

But something had caught his attention, and he needed to figure out what it was. Vero turned to look at him, but he was already turning in the other direction, toward the vendors on the opposite side of the space.

He wasn't sure what it was that had gotten his senses worked up, but he had learned long ago not to question the feeling. The sensation of someone looking at him, studying him, was hard to shake. It felt like he were under a microscope, an unknown entity peering down at him, examining him.

There.

He noticed them—a woman—standing about two hundred feet away, next to a tall concrete pillar that supported a section of the building behind it. The building seemed to be intended for shipbuilding, as he could see two massive cranes poking out above the concrete wall the marketplace was next to, but the woman herself was standing just inside the market.

And she was clearly intending to stay out of sight. Jake spotted her looking in his direction, and then retraced his and Vero's steps in his mind to figured out why he'd noticed her.

They had been walking along the stalls and he'd seen her pass them once already, their eyes meeting for a brief moment and the woman then giving Vero the once-over. He'd not thought anything of it—she had seemed like nothing but a shopper, much like he and Vero. Just two strangers passing by in a public space. There were hundreds of other people around, and she had done nothing suspicious.

But she must have doubled back around, behind the vendors' stands and display cases. She'd hustled to get there before Jake and Vero arrived, then posted up behind the concrete pillar and waited for them.

While Jake's subconscious mind analyzed the data provided to it by his peripheral vision, the recognition of seeing the exact same woman twice—both times staring him down—made something in his brain click. He'd gone into detective mode, his instincts on high alert.

He didn't feel they were in danger, as the woman hadn't exhibited any of the telltale signs of becoming an impending threat. No sweaty brow, no widened eyes, no stiff posture.

"What is it?" Vero asked, apparently noticing that Jake's entire demeanor had changed in the span of two seconds. She pointed her face in the direction Jake was looking, trying to see what he had seen.

He didn't answer. He watched the woman—now feigning disinterest as she shuffled through her purse, her eyes down. She pulled out a pair of sunglasses and placed them on her nose. It was an odd choice, considering there was no direct sunlight in the market, and she was standing in the shade.

After a few seconds, the woman pulled a phone out of her pocket and turned to the side. Jake waited as she dialed a number. He wondered if she was still putting on an act, trying to make it seem as though she didn't notice Jake's interest.

The woman pulled the phone up to her ear and started walking, back in the direction she had come from, making a line parallel to their own position. She moved out of sight while walking behind a fishmonger and his team and their display case, then came back into view. Her face was still staring straight ahead, her eyes concealed by the glasses. She was talking on the phone.

"Jake?" Vero asked.

"Sorry," he said. "I thought I saw someone I knew."

"Here?"

"Yeah, that's why it surprised me. Thought I was going crazy for a minute."

"That is strange. You okay?"

He sniffed, then shook his head quickly. "Of course, sorry. Just caught me off guard."

She laughed. "I would have thought it was the FBI chasing you, the way you froze up. Must have been an old girlfriend." She winked at him.

He smiled. "Yeah, well, if it was, I don't think she'd mess with someone like you."

"And what is that supposed to mean, Mr. Parker?" Vero stuck out her bottom lip in a fake pout that worked exactly as she'd intended it to. He couldn't believe he was even thinking it, but this woman was *hot*.

Pull yourself together, man, he thought to himself.

And, before he could stop himself, the thought continued. *But damn if I wouldn't like to get to know her better.*

He was about to deflect her flirtatious advance and start walking again when she pulled him closer to her. Suddenly their lips were touching. Suddenly she was kissing him.

And suddenly, he realized, he was kissing her back.

It felt good—*too* good. He straightened up to his full height, his mouth down and meeting hers and pulling her back to him as his arm reached around behind her back, catching her sundress and sliding it a bit as his palm nestled into the small crook just above her waist.

They stayed like that for a few moments, an hour or a second, time now lost on him, and he enjoyed every unknown second of it.

His mind wandered back to the resort, to the hotel room, wondering which floor she was staying on and what else he had to do today and how quickly a driver could get them back—

And then, just like that, it was over. She pulled away from him, her forehead now resting on his chest. Passersby split as they passed on either side of them, no one giving them a second glance.

He opened his mouth to protest, or to thank her, or to say something equally awkward and unnecessary, but she spoke first.

"What are you thinking, Jake Parker?" she asked.

He paused for a moment, still lost in her eyes, and then finally spoke. "You sure do know how to leave a guy wanting more."

CHAPTER 39

The woman reappeared on the other side of the market. After their kiss, Jake and Vero continued walking through the main aisle of the open-air market. He had to diligently focus on the task at hand; his mind kept wanting to return to the past: the kiss with Vero, but also his relationship—whatever remained of it—with Eliza. Ultimately, he had to decide what he wanted. Was there something here, with Vero? Or should he try to patch things up with Eliza? Or was there a third option—to stay single for the time being?

When they'd reached the end and started to turn around to head back in the other direction, Jake noticed the woman again. She was standing near an aquarium filled to the brim with live shrimp, the owner and seller busy piling pounds of the shellfish over ice and weighing the bags as he conversed with customers.

Jake met the woman's eyes and noticed that this time she wasn't alone. She didn't point, but he could see a slight nod of her head just as a man standing beside her began to open and close his mouth. They were too far away and drowned out by the noise for Jake to hear what he was saying, but he got the sense the woman was pointing him out to her partner.

For what purpose, Jake wasn't sure. But he wasn't about to assume it was simply a coincidence. Whoever they were, they had business with him and Vero. He wondered if he shouldn't just walk up to them and ask, but he was worried about things getting out of hand. He had his pistol, having retrieved it before the rental company had come to take his car. But, as he always had, he viewed the weapon as a last option. A defense against attack, if things got heated.

He wasn't sure what to do with Vero. She seemed strong and capable, but he doubted she had any real self-defense training or experience. Adding to that anxiety was the fact that he was carless—they would have to hail a taxi or call for a ride-share if things got heated, and he didn't want to have to cut a chase short in order to wait for a cab.

Vero started to ask him a question, but Jake pulled her to the side and yanked her toward a space between two stalls.

"Jake! What are you doing?"

"Someone's taken an interest in me," he said. He turned back to see the woman moving her head from side to side. She'd lost sight of them in the mess of people and fishmongers, but he knew now that he had been right to be on high alert. There was no doubt she was looking for him.

Worse, the man who had been standing next to her, quietly conversing with her, had vanished.

Jake brushed his hand behind his back, a learned habit that told him, in a subtle, secretive half-second, that his pistol was still there. It was a fresh cartridge, one of the extended magazines that held seventeen rounds. He hadn't placed one in the chamber yet, and he hoped he wouldn't have to.

He flicked his head left and right, looking for the man who'd left the woman's side. He wanted to get a read on him. Had he been the woman's sidekick? The man doing her grunt work? Was he Dominguez? If so, Jake should be able to spot his tattoo, as he had been wearing a short-sleeved, buttoned Hawaiian shirt.

Jake felt his mind ramping up to full speed. It was an odd sensation, like adrenaline, that fueled a certain kind of focus. His senses were heightened, as if he had just walked into the marketplace as a new man. He smelled and felt the air around him, the humidity carrying with it the pungency of fish and saltwater and, from some direction, fried food. He could hear the voices of the people around him, the shouts of the fishmongers as if they were five feet away.

Something tugged at his arm. He whirled to the side. It was Vero, and her eyes were wide. "Jake, what is wrong? You seem like you have seen a ghost."

He turned a slow circle, taking a few steps toward a large display case full of blackfin tuna and tarpon on ice, the dead eyes wide and staring at Jake as he approached. He noticed the man behind the counter begin to talk in his direction, but the words were lost on him.

Where did he go? he wondered. It could have been a game, a mistake. Nothing but a coincidence—the woman perhaps looking for the man and finally finding him, Jake simply noticing a lover's rendezvous or a lover's quarrel.

But something told him these two people were colleagues, not lovers. And something told him there were more just like them, scoping out the marketplace and watching for people.

Watching for *him.*

He realized his mistake. *Everyone here either works for Dominguez or knows someone who does.*

The driver. Jake had asked one too many questions, specifically about Fitzsimmons. Specifically about the target of Dominguez's next attack.

He once again batted the air behind his back, feeling the end of the pistol with his pinky finger and running through his knowledge and experience with the weapon. He didn't prefer the Beretta, but it was a damn good pistol, and he'd fired a thousand rounds through it on the range. A full draw and aim would take a full second, but there was no safety on his model, no additional prep work to be ready to fire. Call it a second and a half to line up a shot.

He was accurate as well. He could drop a paper range target from forty-five yards out in a relatively closed space like this, but with the number of civilians strolling around here, he wouldn't fire at anything farther away than twenty. Make it fifteen, to account for the fact that anything he fired at would be moving.

To his left, another man came into view, standing amidst a large group of shoppers walking in both directions. This man was larger than him, with a beefy, barrel-shaped torso and tree-trunk arms. He looked oddly familiar, and Jake wondered if he'd noticed him subconsciously earlier during their market stroll. The man was casing Jake like a house to be broken into, and Jake could almost feel the man's anger toward him.

He took another step to his left, toward the tarpon display case, pulling Vero along with him.

The bear of a man yelled something in Spanish. Vero looked toward him and then turned back to Jake.

"Jake," she said. "Whoever that is, he is wanting us to stop. To ask us a question."

Jake nodded, still staring at the advancing man. He was twenty feet away, well within firing range but still stuck in the center of a throng of people. "Yeah," Jake said, his voice low enough for only her to hear. "Thing is, I don't think they're actually interested in the answer."

Before he finished the sentence, the man's arm rose. Jake saw the pistol at the end of it, held within a massive hand.

Pointing at him.

Jake pulled again at Vero's arm, yanking her toward the ground.

The man pulled the trigger.

CHAPTER 40

The two shots seemed to hang in the air before landing, as if all the noise had suddenly been sucked out of the marketplace. Everyone froze, only the gunman and Jake and Vero moving. The first shot was wide and high, but the second was only high, sailing inches over Jake's head as he and Vero toppled to the ground.

One round struck the concrete building behind the fish stands, causing dust and debris to splatter outward and down to the ground, while the second round whizzed through the plexiglass front of the fish case and came to rest somewhere inside the lifeless body of a tuna. The man behind the counter screamed in surprise and fell to the ground.

More screams rang out through the space, but not everyone in the near vicinity knew what had happened. They were the typical reactionary responses of people who felt trapped, scared. They had screamed because they had heard screams, or a gunshot, or both. It ramped up the chaos and confusion.

Jake found himself on top of Vero, crawling over her body as if it were merely a speed bump on the road, but he no longer cared about her comfort. He needed to keep her safe. He planned to stay there, to watch for the attacker until it was safe to move.

But, to his surprise, he felt his upper body being lifted from the concrete floor by her small hands. She thrust upward, rolling him up and to the side. "Get off me," she said, grunting through forced breaths.

"Are you okay?" he asked.

She ran her hands down the front of her shirt and rolled to her side, rising to a crouch. "For now, yes. But not if you sit on top of me, Jake Parker. Whoever just shot at us is not going to back down."

Jake couldn't help but smile, even as he knew there was still a deadly threat bearing down on them. For Vero to have this amount of calm and collectedness during a gunfight was not just abnormal, it was breaching into the realm of insanity.

He followed her toward the concrete wall against the side of the marketplace area, crawling on hands and knees a few feet toward the wall, until they were even with the refrigerated fish displays on this side of the market floor. He hadn't seen the man again, but that was a good thing. It meant there were still people between them—tourists and local shoppers—and Jake doubted the man would simply shoot through them all to find him.

When they reached the space behind the stands against the wall, Jake turned around and watched the main aisle. He saw scores of men and women, some still standing, confused and looking around, most on their knees or crouching down with their hands over their heads.

He didn't see the gunman.

What he *did* see, however, was the first man he'd noticed, the one who had been talking to the woman. The woman was still missing, but this man had apparently noticed what his coworker had been shooting at and was now sprinting across the open space.

The running man was armed, holding a tiny .380 in his left hand, but Jake knew he had the jump on him. If Jake tried to line up a shot, the man would be able to close the distance to about ten paces away and pull his own weapon up by the time Jake pulled his trigger. That was too close for comfort, so he chose a different strategy.

The stands weren't tall, but it would take an Olympic high jumper to clear them, so he pulled Vero close to him and placed their backs to the rear side of the stand they were behind. The owner of the stand was doing something similar, his wide, terrified eyes watching Jake as they came closer.

The bearlike man suddenly appeared again, this time to Jake's immediate right, about a hundred paces away and closing fast.

Two men approaching. Both armed. One already willing to take a shot at them in a high-density area.

Jake and Vero were now vulnerable, and Jake didn't like it. He could take out one of them in a space like this without trouble, but two men, even untrained, would prove to be a challenge.

"Vero," he said. "On my mark. We're heading back toward the entrance. Stay behind this line of stands, and stay low."

She nodded, then swallowed, but she seemed to be cognizant of the order.

Jake counted to three quickly. When he finished, he shouted for her to move. She immediately leapt up and began crouch-running behind the stands.

Jake stepped up and forward, placing himself between the oncoming attacker who'd shot at them and Vero's retreating back. He lifted his pistol and fired two quick shots, hoping that his elevated heart rate wouldn't cause the shots to fly wild above the man's head.

One did, but the second was closer to the man's center mass, clipping him in the shoulder. He winced and stumbled, slowed but not at all out of the fight, but it was all Jake needed to get moving. He whirled around and stood to his full height as he started to run. As he did, he caught sight of the second man pacing quickly in front of the fish display, his gun out but hanging by his side.

Jake saw his exposed arm, and the small frog tattooed on it.

Dominguez. Just as I thought.

So the gang members were here for him. Somehow they'd seen him, recognized him as a threat to their plans, and decided to take action.

He slowed to a stop, aiming for the man, but something else caught his attention before he could fire. Another man, running toward the chaos in the center aisle. Gun drawn, but clearly not Dominguez. This man was American, and Jake recognized him immediately. Built like a soldier, running smoothly and staying low, no stranger to active gunfire.

Running until he saw Jake. He stopped, frowned, and then started up again. But the man he recognized was not coming from the right direction—he should have been *outside* the marketplace, coming in. Not the other way around. This man was *inside* the space, coming from the same place the Dominguez people had been.

What the hell?

Jake didn't want to believe it, but there was no denying it. The two Dominguez men who had been chasing him and Vero though the marketplace had been joined by an American soldier. One Jake recognized, because he had met him and shaken his hand only a day ago.

One of Holland's men. Delmonico.

CHAPTER 41

Jake didn't know why one of Holland's team was here in the market, nor how he'd known to find Jake. It seemed clear to him, however, that the man knew exactly where to go, and how to find him. On top of that, Jake knew it was more likely that Holland would know Jake's whereabouts than the Dominguez gangsters, which meant only one thing.

The two parties were working together.

He didn't want to believe it, but there were only two other options: either their presence in this market was a complete coincidence, or Holland's group *and* the Dominguez group were there to keep tabs on Jake. Previously, he had no reason to suspect that Dominguez even knew who he was, but if anyone from the kid's house had logged his license plate, they would have been led to the rental car company, and then finding his name would have been easy. Add to that the suspicious interaction he'd had with the driver, and Jake had a feeling Dominguez now knew *exactly* who he was.

But why would Holland be trying to keep tabs on him? Why had they been tracking him without telling him?

It left the only option that made any sense: Holland's team wasn't in the marketplace to track Jake—they were working with Dominguez.

He needed time and space to think this through. He had no qualms about shooting at the Dominguez men—at least they had fired first, and he had plenty of evidence to know that they weren't innocent. The men working with Holland, however, were more of an enigma. What was the nature of their relationship with Dominguez? Why had they tracked him and Vero to the port, and how?

Jake would need to check their persons for tracking devices, even though he knew it was an unlikely move. He hadn't imagined an old-school guy like Holland would have the technological capabilities back at the safe house to run a 24/7 monitoring alert on a GPS-enabled device, but he had no idea about his men. Besides, Jake was confident any battery-powered device placed on him would have died hours ago. He hadn't been in contact with anyone on Holland's team since he'd picked up his weapon.

Jake also wondered if there were any Navy personnel still around, and what—if anything—they'd do after seeing the action. Shots had been fired, so it was plausible that there was already a phone ringing in some commander's cabin, or at least in the local port authority office. But Jake hadn't seen any officers out here—just young enlists who were most likely out for a quick late-morning stroll. If they had been warned of gang violence and told to keep their eyes open, they might also have been warned to not interfere. To wait it out and let the police do their jobs.

Delmonico slowed, seeming to be more interested in how the fight played out than in fighting himself. Jake wanted to keep an eye on him, but for the time being it seemed as though the Dominguez crew was the direct enemy.

He lifted his pistol just as the man rounded the corner and started toward him. *Good,* Jake thought. *Now you're out of the way of collateral damage.* He aimed and fired, a single shot.

The man wasn't hit, the bullet glancing off the metal top of the display case and sailing high, but it was enough to scare him. He fell to the ground, dropping his pistol a few feet away.

Jake shot a glance over his shoulder and saw that the first man who'd shot at them was recovering quickly, still advancing toward him, albeit more slowly. He had the gun in his injured hand but was holding his shoulder with his other. Jake could see blood pooling beneath his shirt.

Time to get out of here, Jake thought. He ran again, catching up to Vero just as she reached the edge of the marketplace's entrance. She started rounding the corner as he caught her and grabbed her elbow. Together, they turned and ran down the small slope leading to the road.

The gunmen would be a few paces behind them now, but they would be firing blind around the corner. Still, Jake wasn't interested in a standoff.

"Get to the other side of the street," he told Vero. "Call for a ride, or flag someone down. Doesn't matter who. We need a car."

She nodded quickly, and moved toward the street. It was lined with cars, all sliding through the intersection. A few sets of brakes squealed as the drivers realized that Vero wasn't slowing down, and more than a few cars honked in argument.

Jake maneuvered behind a large concrete barrier that had been placed to mark the edge of the entrance and waited for another three seconds, his pistol up, and aimed toward the entrance. He wanted them to show themselves, to step into the midday brightness and be blinded by the sunlight. He could take them both down now without trouble.

But they didn't show. No shots were fired, and he heard shouts of people deep within the market. No sounds of the gunmen or their commands to one another.

He knew they were still there. Waiting. Hoping he'd return. But Jake wasn't interested. He backed down the slope, holding his weapon steady. A few cars slammed to a halt as they noticed him, an active shooter working his way toward them. Only at the actual intersection did he stop and turn around, running full tilt across the street.

Vero was there, already inside a car and shouting at him to hurry through an open window. It was an SUV, the driver's eyes wide and a confused expression on his face. But he wasn't arguing, and for the moment it seemed he didn't care that he was about to transport a gunman and his crazed companion through the streets of San Juan.

As he entered the vehicle and it pulled away from the curb, Jake saw Delmonico step into the light, still ducking and hiding behind a concrete support pillar. He looked at Jake, and the two men locked eyes. Jake felt the car accelerate through the green light, heading back toward the Puerto Rican mainland.

He finally released the breath he had been holding, and turned to the other passenger in the back seat of the SUV. Vero was staring at him, and he could immediately tell something was off. It was fear, but he realized she wasn't scared of him, or scared of anything, really. It was some other kind of fear, the visceral, intense burning of worry that he'd experienced when he'd gotten the news about Mel's death. It was a new look in her eyes, something he hadn't seen in her before. Something pained.

Something he knew was going to change the game.

CHAPTER 42

"What the hell are you talking about, he's in on it?" Holland shouted into the phone.

"I mean exactly what I said. It's bigger than us, boss."

Holland waited for Delmonico's answer, hoping he wouldn't have to pry it out of the young man.

"I saw him there, at the marketplace. He was with Dominguez."

Holland paced over the tiny apartment's living-room floor. Thompson was napping in the bedroom, while Jacobsen was messing around on the computer. Holland wanted to snoop around on the south side of the island soon, where they believed Dominguez had a stronghold set up.

He straightened his back, once again being reminded of his two-decades-long service. "I thought you said they *shot* at him."

"I did," Delmonico hastily replied. *"But he was with a woman. Looked like a Puerto Rican local. They might have been shooting at her."*

"Then why do you think they are working together?" Holland trusted the kid's instinct, but he also wanted to verify the information he was receiving, parse it as best he could, and not just take anyone's opinion at face value.

"They seemed to recognize each other, and I saw Parker and the woman pass a couple of Dominguez members who didn't seem to care about them at all. My guess is it's like the Bermuda situation—two different factions, vying for control."

Holland nodded. "And you think Parker's helping with one faction? Trying to get into the port for some reason, because that's where the attack will be?"

"Yes."

Holland didn't need to be reminded about the Bermuda incident. They'd named the event jokingly, as a way to lessen some of the tension around the incident. The boat *Bermuda* had docked in San Juan about six months ago, the two passengers on board claiming to be expatriates from Cuba, running from a drug cartel that thought they had stolen from them. Holland's team had helped the local police somewhat with the investigation, but after the Cubans had been there a week, one of the police officers had snuck into the precinct at night and shot both travelers.

It had taken Holland's team by surprise, especially since the backlash had been minimal. As it had been explained to him later, the police on-island largely fell into two camps: those who were involved with the Dominguez gang, and those who were not. The two camps coexisted well, for the most part, turning the other way when they saw something they wouldn't normally condone.

It was a strange, twisted truth that Holland and his men had had to learn the hard way. Just because a unified body claimed to be for or against something, here in Puerto Rico there could be multiple factions within that unified whole, each working toward a completely opposite goal.

"That checks out," he said. It was, strangely enough, the most plausible explanation. "Parker just showed up on our doorstep a few days ago. Hell, I didn't know he was coming until four days ago. All this right before this alleged attack, and McDonnell's been keeping us in the dark."

"Seemed fishy to me too, boss," Delmonico said.

Holland knew that there were far more factors at play here than "for Dominguez" and "against Dominguez," and the pharmaceutical company's involvement in the mess was one such example. He still didn't understand why they were the target of Dominguez's terrorist attacks, but his plan was to figure all that out later, after they'd caught the perpetrators.

And now, it seemed, one of those perpetrators might be on their doorstep.

"We need to bring Parker in," Holland said, suddenly feeling a burst of energy. *This could be the lead we need.* He had no idea how to get through to a guy like Parker—he would be trained, obviously, but it was worth a shot. Holland saw the beginnings of a plan forming in his mind. "No one contacts him but me. I want to talk to him first, face-to-face. If you see him, call it in and follow him, otherwise we'll wait for him to come back to us. Did he see you?"

There was a pause. *"No, I don't think so,"* Delmonico said. *"He was running out of the marketplace with that woman, but I'm not sure if he noticed me."*

"He's a sharp guy," Holland said. "Hell of a detective, it seems. We need to assume he knows you were there."

"But we can't follow him? I might be able to get a jump on him, and bring him—"

"*And* he was a soldier, Delmonico. A good one, from what McDonnell said. Don't engage. If you don't shoot yourself in the foot, he might do it for you."

"Understood. What about McDonnell, speaking of him?"

"He placed Parker on the case, which means he smells like a fish's asshole as well. I want to trust him, but these political types are so far removed from their fighting days, it wouldn't surprise me if he's playing us to get himself into an even better position. This could have been a long game from the start, with nothing to do with Dominguez."

"Right," Delmonico said. *"I'll forget about it, then. Wait for your signal, I guess. Boss, this feels off. Something's a little strange about the whole thing."*

"Son, you've got a gang that's got gangs *within* it, pharmaceutical companies fighting like high-school girls over the quarterback, and a US government that doesn't really care who gets bent over a barrel as long as it lines their own pockets. Ever since we set foot on this hot-ass island, it's been strange."

"True, but this Parker guy doesn't really fit into the equation."

"Sometimes they don't, until they do. We'll figure it out, but we'll let Parker make the next move."

It was a lie—Holland was going to make a move on Parker first—but he needed Delmonico to understand the importance of allowing Jake to act without fear that his own team might be working against him. With any luck, Parker hadn't seen Delmonico in the marketplace.

He hung up the call and walked toward the back bedroom. He had no idea what Jake Parker was doing, but it was clear they had not agreed to any sort of direct confrontation with Dominguez, nor was Parker to surveil the gang without his approval. There should be no reason Parker would be at the port with another woman, unless he was on a date.

And most people on dates didn't attract the attention of a massive gang and proceed to get shot at.

Holland sighed, then knocked on the door. "Thompson, we're out in five. Be ready."

There was a muffled response from within the room, and Holland returned to the other room to address Jacobsen.

Time to get ready to fight, he thought.

CHAPTER 43

"You knew that man," Vero said.

Jake nodded, offering no other information. "You also knew him," he said.

She paused for a moment, her throat catching. "No," she said. "I did not. I saw the recognition in your eyes, and—"

"I saw the *same thing*, Vero. *You* knew him!"

Jake felt his blood starting to heat, his insides churning as the adrenaline fought with reality and the unknown fought with instinct. He knew what he had seen. She not only knew the man, she knew him *intimately.* "Don't lie to me," he said.

"If anyone has been lying, it is you."

He wanted to scream, but instead he forced his breaths slower, knowing his heart rate would eventually follow suit if he could keep up the purposeful cool-down. "Look," he said. "I have not been lying to you. Withholding the entire truth? Sure. I was a detective, Vero. It's part of my nature."

"Somehow I think you still *are* a detective?"

He waited, hoping she would continue and forget about the question. Instead, her eyes told him that it was indeed a question she expected an answer to.

"Okay," he said. "Question for question, deal? No lies, no bullshit."

The side of her mouth lifted slightly in a tiny grin. "No 'bullshit.'"

"I *was* a detective, and everything you read about me is true. But I'm still taking cases apparently."

"Apparently?"

"Yes. Friends, acquaintances, I guess. People who need answers to big, difficult problems. They call me. It's a new thing, and I guess I'll need to get some business cards," he said wryly.

"Okay, that is what I thought," Vero said. "And you have a job here in Puerto Rico?"

"Yes," he said again. "I'm working for the US government. It's related to drugs and terrorism."

"So it's related to Dominguez and pharmaceutical companies."

"Yes."

"And it's related to *my* company."

Jake shook his head. "Probably not *just* APHINT. I'm not sure of the connection yet. Your finding me in the hotel restaurant? Just a happy coincidence. And if you recall, I was *more* than happy to just eat subpar food and hit the sack until you walked in."

She smiled wider.

"So no, it's not just about APHINT, and meeting you was just a nice upside. Fitzsimmons seems to be the most vocal about terrorism on the island as it affects them, but that makes sense—it's the biggest fish in the fight. Charles Lafleur has been fighting US Congress for more security and defense presence to help keep the port safe. It's why I wanted to see the port for myself."

"That makes sense."

"That's because it's the truth," Jake said. "Now, my question: if you didn't recognize that guy at the market, why'd it look like *you* just saw a ghost?"

Vero looked out the window as the driver changed lanes and started to head over the bridge, then closed her eyes for a few seconds. When she opened them, there were tears forming on the outsides of them. "Those men, Jake. The two who were firing at us?"

"Yes. Both Dominguez, I assume, from the tattoos on their arms."

"Yes, both Dominguez."

"You know them?"

"No," Vero said. "I have never seen them before. But it was not them I was surprised to see."

"The woman?" Jake asked. "She disappeared, but I noticed her first—she was on her phone, probably calling the two grunts to move in and make the kill."

"Not her, either. She was also Dominguez, but no. I noticed someone else."

Jake couldn't imagine what—or who else—she'd noticed that would make her stop short. Someone who would bring tears to her eyes. It had obviously affected her, and Jake hadn't even realized it until he'd gotten into the car.

Now, she was acting strange about the whole thing. Sure, they'd just been shot at. Sure, they'd just been chased by professional gangsters. But she didn't seem to be affected by that. She didn't seem fazed by the fact that her life might be in danger.

Jake wanted to ask if she'd been shot at before—if this sort of crime was something more normal to her than anyone else he'd ever met. But he held his tongue. She was going to talk, he just needed to give her space. She needed time to process whatever—*whoever* it was—she'd just seen.

After a second, Vero spoke. She turned in the seat, faced Jake, and whispered. "That was a Dominguez member."

"You know him well?"

She nodded. "At least, I used to. It was my brother."

CHAPTER 44

Her brother? Jake's mouth began to move, the words already forming on his lips, when his phone began to ring. He pulled it out of his pocket. As the driver crossed the bridge into downtown San Juan, Jake looked at the number on the phone.

McDonnell.

"Who is it?" Vero asked.

Jake didn't answer her. Instead, he answered the call and held the phone up to his ear.

McDonnell was irate, and started laying into Jake the moment the call connected. "*The hell have you been doing? Where are you? What's going on down there?*"

"Whoa, whoa," Jake said, trying to use the calmest voice he had available. It was difficult, as he hadn't quite calmed down himself from the shootings in the marketplace. He involuntarily leaned up and over to check out the rearview mirror as he spoke. "What are you talking about, McDonnell? What happened?"

"*Holland just severed all communications with my office,*" McDonnell said.

"Severed all—what?"

"*He's gone rogue.*"

Jake closed his eyes and hung his head, shaking it slowly. It was exactly what he'd feared when he'd seen Delmonico in the market. Holland was not the man he thought he was—he was playing him and McDonnell both.

Jake opened his eyes and saw Vero staring at him from the opposite seat. Even the driver seemed to be checking in on them from the front seat, curious. She reached her hand out toward the center of the space between their seats, but he didn't take it. He wasn't interested in comfort, and he wasn't interested in whatever false sense of security she might provide.

"All right, McDonnell," Jake said. "Slow down a bit, and start from the beginning. What do you mean, Holland 'severed all communications with you'? He's gone off the grid?"

McDonnell cleared his throat. Jake had never heard the man worked up, even when they were younger and hotheaded on the ice after a nasty hit. He had always been like Jake—cool, collected, unflappable. *"I had Smith reach out to Holland's man Thompson about an hour ago. She told me she couldn't get through to him, but I knew they were working on getting downtown later today. I still hadn't heard anything about twenty minutes ago, so I had her try to reach the rest of his team. All of their phones were off—disconnected. I didn't have her leave any messages, but I called Holland directly from my personal cell phone, not the encrypted device we have here at the office."*

"I'm guessing he didn't answer?" Jake asked.

"Your guess is correct."

"Does he usually answer?" Jake asked.

"Every time."

"Strange," Jake said. He thought of mentioning the Delmonico sighting in the marketplace but decided against it. "I am down at the port, just outside San Juan. Looking into pharmaceutical arrivals and deliveries, trying to make sense of their schedule and trying to figure out if there's any connection to the terrorism."

"The impending attack," McDonnell said. *"Do you still think it's going to happen tomorrow?"*

"I have no reason to suspect otherwise," Jake said. "But I also don't have any solid leads as to *what* we're looking for. There are no Fitzsimmons ships in port right now, so I need to know the arrival time for anything of theirs later this evening or overnight. My hunch is that our terrorist friends will target their ship."

"Way ahead of you," McDonnell said. "There's an ambassador from the FDA meeting with Fitzsimmons tomorrow morning, and they are scheduled to arrive early tomorrow. I'm not sure what dock they'll arrive on, or any of the pertinent details, but Bolivar will be able to dig that up in a few hours."

Jake nodded as he listened. "Okay, that's good. We don't have much time before Dominguez makes their move, so anything you have I'll need to know as soon as possible."

"Noted," McDonnell said. *"Especially since Holland's team is no longer reliable."* There was a pause, and when McDonnell's voice returned, Jake heard the slight hesitation, the lowered decibel level of his voice. *"Jake, do you think Holland's been playing both sides?"*

Jake looked at Vero. She couldn't hear the conversation, but he knew that she was far more knowledgeable than she had let on. He wasn't sure she was directly involved in any of this, but it was now clear that she wasn't completely out of the loop. Her own brother was Dominguez, and he had been in the marketplace.

"I don't know," Jake said. "It's impossible to tell based on that alone. In my experience, anyone wanting to go undercover has something to hide, for better or worse."

"That's what I'm thinking. And I'd sure like to know if it's going to have an effect on completing this mission."

"It will *absolutely* have an effect on the mission," Jake said. "I'm getting antsy, McDonnell. Holland knows it, so I don't think it's a coincidence that he chose this moment to cut us out."

From the other end of the phone, Jake heard the sound of a fist slamming against a hard surface. McDonnell was pissed, and Jake couldn't shake the feeling that it was his fault, in some way or another. He hadn't intended to come across Delmonico in the marketplace, but there was no doubt in his mind that the man had seen him.

But the timeline didn't match up. If Delmonico had seen Jake, called it into his boss, and *then* Holland had decided to sever his chain of communications, McDonnell would have known about it only a few minutes ago, as he and Vero had just gotten into the cab at that time. Instead, Holland had told Jake it had been about an hour since Holland had cut him off.

Did that mean Jake was off the hook? That it wasn't *his* fault Holland was now going rogue and advancing the timeline? Or was he simply confused about the loyalties of the parties involved? Had he decided to double down on the mission and cut everyone out but his own team? It wouldn't be the worst strategy—cut out anyone he didn't fully trust.

"Listen, McDonnell. I've got a *tiny* lead. Maybe more than one. But I'm going to need an hour at least to track it, and I might need some help. Have Bolivar and Smith standing by, and be ready to answer the phone."

"Holland's not talking to me, so there's no one else down there I could *answer the phone for,"* McDonnell snapped. "Jake, I trust you. But, by God, if you are playing me for a fool, I will—"

"No need to get antsy, McDonnell," Jake said. "You *know* me, and you know you can trust me. You brought *me* into this whole mess, remember? I've got nothing to gain from this except finding who killed Mel. *That's* my mission. Always has been, always will be."

"Your mission is to figure out who the hell these terrorists are targeting, and why. If Holland's team can then bring them down, great. But—"

"I feel like I'm getting closer, McDonnell," Jake said. "And while I know I'm good at what I do, I know I am also only good at doing it *my* way. You have to trust me. Because if you don't, you're on your own." He took a breath, gripping the phone tighter. "Just say the word and I'll come home, otherwise let me do my job and be ready to provide support. I'm watching this unfold with my own eyes, on the ground. Holland is doing the same, and I'll keep an eye on him as well. You have my word."

McDonnell sighed, a long, breathy thing that reached Jake's ears even through the phone. Finally, he spoke again. He sounded weary, tired. *"Fine, Parker. Don't make me regret this."*

The call disconnected. Across the backseat, Vero met Jake's eyes. She had retracted her hand, resigning herself to looking out the window until Jake ended the call. Now, however, Jake sensed something different in her eyes. She wasn't unhappy, but there was an unsure expression on her face. Where before there had been a flicker of pain—the manifestation of the recognition of a loved one getting involved in something she didn't want to be a part of—now there seemed to be a look of disbelief.

The face of someone who had been betrayed.

CHAPTER 45

They had pulled over at a stand to get food, and while Jake was concerned they were being watched, Vero seemed far more relaxed. In fact, she had ordered extra food from the owner. He wasn't sure who it was for, or whether she was just feeling extra hungry, but he didn't have time to ask.

She began to argue with the owner when the man said it would take twenty minutes to cook. He watched as they haggled over something in Spanish, then, frustrated, she turned back to him.

She got in the car, took a few breaths, then looked at Jake. "The food will take a while."

"Fine," he said. "Who's it for?"

She didn't answer, and Jake decided to change the conversation back to their previous spat. "Vero, I didn't lie. I—"

"Do not speak, Jake Parker. *Technically,* you have not lied to me, but that does not mean you have been telling me the truth. You are involved in this case, and you have been from day one. From the moment I met you, you have been working me."

"Vero, that's not true. I didn't *know* you. Hell, I *still* don't know you."

"Are you not here to try to bring people like my brother to justice?"

He sighed. "Yes," Jake said. "That… that part's true. People like your brother—people who are involved with Dominguez, in any way—they deserve to be brought to justice. I'm trying to figure

out how they're involved in the terrorist attacks here, the ones
that target places like your company. If your brother's involved
in that in some way—"

"I do not disagree with you about my brother," Vero said.
"However, what has happened here in Puerto Rico is as much a
cultural event as it was a societal shift. Dominguez is not a gang. It
is not an organization that can be toppled or defeated or brought
to justice."

"Organizations can absolutely be brought down, Vero. Even if
they're bordering on becoming institutions."

"This is different, Jake. You have seen the tattoos yourself, I am
sure of it. The coqui frog. A symbol of Puerto Rico, the symbol
of a people."

Jake nodded. "Yes," he said. "I've seen them. All Dominguez
members have them. Other people as well, right?"

"No," Vero replied, shaking her head. "While it has always been
a symbol of the Puerto Rican people, the only people wearing
this tattoo are members of the gang itself. It is not something we
stamp upon our bodies unless we vow to fight for Dominguez."

"And your brother?"

She nodded, looking back out the window for a moment. "Yes.
He has always been difficult. Intelligent, stubborn, driven. More
so than me." She started to grin, then her eyes fell down to her lap.
"For the past five years, I have not heard from him. Our parents
were worried at first, but we understood that he had become more
and more involved with the group. He has always had a soft spot in
his heart for the people of this island, and Dominguez is, ultimately,
about the people. To them, *we* are first. And to my brother, that
means Dominguez is his best opportunity for success."

"Okay, so he has a cause he thinks worth fighting for," Jake
said. "But what cause is that? What is it he thinks he's *actually*
fighting for?"

Vero scoffed and then let out a bit of laughter. "Do not be naive, Jake," she said. "He does not think Dominguez stands for one singular thing. Just like any political party, the gang is a broad and wide group of Puerto Rican individuals. Businessmen and women, politicians, even well-known pharmaceutical executives—they are all members. They are all Dominguez. It is not one thing, and yet it is a collective. One idea, pursued at once by multiple threads that all want slightly different versions of the same outcome."

"And what outcome is that?" Jake asked.

He watched the buildings pass by outside. He had given the driver an address after they had gotten into the car after seeing Delmonico in the marketplace. He was tracking their progress using the GPS app on his phone, as he wanted to be sure they were getting there as quickly as possible. While the man certainly knew the streets of downtown Puerto Rico better than he, Jake wasn't going to second-guess a computer-assisted location app based on algorithmic data of constantly updated traffic patterns.

Vero turned and waited for Jake to look up at her before she answered. "I feel you know the answer to this already," she said. "It should be obvious, as it is the one thing all Puerto Ricans have an interest in. Dominguez or not, it is something we have *all* fought for and argued about over the decades."

"You think Puerto Rico is grappling with the question of freedom," Jake said.

Vero nodded. "I do not *think* this. It is a *fact*. There is only one thing on the minds of the men running the Dominguez organization. And that question is a simple one: what do we have to do to free Puerto Rico?" Vero looked over at Jake and then down at his phone, where the cab's progress through the city was displayed by a tiny blue dot superimposed on the map. "Where are we going?" she asked him.

"I have to get you someplace safe," Jake said, not looking up from the map. "I need to get you to—"

"A police station? No, I know where we should go. Turn left at the light," Vero said, leaning forward in the seat, directing the driver.

The man in the driver seat raised an eyebrow, but then gave the slightest nod of his head.

"Turn around on 22 and get on 18, heading south," Vero continued.

"Vero, I—"

"Wherever you would try to take me is going to be somewhere Dominguez can reach us," she said. "You think they are a large organization, but I know the truth. They are not just large: they are an entire *culture*, a way of life for the people here. There is no separating Dominguez from the Puerto Rican people. In some ways, it is subtle, and in other ways, it is obvious. No matter where we go, they will find us."

Jake felt himself torn between two truths: one, that he trusted his instinct. Two, that he trusted Vero. He didn't think she was interested in sabotaging him. If she had been, she would have turned him in back at the marketplace, allowed him to be caught, or worse. She had seemed just as scared as he had been when the shots had started flying, and she had seemed genuinely concerned when she'd spotted her brother.

That did not mean, however, that Jake would trust her blindly. He didn't get the feeling that she was playing him, but he also was not about to let his guard down. Holland had already pulled the wool over his eyes, so it was possible it could happen again. If Vero knew of a place they could go that was safe, Jake would assess the situation before allowing either of them to walk through the door.

"Where is it?" he asked.

"A small village outside of San Juan. Near El Yunque National Forest."

Jake shook his head. "Vero," he said, "I don't think that is such a good idea. I know that area is—"

"No, Jake Parker. You know nothing. You think you know me and my people, and you think you know this gang. What you do not know is that these people value family above all. They value Puerto Rico above all. There is an unspoken set of rules, a barrier across which they will not tread. No one will think to look for us there, because no one will suspect that you are that close to me. They will look for you, so if you popped up at the resort or the restaurant or literally anywhere else on the island, they would find you in minutes. But where I am taking us, no one will think to look."

"Why is that?"

"Because there would be no way you would know how to get there."

"I see," Jake said. "And… are you going to tell me specifically what this wonderful place is?"

"Sure," Vero said. "We are going to my childhood home."

CHAPTER 46

Vero's parents' home stood in the center of a copse of trees abutting the edge of the National Forest on the northernmost side, about an hour from San Juan.

Her father and mother toiled on the land as local organic gardeners. As she had explained to Jake, her childhood had been tumultuous: while her parents were loving, and life was generally good, the financial situation of the family was precarious at best. For most of Vero's childhood, her parents worked harder than anyone she knew—and brought home less than anyone she knew.

After a few decades, however, the world seemed to appreciate the idea of free-range, locally grown animals and organic, small farm foods. What her parents had been doing since before she was born had quickly become a trendy fad, and their expertise, knowledge, and reputation allowed them to suddenly raise the prices on all of their produce in order to compete with the growing chains of grocery stores dotting the island.

Her parents, however, seemed to hardly notice their increased net worth over the last few years. They operated the same way they always had, in a frugal and nonchalant manner. They brought their food to the market, sold it, and returned home, day in and day out, season after season. Vero and her brother Cecil had grown up, used their educations to get good jobs and begin their own adult lives, and their parents remained humble and living well below their means in the same house both children had been born in.

The house itself was set back from the street about a hundred paces, a narrow cobblestone path nearly overgrown with brambles and rainforest ferns was the only route up to the house. The foliage around was dense enough to be impenetrable and no doubt full of nasty creatures and critters.

Vero led Jake up the path until the entirety of the house was in view. It was a quaint little thing—well-constructed and thoughtfully appointed. It reminded him of a Hobbit hole, except above ground and set in the rainforest. A hill rose behind the house, and Jake immediately felt at home. The way the house sat halfway up the hill reminded him of where his grandparents had used to live. Theirs had been a single-story, two-bedroom affair that was nothing special from the outside, but inside was filled with wonders and trinkets that let a young child's imagination run wild. He had spent many late nights there with his grandfather, working on puzzles or logic problems by candlelight—not because they didn't have electricity, but because his grandfather seemed to think he thought better when aided by "nature's illumination."

As he walked up and reached the front door with Vero, Jake smiled, his mind harkening back to his younger years.

Vero spoke, snapping Jake out of the past. "My father will pretend to be intense and intimidating," Vero said. "He is not. Just allow him his indulgences and be sweet to my mother, and you will not be chased out."

Jake laughed. "Okay then. Meeting the parents—didn't think this was a 'second date' sort of thing."

Vero elbowed him in the ribs and then grabbed his hand. "So, you think we are on our second date?" She asked.

Jake shrugged.

"…And you think taking me to a market and letting me get shot at by gangsters is a *first* date?"

Jake's mouth opened in response.

She spoke before he could. "If it was a date, that was the *worst* first date ever. And since we are technically still on that first date, you are meeting my parents in spite of—not *because* of—it."

Once again, Jake started to respond, but suddenly a tiny light bulb next to the door turned on and the door itself opened.

The smallest woman Jake had ever seen appeared on the stoop, a deep and angry frown on her face. "Vero? Is that you? Why do you bring another boy to my house?"

"Another?" Jake asked. He was met by an elbow to his side.

"Mama!" Vero said. "This is my friend, Jake Parker. We will be staying the night. We brought food, too. It's cold now, but I can heat it up."

Her mother's eyebrow rose, and Jake suddenly saw Vero's own personality on the woman's face. "Oh, you will be staying? Well, good, because the last time you stayed, you did not clean the sheets. They are still on your bed, in your room, waiting for you to wash—"

"Vero?" a new voice asked, from farther inside the house. "Verónica, is that you? What is your mama saying? You can stay here as long as you'd like. You should live here, it is far cheaper and a much better situation then whatever your roommates want you to believe down at—"

"Stop talking, old man!" Vero's mother said, snapping her fingers in the direction of the man's voice. "She brought a friend with her, can't you see that?"

Jake suddenly bust out laughing. He couldn't help himself. After a second of laughter, he cut himself off, noticing that both women's eyes were on him. Then suddenly, the door opened wider and Jake saw a man, six inches *shorter* than the woman, appear.

CHAPTER 47

He couldn't believe it. Cecil's eyes must have been lying to him. Yet his mind knew the truth. The recognition was unquestionable, but it still seemed impossible.

Vero had been in the marketplace.

Cecil had traveled to San Juan an hour earlier, heading for the port to watch the bay and look at the arriving and departing ships. He had wanted to go mostly to clear his head and try to forget the habit-forming monotony of his temporary day job in the mailroom, but he also wanted to see if Dominguez was, in fact, going to make a play against the FDA ambassador who would be arriving in Puerto Rico tomorrow.

He wasn't sure what the situation was—if this would be the usual type of attack or just a reconnaissance mission—but he was starving for information.

Over the past few days, his life had been turned into a roller coaster. The leader of Dominguez, Mr. Diego, had personally summoned him from his work in the United States, getting his hopes up that he might be destined for a promotion in the organization. He had put his entire life into Dominguez, and he had felt that his opportunity had arrived.

But in the Fitzsimmons mailroom his hopes and dreams had come crashing down. His life had come to a halt. He was nothing but an errand boy, a grunt day laborer. He had wanted to be a *soldier*, a man on the front lines of the victory coming to Dominguez. He had wanted to *lead*, to guide others into battle.

Instead, he had been served a plate of humble pie, and it did not taste good.

But he was not an intelligent, bullheaded young man for no reason. He had been created to strive for power, attention, *true meaning*. And he would find it.

He had performed his role admirably, allowing Dominguez a small step toward whatever it was they were planning. And so he had decided to award himself a small victory as well: he would do his best to find out what it was his organization was planning.

Visiting the port had seemed like a good idea—it was public, so if there were other Dominguez members there, his presence wouldn't seem terribly suspicious. And it was where the FDA ambassador was scheduled to arrive, so whatever was happening would be visible to Cecil.

He had chosen the old marketplace north of the port on the San Juan Island as the place to sit and watch. He could grab a bite to eat, see the tourists and business owners and fishmongers all fighting for attention and money. It was an exciting, thriving place to be, and it was familiar: Cecil and his family had visited the market here a couple of times when he was younger, his parents hoping to sell their homegrown vegetables and fruits in one of the many stalls. While the day rates had been far too expensive for his parents to set up shop there regularly, when the local economy was booming with tourists and cheap gas prices, they would pile into their old station wagon and head over the bridge for a day.

Cecil smiled when he remembered it. It was a simpler time, to be sure. But if he had known then what he knew now—if he had had the knowledge he had gained working for Dominguez and through his studies at university, he could have helped his parents with their business. Things may have worked out differently. Rather than see his parents scrape out a living from the land they didn't even own, struggling to feed growing children and put them through school, only to have it all wasted by sweeping changes to agricultural laws and new United States FDA regulations, Cecil could have helped them navigate it. He could have helped them price their wares appropriately to generate profit, build a brand and grow their business.

He saw ways to use the land more efficiently, to produce twice or three times as much as his parents currently did, but he knew they wouldn't listen. They were stubborn—he and his sister had learned the trait from them—and would simply complain that they didn't want to overcomplicate their little farming business. They would ask him to go his own way, to leave the farming to the boring old parents.

And so he *had* found his own way. Puerto Rico needed to be freed from the United States' stranglehold on it, and Dominguez offered a way for that to happen. Sure, it was a brutal, tough-love approach, but Cecil had never been one for diplomacy and wishy-washy meandering. He liked the blunt, direct approach.

The *power* approach.

The marketplace had been quiet for most of the morning—there were fewer tourists there than he'd remembered—but he had seen two Dominguez gang members after about an hour. They were walking side by side, a man and a woman, and he recognized the man as someone he had spoken to once, long ago. He couldn't remember their names, nor could he remember what their position in the organization was, but it didn't matter. He wasn't about to speak with them or call attention to himself. He had assumed that they were here to do a job, and he wasn't going to insert himself into their mission and get any of them in trouble. No, he would watch, see what they were doing, and simply appreciate the day.

It was evident after about five minutes of watching them that they were part of a larger team. The woman had checked her phone a few times, glancing around at the stalls of fish and seafood. He had noticed another man, younger, with a coqui tattoo on the inside of his left wrist, and realized that they were all here to case the marketplace.

They were looking for someone.

Intrigued, Cecil had walked closer to the woman, staying hidden behind the rows of fishmonger stalls and ice chests. He had watched when the man left her side and walked back in the other direction.

Then he had seen them: the man and woman the Dominguez team was apparently interested in. Their backs were to Cecil and the Dominguez woman, but they walked arm in arm through the market, laughing at each other's jokes, the not-so-subtle flirtation apparent on both their faces. The man was American by the looks of it, his slightly curled hair barely lapping at the tops of his ears.

He had pulled the woman in close, and then they had kissed.

And then she had pulled away from him, and Cecil had felt his heart rate quicken.

No.

It couldn't be. There was no way—*how* could it be true?

He had seen her face clearly, then. She'd even looked in his direction, but he didn't think she'd noticed him. If she did, she didn't react.

But it was unmistakable. He knew the face better than any other on the planet. His mind had reeled with the possibilities, with the realization that what he thought had to be wrong, and then his better judgment, trying to convince him to leave, to run away and forget he'd seen anything.

But who was the man? The American? Why were they together? What were they doing here? And, most of all, why was his *sister* in the marketplace, being watched by the Dominguez group? What had she gotten herself into?

He had rubbed his temples as he thought, a nervous habit. And only when he'd stood up fully and started toward the exit to the marketplace did the shooting begin.

He couldn't be seen here. He'd started to run, fitting in with the people screaming and heading for the exit.

What are you doing, Vero? He'd thought. He hadn't looked back. He hoped she was okay, but he also hoped she knew what it was she had gotten involved in.

The shots had continued as he reached the street, but he had ignored them as he turned left and headed back toward the bridge.

CHAPTER 48

"Who is this? Vero, you have brought another man into your mother's home?"

Vero pushed past her tiny parents and into the kitchen of the house. "Come on, Jake, ignore them. Mama, Papa, stop heckling my friend. You know as well as I do, I have not had a boy here since—"

"Hector," both parents said in unison, their voices abrupt and forceful.

Vero sighed and rolled her eyes as Jake sheepishly walked in and joined her. "Hector was just a friend, just like Jake is."

"Hector slept in your bed," her father remarked. "And you did not clean the sheets after. Your mother has left them for you, and I hope—"

"*I know* that Mother has left them for me, Papa," Vero said. "She *always* leaves them for me, no matter who is sleeping in them. And I will have you know, Hector slept on the floor *next* to my bed."

"Good," her father said. "That means they will not be nearly as dirty. It should take you less time to clean them."

Jake knew he was wide-eyed and slack-jawed while listening to the comical, almost unbelievable exchange, but he couldn't help it. These people were hilarious and yet loving and kind, and he immediately felt himself endeared toward them, even though they had barely even looked his way.

Vero tossed the food from the Styrofoam containers onto a skillet on the old range top and heated it. They exchanged pleasantries, but it was clear to Jake that her parents thought nothing of him other than that their daughter had simply picked up a hitchhiker she was now friendly with.

They ate slowly, taking nearly a full hour to get through her parents' barrage of questions and comments on the quality of the food. Vero and Jake sat in the kitchen at the table, Vero doing her best to dodge their questions of work and life and boyfriends.

After they had finished, Vero pulled Jake through the kitchen and into a tiny living room, full of televisions. He counted three on a television stand and table that had been set up side by side, then saw a fourth—a tiny black-and-white 7-inch thing—against the far wall. All of them were on, all of them quietly pumping noise into the tiny room.

"They can never decide what to watch," Vero said, then yanked him along as if she'd just explained everything sufficiently. "Come on."

Jake let himself be pulled farther back into the house, noticing pictures on the walls of a young Vero and a boy, up until their high school years. There was a picture of both children, Vero considerably older than her brother. After what looked to be a high-school senior portrait, there were no more pictures of the boy.

"That your brother?" Jake asked.

Vero nodded, not offering anything else. He didn't press it. They were walking towards a back room, so he figured she'd want to close the door and make sure her parents couldn't hear before they'd start into debriefing the events of the past few hours.

"Your parents speak English well," Jake said.

She nodded. "They speak it at the market, so they're fluent. And whenever I bring guests who look American, they slip into English for their sake."

Jake grinned. "So that was all for me?"

"They are characters, no? They do enjoy drama."

Jake laughed, thinking of his first encounter with Vero. *The apple must not have fallen far from the tree.*

Vero pulled Jake into a bedroom that had a rumpled, unmade bed in the center against the far wall. It was a twin-size, and the sheets were plain and unfurled, the comforter piled up in a ball at the foot of it. There were no pictures in this room, but a dresser sat on one side and a small vanity on the other. Both were worn, likely older than the house itself.

"This is your childhood room?" Jake asked.

Vero shut the door behind him and then waved her hands around. "Yes, this is it. Everything you see has been here since I was a child. I took some photos when I moved out, but my parents are still harboring some crazy dream that I will move back in with them and we would forever argue about my boyfriends."

Jake chuckled. "Speaking of your boyfriends, tell me more about Hector."

She shrugged. "What's to know? He was really just a friend. We tried to see if it could be more, but it couldn't. He was immature, not ready for commitment."

Jake waited, but she didn't offer more. "And you are?"

She shrugged again, then walked over to the vanity and pulled out a tiny chair and sat on it. "I don't know, really. I was very involved with my career—I *am* involved with my career. I love it."

"But…"

"But APHINT is dealing with a lot right now. It seems like my job is getting to be more and more about politics than it is chemistry. I miss the *work*, the fourteen-hour laboratory days, the discovery. We are doing very little of that now, it seems."

"Why? I thought that was what your company did? How can they sell pharmaceuticals if they're not spending as much time making them?"

"I explained a bit about it at the restaurant—they are doubling down on new treatments for Lewy, but they are also selling their products to new markets. It has become more about marketing than research and development."

"And with the attacks, and what you've told me about the medication—Chemical X—you're working on, I'm sure it's only going to upset things more," Jake added. He wanted to get the conversation back to the marketplace, to ask her about her brother and his involvement. Anything she could help him with might bring him closer to his own goal.

"Yes," she said. "Of course. Chemical X, the drug we're working on, it will only get us in trouble when the FDA figures it out. I'm not sure there will be a way to deny it. And yes, the attacks are gang-related, but no one knows why they are doing it. After the Puerto Rican pharmaceuticals got their billion-dollar bailout, the companies have all been—"

"Wait," Jake said. "Their what?"

"The bailout," Vero answered. "A couple of years ago. The terrorist attacks started getting more frequent—bombs, kidnappings, ransoms, that sort of thing, all related to the pharmaceutical companies—so the FDA dumped some ungodly amount of money into corporate interests here to try to curb the attacks and keep the economy balanced."

"They gave the companies money to help fight terrorism?"

"Well, it was all sold to the nation as a legal avenue for injecting money into the local economy. No one really cared—we knew we weren't going to see a dime of it. But if the crooks at the top of these companies get their pockets lined, I guess they have enough to pass around to pay off whoever's interested in attacking them."

Jake whistled. "Wow, that seems like a really good way to *increase* the amount of terrorist attacks. I mean, if you know the bigwigs have a bunch of extra cash, wouldn't you target them even more?"

She shrugged again. "Who knows why they're doing it? Dominguez has never admitted to any of the attacks, but—"

"But we know the materials used in the attacks are originating in Puerto Rico," Jake said abruptly.

She paused, then leaned back against the vanity. "How do you know that?"

Jake swallowed. He hadn't meant to blurt it out, but it was nagging at him. "Bismuth. One of the main products your company produces."

CHAPTER 49

"Bismuth? As in, bismite?" Vero asked.

"Yes," Jake said. "The element."

"Well, sure," Vero explained. "It's a byproduct of what we do. But most of the pharmaceuticals use it during at least some part of their process. It's difficult not to. Why?"

"Well, I'm here in Puerto Rico investigating the attacks. The explosions, specifically. We think there's going to be another one tomorrow, and—"

"We? Who's we? Jake, I need you to tell me everything."

"Sorry," Jake said. "I mean the team I'm working with." He thought of McDonnell, and considered how much he wanted to reveal to Vero. "They're not here—I'm just helping out, as a consultant."

"Okay, fine. Go on."

"Well, there have been attacks in several countries, including the United States, but one of the reasons we had Puerto Rico pinned as the epicenter is that they're using bismuth in their bombs."

Vero frowned. "That seems unnecessary."

Jake nodded. "It is. It's totally unnecessary, and there's not really any benefit to adding it. Besides that, the explosive debris that we've identified that has bismuth in it is appearing in a few spots around the world, but it's mostly confined to the United States and Puerto Rico. *Heavily* on Puerto Rico's side of things."

"I know that," she said. "We all know that. And you already know that Dominguez is behind the attacks."

"Right," Jake said. "But *why*? It's not really about targeting the pharmaceutical companies as a fear tactic, because why would they use bismuth in the explosives? If they wanted to go under the radar and shake things up, scare the pharmaceuticals and the powers-that-be, why wouldn't they do it more secretively?"

"Because they want people to know it's them."

"Exactly," Jake said. "The explosions are caused by bombs made by Dominguez, or at least related to the gang somehow—they might be making them themselves or they might be paying people to do it. But they're building them similarly, using bismuth as a sort of token—a calling card, one that remains at the scene long after the explosion."

"As I said, they *want* people to know it's them," Vero said. "Why is that a problem?"

Jake shrugged, then looked out the tiny window near Vero's vanity. "I don't know. Maybe because no one's doing anything about it? The local police here seemed completely disinterested in helping me—"

"Seemed?" Vero asked, frowning.

"I was looking into an incident. Talked to some police officers, that was it. I wanted to see what was being done to keep Dominguez in control."

Vero scoffed. "I told you already, Jake Parker, there is no 'keeping Dominguez in control.' *They* are in control. *They* run this island."

"Right," he said. "All the more reason I think it's strange they want everyone to know the bombs are theirs."

"How so?"

"Well, typical small-time gang warfare is highly competitive. There aren't any rules, of course, but each side wants to show up the other side, in a dangerous game of 'keep up with the Joneses.' They leave behind items as a way to 'prove' to their opponents that they're better than them. We've seen playing cards, scarves or handkerchiefs, caps, all sorts of things."

"So you are saying that this is done by a gang to mark their territory."

"Yeah, something like that," Jake said. "Sometimes it's about claiming territory, sometimes it's just to send a message: 'this is ours,' or something like that."

Vero nodded, and Jake knew he was getting through to her. She looked away, then her eyes snapped back and stared into his. "That means Dominguez is trying to prove a point," she said. "And since there is no 'territory' up for grabs…"

"Right," Jake said. "You said it yourself: Puerto Rico is all but controlled by Dominguez. It's their island. There *aren't* any other gangs around. Sure, there are factions, different microcosms within the whole of the organization, but that's normal. And we can tell it's not an intra-organizational feud because we've only ever seen this one side of it. Like, if two or more factions were battling it out and trying to leg up on another, we'd seen one side using bombs with bismuth in them, and another side using bombs with some other chemical. Or something else entirely—killing people and marking them somehow."

"But that is not happening," Vero added.

"Nope, not at all. It's *all* been Dominguez-based. Yet they still mark their crimes, they still leave a fingerprint. Why?"

"Because there *is* another side. There *is* someone they're against."

"Who's that?" Jake asked, already knowing the answer to the question.

Vero confirmed his suspicions. "The United States."

"That's like biting the hand that feeds you, isn't it?"

"Well, Dominguez doesn't get any of the benefit the pharmaceuticals do. The bailout money from the FDA doesn't line their pockets, at least not directly."

"I see," Jake said.

"And I know my brother joined Dominguez because they want what he wants: a free, self-ruled Puerto Rico. One that is not beholden to the United States."

Jake nodded. "That's what I'm taking from this, as well. Dominguez's *true* target isn't the pharmaceutical companies, it's the United States itself. They don't want the government bureaucrats showing up and bossing them around. And the best way they've found to hit them where it hurts is by attacking the pharmaceutical companies."

"Yes, exactly," Vero said. "I never thought of it that way, but it makes perfect sense. If people like me can't do our jobs because our companies are under constant threat of attack, the companies cannot be in business. The United States will lose the pharmaceutical companies and then its hold in Puerto Rico will slip."

"And, ultimately, the United States will no longer get the sweet deal they've gotten: essentially free pharmaceuticals—drugs and medications it can sell at a massive profit—produced by a low-cost workforce in a place it barely has to secure."

Vero stood and started pacing. Jake was pleased to see her excitement, but there were still questions to answer. It was as if the pieces of the puzzle had been shaken out of the box and were now scattered all over the floor. They were all there, but they needed to be placed in the proper configuration.

"There's one more part of this that really sells it for me," Jake said.

"What's that?"

"Well, Dominguez is a gang. An organization—a *business*, if you will."

"Of course."

"And businesses need to make money. They have operating expenses. Overheads. They're playing around with terrorism, which, not surprisingly, costs money. Equipment, training, ingredients for the explosives. So where are they getting the money?"

Vero frowned. "That is the part you don't understand?" she asked.

"Well, I don't have any evidence to prove it yet, but I'd bet that just like many gangs in the States, Dominguez has a pretty steady income stream selling drugs."

Vero nodded, then her eyes fell. "Yes, of course. That is true. It is said that any drug in Puerto Rico starts as a legal product of one of the companies, then becomes illegal when it is stolen by Dominguez."

"So they're making money off the backs of workers like you," Jake said. "But even more, they have a common enemy with the United States. They're not just targeting the pharmaceuticals to get to the US and the FDA, they're targeting them because, in the short-term, putting companies like APHINT and Fitzsimmons out of business means less *competition*."

Vero confirmed. "Yes, that is right." Her eyes were no longer on Jake, and he saw that she had her phone in her hand. It was ringing, and Jake suddenly noticed the steady vibration emanating from it. He tried to peek over her hand and see the screen, but she answered it before he could glance at it.

Surprisingly, she pressed the speaker button on the phone and held it out so that Jake could hear the conversation.

"Vero?"

It was a man's voice, crackling through a poor connection. Deep, but not terribly low. He sounded distressed, and Jake could hear voices from far away somewhere around the man on the other end of the line.

"Yes," she said. "Cecil, is that you?"

"Vero, they are coming. Run."

CHAPTER 50

"Jake, we need to go. Now."

Jake looked at Vero and saw the fear in her eyes. There was confusion there as well. Jake had heard the words over the phone just before her brother, Cecil, had disconnected the call.

They are coming. Run.

Jake might have been a trained detective, but he knew it wouldn't take much investigation to know who the man was talking about. "That was your brother?" Jake asked. "He warned you about Dominguez. Why?"

Vero threw her hands up, exasperated. "He is my brother, Jake. He loves me."

"If Dominguez is like any other crime organization, he will get in serious trouble when they find out he snooped."

"We can't worry about that now," Vero said. "Hurry."

Jake wasn't planning on *worrying* about it now, but it was worth mentioning. Cecil—and by extension, Vero—was implicated. They would have to be careful from here on out.

There was a knock at the front door and a voice—a man's—shouted something in Spanish. Jake couldn't understand it, but it sounded urgent. "Your parents," he said. "I need to go make sure they'll be—"

"No," Vero said gruffly. "They have lived here their entire lives; they know this place and the people. Dominguez won't harm them."

"And if it's Cecil?" Jake asked.

"It's not," she answered. "He called me to warn me; if he was here in person, he wouldn't have needed to. It's Dominguez, but they're not going to harm my parents."

"Even to get to us?" Jake asked.

"No."

Jake could hear the hesitation in her voice, he could see it spelled out across her face. To her credit, however, Jake knew she had made the decision and would stick to it, no matter how scared she might be. She wasn't going to back down now. If Dominguez wanted trouble, there was nothing they could do about it. The best option they had was to sneak out a back door and hope that Vero's parents lied and said they were never here.

"There is a side door," Vero said. "Go out and head up the hill. You will be able to stay out of sight in the trees and bushes. I will be one minute behind you."

"What are you going to—"

"Go!" Vero shouted.

She ducked and ran out of her bedroom, turning back into the hallway toward the living room. Jake wanted to chase after her, but he knew there would be nothing he could do to help her. If it came to having to fire on someone, he'd rather be in an open space, away from Vero's parents. He felt the weapon still seated behind his waist, tightly secured with the safety on.

Jake turned to the left as he exited the room, aiming toward the back part of the house. He saw a bathroom with its door open and another bedroom—probably the master—to the right, so he reached the end of the hall and turned the opposite way. There he found a utility room with a tiny washer and dryer stacked on top of one another against the wall. And next to the washer and dryer was a storm door. He pushed it open slowly and quietly, his hand grasping around the grip of the pistol.

He listened for any unnatural noises, but all he could hear were the sounds of the coqui frogs and crickets singing their early-evening song. He pushed the door open wider, then glanced left and right. The side yard was a mere strip of land, mostly mud and some pressed-down leaves where someone had trod over the area many times. Just feet away from the door was a wall of foliage, thick enough that he didn't think he could cross through it if he wanted to.

He turned to the right and headed up the hill just as Vero had directed. He wasn't sure how far he was supposed to travel, but he knew that his best chance at defending himself and Vero, as well as her parents, would be to get away from this place. Dominguez were chasing *him*, not her. He was their target, and if they were smart, they would breeze past Vero's parents' house and keep looking for him before the trail went cold.

The hill rose steeply, then tapered off to a shallow incline for about fifty more feet until the wall of foliage curved around the back of the property and created a natural barrier directly in front of him. Jake pressed himself into the woods, feeling the damp, cool fronds and shoots of bushes and tree branches against his body. He had to work to get through, but after about a minute, he was able to crawl a couple of feet into the dense rainforest. He shifted and turned around, facing down the hill, where he could see the entire backside of the house.

Vero appeared at the side door and turned toward him. She was crouching, hustling up the hill while staying close to the tree line, just as he had. Jake heard the sound of a car rumbling down the street in front of the house, but they were too far away for him to see them.

After another minute, Vero joined him.

"What did you have to do?" Jake asked her.

"I had to get something. I think it will help us out."

"Okay," Jake said, nodding. "I appreciate all of this, but I have to admit—I'm not used to running around while people are shooting at me without a plan. What did your parents do? Did they answer the door?"

"I'm sure they did, but they know better than to tell strangers where their children are. I'm sure they concocted a story about how I've been off in some unknown place traipsing around with some unknown boyfriend, just waiting for me to return home so I can finish doing my laundry."

Jake couldn't help but laugh. "Yeah, you know what? I can see that."

"Trust me, we are fine," Vero said. "For now. We do need to get to the water, though. There is a road that winds around the village and down toward the waterline, and if we start now we can get there in half an hour."

"Half an hour?" Jake asked. "We need a vehicle, there's not enough time."

"Not enough time for what? Dominguez is everywhere, Jake Parker. If they are checking at my parents' house, they will also be checking my home back at APHINT's campus, as well as at the hotel. The manager of the hotel is probably fielding phone calls right now from people working for Dominguez. There is nowhere on the island we can go to hide from them, Jake."

"Okay," Jake replied. "So where are we going to go?"

Vero smiled as she yanked Jake out of the rainforest. He stumbled on a root, but then caught himself and prepared to start moving once again.

Vero had other plans. She waited until his face was clear of the forest and then leaned in and kissed it. It was short, no more than a quick peck, but it reminded Jake of everything they had been through together over the past couple of days. It reminded him of his blossoming feelings for this woman, someone he had only just met.

And, of course, it reminded him of Mel. Strangely enough, he realized that it reminded him of Eliza, as well.

When she pulled back, she kept his face in her hands. Her silhouette was framed by the dying early-evening light, making her face dark and mysteriously unreadable. A flicker of sunlight caught her face, and he noticed her eyes had narrowed. She was smiling. "Jake Parker, I am scared as well. But this is my home. These are my people. Trust me. I know that it is not easy for you to do, but I will not let them get to us."

"Yeah, but—"

"But where are we going?" Vero asked, finishing the sentence for him. "As I said, there is nowhere *on the island* we can go to hide from them, so we'll leave it."

CHAPTER 51

The road leading down to the water on the other side of the town was really more of a path, just two lines of muddy rainforest floor twisting and winding around the outskirts, meandering slowly toward the coast.

Vero had changed at her family home from the sandals she'd had on before into slip-ons that more closely resembled tennis shoes.

Jake was glad she'd had the foresight to know exactly what type of "road" they'd be traveling on, as they were both jogging down the path, trying to elude the largest of the muddy puddles. She hadn't grown tired yet, judging by the fact that she had not slowed in almost twenty-five minutes.

They reached the edge of the forest, and the path rose upward for a few yards and then dropped steeply down onto a beach. Immediately, the air felt different, with a slight metallic taste to it. Lighter as well. A few birds squawked and flew toward the water, searching for dinner as the sun began to set to the left of Jake's view. It was getting dark already, and the shadows cast on the shoreline were long and deep, making it difficult to see the details of the terrain. He could see that there was a tiny stretch of sand adjacent to a tall pile of boulders to his left, but the sand curled around the front of the rock wall where it ended against a man-made structure.

It was a dock, and at the end of the short dock were small single-motor fishing boats, moored to the posts sticking up from the pier.

"The families of the town own these," Vero said. "We each help keep them maintained, and in turn the people who fish from them keep the families supplied with fresh fish and seafood. There are a bunch more around."

"That's a pretty good arrangement," Jake said, barely able to talk above his panting. The sweat and humidity had reached an equilibrium, so while his shirt was damp, it was not overwhelmingly so, and he knew that after a few minutes of steady, deep breathing to get his heart rate back down, he would start cooling off a bit. And, if they were going to go out on this tiny boat, the ocean spray forming around him would only help.

"Get in and I will take off the line," Vero said.

"You're a pharmaceutical chemist, who was raised by organic farmers, whose brother is in a gang, and now you tell me you're an expert boatswain?"

"I am certainly not an expert, but I know my way around a fishing boat. We used to go out a lot, before I moved out. My father loves to fish, and my mother loves to eat it. Cecil and I would take turns driving the boat. We were never much for waiting around for fish to bite, but getting the engine open out on the water, navigating between swells was always a thrill."

Jake stepped into the small watercraft as Vero untied the line and tossed the rope into the boat. She stepped in and grabbed Jake's arm to steady herself. When they were both seated, she pushed off the dock and allowed the boat to slide gracefully toward open water. She waited a few more seconds and then pulled the ripcord on the engine. It sputtered to life, choking a few times until starting to purr like a brand-new motor. She grabbed the handle and deftly maneuvered the boat around the breakers and toward open ocean.

Jake was facing her in the boat, and over her shoulder, he could see the shoreline they had just left. Suddenly he saw lights in the distance, and then the single illuminated circle became two pinpricks of light.

Headlights.

"Looks like we have company," Jake said over the noise of the motor.

The car came into view over the road. It was in a hurry, bouncing haphazardly over the tiny road and swerving to a halt as it struck the sandy beach. The lights were now facing northwest, brightening the dock they had just left from, and because of that Jake could see three men piling out of the car. Another man, the driver, opened the door and came out the other side.

Jake felt the rush of adrenaline and he reached back for his pistol. Against the shadows and dancing light, Jake saw the unmistakable shapes of submachine guns in the men's hands.

"Hey, does this thing go any faster?" he asked.

Vero looked over her shoulder just as the first man opened fire. Tiny splatters flicked water upward as the line of hot bullets raced toward the boat.

"Vero, left, now!" Jake shouted. He lurched forward and fell on his knees into the center of the boat, using the side of it for balance, his other hand drawing his gun.

Vero pulled the rudder hard and the boat jumped sideways, catching the crest of a wave and then smacking against the bottom of the next. Jake's knees were crushed against the hard metal hull of the craft, but he gritted his teeth and ignored the pain. He lined up a shot and fired three times.

The shots all went wide, the combination of the rocking boat speeding away from the shore and the distance from him to the shooters too much for the small handgun. He lined up again, hoping Vero would keep the boat between the crests of the waves for a few more seconds.

The other men fired at the same time, their rounds also sailing wide and landing behind the boat.

Suddenly, the boat flew upward, Vero turning back toward the open ocean and sending the boat flying over another crest. This time, the vessel got air and there was a momentary sense of weightlessness as the boat and its passengers all reached the apex of its short flight.

When the boat landed this time, Jake's knees had had too much. He groaned in pain, pulling the pistol back in and then sitting back down on the strip of wood that formed the seat.

"Sorry about that," Vero said. "I was more interested in getting away than in your comfort."

Jake shook his head. "No need to apologize. Bruised knees are far better than gunshot wounds."

Vero smiled and then yanked the tiller handle sideways once again, immediately causing the engine to strain and pull the opposite direction. It was a smart move, trying to put as much distance between themselves and the shooters while also making themselves a harder target, but anymore such maneuvering and Jake was going to vomit. He wasn't prone to seasickness, but every man had his limits.

Rather than trying to line up another shot, Jake decided to conserve ammunition and simply hold on for dear life. He heard the pattering of far-off gunfire as the men tried to land a hit, but the best they could manage was a couple rounds pinging off the hull, the angle too shallow for penetration.

Another fifteen seconds passed and they were safely away from shore.

"Are they going to get in one of the other boats and chase us?" Jake asked.

"If they do," Vero said, "They will have a hard time. The other two boats were in need of repair. My father gave me the keys to this one since he was going to use it tomorrow morning. He told me it was the only one gassed up and ready to go."

"So that's what you were doing," Jake said.

She nodded, winking at him in the dying daylight. "I had to sneak around and whisper while the Dominguez idiots were talking to my mother at the door, but my father was already waiting for me near the hallway."

CHAPTER 52

Vero slowed the engine and aimed the boat toward the sunset to the west, careful to stay far enough away from shore that they would be difficult to spot.

"Your family seems to be very prepared for when gangsters come knocking on your door," Jake said. "My guess is this isn't the first time it's happened."

Vero's eyes fell to the floor of the boat. She shook her head. "No, but I wish you were wrong." She sighed. "When Cecil went off to join them, we thought he would lose interest quickly. This is not like joining a normal gang, if there is such a thing. It's not like you have to just kill somebody or tag something to be initiated. They operate like a business. They make you take tests, there is a training period, the recruits even have a dress code. Plenty of time for an interested newcomer to decide they are not actually interested."

"Wow," Jake muttered. "Sounds like a cult. And Cecil was interested?"

She nodded. "To be honest, it seems like a good fit for him. He is very smart—very business savvy. But he has always been the kind of person to want to make his own way. He has no interest in doing anything the traditional way. Dominguez offered him a way to climb a corporate ladder of sorts, to give him the structure and something to achieve, all while feeding his desire to find his own purpose and giving him the freedom to discover it."

"Sounds like you talk to him a lot."

She shook her head. "I used to. I do not know when it happened, but after he had been a member for two, maybe three years, it was like they cut him off. I have not spoken to him directly since then."

Jake nodded as he listened. "Sorry to hear that. I do understand the appeal of the overall big picture, though. That's what the military was for me—at least, that's the promise."

"You were in the Army, yes?"

Jake nodded, remembering that she had done a bit of research on him after their first dinner. "I was. Went to West Point, wanted to go pro as a hockey player but got injured my junior year. The Army offered me a deal I couldn't refuse: I got to travel the world, while saving it at the same time."

One of Vero's eyebrow rose on her forehead. "And did you get to save the world, Jake Parker?"

Jake smiled from the side of his mouth. "Verdict is still out on that."

They sailed on, puttering at half-speed to the west. Jake wondered what the plan was, and he was about to ask when the engine began to sputter intermittently.

"Out of gas?" he asked.

"Yes, but there are two more five-gallon canisters in that compartment next to the engine." She tapped with her heel at a closed wooden box next to the motor. "Besides, we are almost there."

"Yeah—about that," Jake said. "Where is 'there,' exactly?"

"This is a place my father and I discovered a few years ago on one of our fishing trips. We are too far away from shore for anyone to see, but there is a spot just up ahead where we are in range of the cellular towers from the east side of San Juan. I figured we could stop out here and throw the anchor down as long as we need to. They may be tracking *you*, but they will have no way to access your personal cell phone, at least not yet."

Jake smiled. It was a genius plan. "That's brilliant, Vero. Unless they're the National Security Agency, they won't have enough on me to know how to find my cell phone. Much less how to track it. We don't need to stay out here all night, just long enough to figure out what the plan is and which direction we need to head next."

"Exactly," Vero said. "The men back at the dock will call it in and everyone around this area will be waiting for us to return. There may be a few paid-off Coast Guard boats in this area, but I doubt it."

Jake smiled. "And they probably don't expect that we've got enough gas to get halfway around the island," Jake said.

"Right. They'll assume we need to get back to shore to figure out what to do next, but if we can do our research from here, we can point the boat in whatever direction we need to go, with enough gas to get there."

Jake sighed, seeing Vero and the sunset at once and the absolute beauty of it all not lost on him. "Vero," he began, "why? Why are you doing all this?"

She frowned. "What do you mean?"

"Well—I mean, your brother. He's part of the gang that wants *me*, right? Not you. The best outcome is that they grab me, kill me, do whatever—and you're in the way. There's no chance they'd be happy with that."

"The *best-case* scenario is we get away, figure out this terrorist attack and who is the target, and what my company has to do with all of it."

"Well, yeah," Jake said. "That would technically be the best-case scenario, I guess. But the question still stands: why are you helping me?"

"I thought *you* were helping *me*?" she asked, her eyes big and droopy, no doubt playing a role.

He smirked, then rolled his eyes. "Right, you're the helpless damsel in distress. Don't forget—*you're* the one who dragged me into all of this. I would have been happily running from Dominguez grunts and getting shot at all over this island just fine on my own until you barged in and interrupted my dinner."

Her mouth fell open. "I *improved* your dinner, Jake Parker. And you looked so bored. So... busy. I thought you needed a break."

He laughed. "You got all that from my computer and an empty restaurant?"

"No," she said. "The truth is that I got it from the fact that you were clearly not a tourist. And right now, the only Americans coming to my island are Americans who want one of two things."

"Let me guess," Jake said, "they want the same two things Puerto Ricans want: either to become a US state, or to become a free, sovereign nation."

"Precisely," Vero said. "And I needed to know which one you wanted. The fact that you are handsome enough to upset my parents was just—how do you Americans say it?—'Cake icing?'"

Jake laughed even harder. "'Icing on the cake,' I believe it is. And you're right about that first part: I have been known to upset quite a few parents."

CHAPTER 53

"So tell me, Jake Parker," Vero said, "why are *you* here?"

The question took Jake by surprise. He looked up from his phone. For the past fifteen minutes, Jake had been looking into the leadership of Fitzsimmons and APHINT on the island, while Vero had been doing research of her own, trying to figure out a way back to the island that would cause as little attention as possible.

"What do you mean?" he asked.

"I mean exactly what I said," Vero said, slyly. "Why are you here in Puerto Rico? I told you why I am helping you—now tell me why you are really here."

"I… uh." Jake didn't know what to say. "I am helping with an investigation, working for an old friend from West Point, who is trying to help end the terrorist attacks here—"

Vero waved her hand around, annoyed. "No, no. I know all of that. That is why you are here, but *why* are you *here*?"

Jake nodded. He figured she had been wondering this—she wasn't ignorant, and he knew his previous answers hadn't been fully truthful. While he was prepared to offer the true, full answer freely, he hadn't expected her to pose the question quite so bluntly. "Well, I guess it's time to come clean."

Vero arched an eyebrow.

"Not that I've been lying to you," he began. "I told you that before, but this goes deeper than just an investigation into some gang-related terror attacks."

"I figured as much."

Jake turned off his phone's screen to conserve the battery and he placed it on his knee. The boat was rocking gently but steadily, the bigger waves now farther toward shore and the sun only a pinprick of orange light. In a few minutes, it would be nearly too dark to see.

"You read about me, right? About my past with Boston PD?"

She nodded. "Your wife died and you left the force."

Jake swallowed. It was blunt, but true. No reason he should interpret her words as insensitive. Still, while he had come down here to find answers surrounding his wife's death, one thing he had not expected to do was talk about it. He hadn't imagined that Holland or any of the testosterone-laden soldiers would want to delve into the emotional baggage of his past. "That's right," he said, clearing his throat. "She died in an explosion. A bomb, planted outside a café."

"An... attack?" Vero asked.

"Yes. An attack exactly like the ones here in Puerto Rico. Exactly like the ones Dominguez has been planning and executing."

"I see," Vero said, her eyes glancing back toward the shoreline. "So, you are down here to find answers about your wife, yes? About why she died in this attack?"

"No—I know why she died," Jake said. "She was just in the wrong place at the wrong time. I've accepted that. Shit happens and there's nothing I can do about it now. She was collateral damage." He said the words with a clipped speech, his teeth gritted.

Jake watched her eyes, which was difficult in the low light. It didn't seem as though she bought his explanation. "But you want to know if there was a reason behind the attack."

He sighed, letting out a deep breath. "Yeah, I guess. I wasn't really thinking about it anymore, honestly. An old friend pulled me in, and that was all the leverage he needed. 'I can help you find who killed your wife,' he said. But I know there *is* a reason, I just never really cared to dig into it. I didn't have the heart for it. Now that I'm here? I just want to know what that reason was. I can accept that she was in the wrong place at the wrong time. I don't think I could have prevented it—no one could have, other than the person who ordered it. But if I can prevent the next innocent death? The next collateral damage? If we can get enough information to know what Dominguez is *really* planning, and why? *That's* why I'm here, Vero."

"But we already know why," she said. "We talked about it earlier, right? These are *terrorist* attacks, so they are meant to bring *terror,* and scare the pharmaceutical companies and politicians enough so that the United States has a difficult time managing them. The long-term goal is—"

"I know that part," Jake said, "and yes, you're right. We know why they are doing it, generally. From a long-term perspective, the goal is to break free from the United States. But my wife was in a café in *Boston,* not Puerto Rico. What does any of that have to do with a pharmaceutical company here? Hell, why was Dominguez even there in the first place?"

"And you know it was Dominguez for sure? That they were the ones who planted the bomb and detonated it?"

He nodded again. "There was bismuth in the bombs—in the residue—just like all the other ones we've been tracking."

"Who's been tracking?"

"The team I'm working with. The old friend from West Point."

Vero nodded. "I see." Her eyes were elsewhere.

Jake continued. "The attacks were less frequent back then, but we know now that the materials at least all originated from here."

"Then what else is there? What are you actually looking for?"

Vero's eyes bored into Jake's, and he could see that she wasn't interrogating him, but working on the problem—as much as he was. It wasn't just his problem, he realized. It was hers, too. It was her past, her future. Puerto Rico was at stake here. He could see that she was struggling with putting the pieces together, trying to figure out how her brother and Jake's wife and all the other people, innocent or not, fit into the larger picture.

Jake knew that the only thing left to do was to come clean, to be completely transparent. "Fine," he said. He took a deep breath. "There was a man caught on camera, in the café. Just moments before the explosion. It's a grainy, low-resolution image, but it is in full color and it's just enough to go off. He had no identification, used no credit card to pay for his food, and he does not appear anywhere else in the city's databases, or on record, before or after the explosion."

"And he was in the café when your wife was? He died in the blast?"

Jake swallowed and then confirmed. "Yes. And we have alibis for everyone else in the café who either died or was injured in the explosion, except for him. No one knows why he was there, and no one knows who he was. He's a ghost."

"So you want to find him."

He shrugged. "Sure, of course. He's my ghost, right? If I find him, I might find some more answers. And they might lead me to the right people, and eventually lead to—"

"An answer."

Jake smiled. "Right," he said. "Something like that."

Vero nodded, then tensed and relaxed her shoulders by rolling them forward and backward a few times. "It just… seems like a difficult thing."

"What's difficult?" Jake asked.

"Being a detective," she replied. "I mean, you were a soldier, too. I understand that part, however. My brother is sort of a soldier. In some ways, we all are. We fight for what we think is right. Some of us are better fighters than others, but that's really what a soldier does."

"Sure," Jake said. "That's about it."

"But a detective—*they* are trying to find answers to questions no one even knows *how* to ask. Or who to ask. You are trying to find things that the rest of the world has stopped looking for."

Jake shrugged once more. "Yeah, that's true. It's not an easy job, but I feel like I'm pretty good at it."

"From what I read about you, Jake Parker, you were *very* good at it. The best, according to some people." She turned in her seat, shifting her position. "And you like it?"

He started to agree, then stopped mid nod. "I used to like it a lot more. Now that I'm solving my own case, it's dredging up memories I thought I had successfully compartmentalized. It was easier in some ways when the victims were other people, you know?"

"But do you like it enough to keep going?"

Jake studied her. The moonlight, now competing handily with the last remnants of sun, made Vero's face and shoulders prominent against the ocean backdrop. He tilted his head to the side a few inches, trying to read her. Trying to understand her question.

He knew he was here for *his* ghost, but what of Vero's? Whatever she was looking for—would she find it? He was still forming his opinions on whether or not he believed in some intelligent higher power. If it were some sort of celestial puppeteer, one that had pulled strings in order to bring him to this place to meet Vero, it seemed a bit far-fetched.

That said, he *did* believe in simple fate. Things happened, and because of that, other things happened. It was a simple explanation, but it worked for him. Sometimes those things were related, either causally or situationally. Sometimes they weren't.

Was it merely a coincidence that his case—his desire for closure surrounding his wife's death—had brought him here to meet another incredibly attractive, amazing woman who had her *own* nuanced problems, ones that involved the same targets as Jake's investigation?

And was this even an investigation? McDonnell had sent him here for what? Jake was physically outmatched by Holland's team, and most likely outmatched in the intelligence arena, as well—he was up against a group of soldiers who had been on the ground for months, men who had been working each angle of the mission and learning to blend in with the locals in a way Jake couldn't possibly do yet.

And, worse, he was afraid those soldiers were no longer on his team—they'd cut out McDonnell completely, and Jake was sure Delmonico had been eyeing him and Vero in the marketplace, no doubt suspicious of him. Why?

He shook his head, trying to find the words to answer Vero's question. McDonnell had sent him here for a reason. McDonnell was a man he trusted, and while he still couldn't be sure he wasn't just some tiny puppet in a larger theater production, he had no reason to believe McDonnell was trying to get *himself* in trouble. If Jake's mission was a failure, McDonnell's would be, and that wouldn't be something the man wanted.

He thought about Vero's question for another few seconds until she began to ask it again.

"Yes," he said, the word blurting out before he thought he was completely ready to answer. "Yes, I do still like it enough. Enough to keep going, at least. Enough to find the answers I'm looking for. Answers that, I suspect, will help *you* find the answers to some things you've been searching for."

He expected pushback, further interrogation from the woman across from him. Instead, she peered into his eyes and smiled.

"Good," she said.

CHAPTER 54

"Mamá," he pleaded, "just tell me where she went. And tell me who they were. The ones who came after they left."

Cecil was pacing around the living room in his parents' home. *His* home, though he hadn't set foot inside in three years.

His father was staring at him calmly, the patience and love present alongside the confusion and anger. He was a more generous person than his wife, but he rarely differed in opinion from Cecil's mother.

"I will tell you nothing."

"Because of Dominguez?"

"Because I know nothing." She paused, nearly in tears, as she looked her grown son up and down. "And because of Dominguez. They cannot come to this house, Cecil. They cannot just show up on my doorstep, trying to intimidate us."

"*Mamá*," he said again, stressing the word. "This is not a game. They are looking for the man she is with, and I am afraid that they will harm—"

"These are the men you have partnered with?" she began. "These men who will harm a woman—your sister—in order to get their job done. My son, you are a smart and capable man. You do not need a group like this—"

"*I do not have a choice,*" he said, the words falling quickly out of his mouth, the singsong lilt of Puerto Rican Spanish no longer there. "This is my life now. I am not playing. They will hurt her. They will hurt *you*."

His mother wouldn't meet his eyes.

"Papá, surely you understand this. It was my choice to join them, and it is my choice to stay. They are focused on a goal that will be very good for Puerto Rico. One that will be very good for us. For you." As he said it, he thought back to earlier, when he had visited the docks and marketplace. Even though his words were steady and confident, he knew the truth was a bit more nuanced. *Whatever their plan is, I have no idea.* Dominguez was a group whose leadership loved to play things close to their chest—it seemed this was no different.

"They kill people," his mother said. "That is not a good group. I will not have anything to do with it."

Cecil was growing frustrated. These were the same stubborn old parents he'd grown up with, the same parents who'd instilled in him the values of hard work, being driven, focusing on a goal. Why could they not understand this now?

He spoke through gritted teeth. "You do not need to have *anything* to do with us, then," he said, his voice low. "We deliver a free Puerto Rico to you. Free of charge. You can continue to do nothing. You can continue to—"

His mother stood and in one lunge was in front of him, her head at his chest. Her hand barely reached, but she brought it back and around and smacked him, hard, across his face.

He was shocked. She had *never* laid a hand on either of them. He couldn't speak. His face was hot, he could feel each of the fingers and palm tracing a searing red mark on his cheek. His nostrils flared, his mouth fell open and closed. No one spoke.

Finally, he took a step back, eyeing his parents, his father seated in his favorite armchair that was older than Cecil, his mother rocking gently side to side in the middle of the living-room rug. He watched them, fascinated, as if seeing them for the first time. Who were these people? This man and woman who had raised him, who had given him a home? Why were they acting this way?

Couldn't they see that he had made the difficult choice for them? He had decided to fight for them—*all* of them—all of Puerto Rico?

He felt the phone in his pocket vibrate. *Not now.* He knew he would have to take it or there would be consequences. For him, for Vero, for his parents.

He could only do so much. The protection he could offer only extended as much as his power within the organization, a power that was but an inkling of the power he knew was possible. His pleading with them would only go so far.

The phone buzzed again, and his hand pulled it out. He saw the number. No mistaking who it was, or why they were calling.

"Cecil," his mother began. "Cecil, I—"

"Leave this house," his father said. "Cecil, you are not welcome here."

"Father, I—"

"*Now*, Cecil."

His mother walked over to protest, but his father was suddenly standing, his chest out. The smaller man didn't sway, didn't move. He stared at Cecil. His mother seemed shocked, dumbfounded for the first time in his life.

Cecil looked at his father as the phone continued to buzz, waiting to see what this quiet man would say.

"The fear and chaos you have brought into my home is unfortunate, but acceptable," his father said. "We are family, we are one. These things are mistakes, accidents. You are young and brash, and this is forgivable."

"Papá, I—"

His father held up a hand. "But you have threatened your sister's safety by involving her as well. You have taken lives that are not your own and placed them into your own hands. We believe you are reckless with your own, and while that is a consequence we will have to live with, we will not condone the consequence of playing God with the lives of others."

Cecil opened his mouth to speak, but his father continued.

"So you are no longer welcome here. Cecil Romero, this home is no longer yours. This place is no longer a sanctuary for you. You are free to go your own way. You have broken your mother's heart by joining this group. But if you cause harm to my daughter, you will break mine."

Cecil's knees felt weak. He had never heard his father speak like this before. He wanted to cry, to explain to them what Dominguez was really working toward. But it would be no use. There would be no persuading these people.

He stepped backward once again, accepting the call just before it went to voicemail. He didn't hold it up to his ear at first, choosing instead to take a long, slow breath and then look up at his parents once again. He nodded. "I understand. Goodbye."

And then he turned to leave, just as the phone crackled in his hand, a voice reaching his ears from the tiny speaker.

"Cecil, hello?"

He pulled the phone up to his ear. "Yes, sorry. I am here."

"We need you to find your sister and the man she is with. We are out of time. If you cannot produce the man, we will take matters into our own hands."

Cecil swallowed as the door to his parents' house closed behind him. He needed no reminder of the threat they posed. *I must succeed.*

The voice continued: *"You have until 8 a.m. tomorrow morning."*

CHAPTER 55

"When your people were doing their research on the Dominguez attacks, how far did they get?" Vero asked.

Jake frowned.

Vero continued, "I mean, they know it's Dominguez behind the attacks, right? And they know there is another attack scheduled—tomorrow morning sometime—but how deep have they gone into the suspects?"

"I'm not sure they *have* suspects, other than every member of the Dominguez organization. Why?"

It was Vero's turn to frown. "Really? That seems like the first thing you would want to do, right? Find suspects"

"Well, yes, but we can't exactly start pulling Dominguez members in for questioning. Besides, the local police are pretty finicky about anything Dominguez related. We've had to operate under the radar."

"But you have a team working with you back in the United States?"

"I do, yeah."

"Okay, and they have not given you any names to look at?" she asked.

"It's not that we don't have *names*," Jake answered. "It's that all of the names are equally suspicious. And these things are complicated. I tried snooping around a bit. Local police stations, public arrest records—but I came onto this case precisely three days ago. I was told to come down to provide support."

"For whom?" Vero asked.

Jake froze. He hadn't mentioned a word to Vero about Holland and his team, nor anything about a team on the ground in Puerto Rico.

"I—well, support for whatever they need, really. I'm a detective, so I figure I'm here to detect things."

Vero laughed, her head falling back and her hair nearly hitting the water. "Right. So the US government has sent you on a… what do you call it—'goose hunt'?—and you do not even have any leads?"

"Well, there have been *leads*, Vero, but they haven't really—"

"Charles LaFleur. José Corazon. Luisa Monteverde Benevides."

Jake knew the names, but couldn't place them exactly. "Pharmaceutical company employees?"

"The CEO and CFO of Fitzsimmons, the largest manufacturer of pharmaceutical exports on the island, and the CEO of APHINT, the company I work for. Also, Roger d'Or, the South African man in charge of a conglomerate that controls three of the other companies. His name is literally *gold*. If anyone's trying to embezzle or cheat my company out of money, it's one of them."

"That's… I'm not sure what that is," Jake said, scratching his forehead. "Vero, that's just Wikipedia information. And just because the guy's name makes him sound like a schmuck doesn't actually mean he is."

"It might be public knowledge, but you did not seem to know anything about the US bailout of the pharmaceutical companies."

"That's true," Jake said. "How does it help the case?"

"Because it is going to happen again," Vero replied. "It is only a matter of time. It is a vicious cycle. The companies argue and fight each other, but when they act like they are unable to increase profit margins enough for a few quarters at a time, the government swoops in and gives them a big bag of money."

"Really? It's going to happen again?"

"Sure," she said. "Why not? That is why the FDA has been traveling here so much. They are working to ensure the pandemic did not slow production too much, but they are also trying to assess whether or not another large payout is in order."

"I guess that could be something," Jake said.

"Well, if that is not enough to make you look twice at the power players, consider that the CEO of APHINT, Luisa Benevides, is the sister of a man known to be quite high in the Dominguez organization."

"Wait, really?"

"Really. Diego Benevides. The story goes he is in charge of the drug operation Dominguez is engaged in, which, not surprisingly, is just about *all* of what Dominguez is engaged in. He is as driven and power-hungry as his sister, and while his involvement in the organization is technically a rumor, no one here denies it. Some even say he's running the whole thing."

Jake sat back in the boat's uncomfortable wooden chair. "Yeah, I'd say that's a pretty big conflict of interest. The head of a massive Puerto Rican pharmaceutical company is the sister of the head of a Puerto Rican cartel that trades mostly in those same drugs. Geez."

"Yes, 'geez,'" she said mockingly. "That could be one word for it. So maybe we start the investigation there?"

"Wait a minute. 'We'?"

"Well, sure. I just gave you a lead. And I can help you follow it."

Jake squeezed his fingers over the bridge of his nose and closed his eyes. "Vero, I already know what you're going to say, but—but this is all really dangerous. I mean, I know you grew up here, and that your brother is involved, and APHINT is the company you work for…"

"Which is why I am the *perfect* person to help you solve this."

"Vero, it's just that—"

"What, Jake Parker?" she asked, her voice rising. "I am not *trained*? I am not a *detective*? Ever since the marketplace, you have been looking at me like I am a scared, lost child. As though you need to protect me, to put your arm around me and be my personal guardian angel."

"No, that's not what I—"

"Yes, it is. I can see it in your eyes. Your face is all concern and puppy love and sadness that you couldn't prevent me from seeing the gunfire."

Jake sniffed and looked out over the darkening waters. He didn't appreciate the tongue-lashing, but he certainly could appreciate that time was running out. The longer they argued out here, the less time he would have to figure out where the Dominguez attack was going to be.

Vero suddenly pulled her dress up, high above her knee. She grabbed her phone with her other hand and turned on the built-in flashlight.

"What are you doing?" he asked.

"Look. Right here." She held the phone up and pointed the light at a spot on the outside of her left thigh, about halfway between the knee and the waist. It was a round, twisted mark of flesh, shiny and pink.

"A bullet wound?"

She nodded. "Yes. And I have one more just like it on my back. A .22, so the rounds didn't get very far. They cut out most of it, but there is still shrapnel in there."

"That's... Vero, I'm sorry. What happened?"

"I was nine. Riding my bike. My brother was only a baby at the time, inside with my mother. My father was working in the field, so they were not around to see the danger. It was a Dominguez gang, young boys, maybe only twice my age. "I was collateral damage," she paused. "There was a big attack that month, in a marketplace much like the one we were in. Dominguez claimed credit for it, but they weren't actually the perpetrators. It came out later that it was an accident, but the young members wanted a turf war, so they drove through my town and saw their target."

"They shot a nine-year-old girl?" Jake asked.

"I was not who they were shooting at. They were trying to hit someone's kid, I guess in a rival faction or a small upstart gang or something, or someone related to a pharma executive, I do not even remember. But I was there, standing in the way. One of them fired a couple of shots, and they hit me. My mother ran out and found me. I almost bled out."

"That's terrible," Jake said. "And it's exactly why I want to find these Dominguez assholes and make them pay."

"Well," Vero said. "It turns out, they did pay." She looked at him meaningfully.

"Dominguez paid off your family?"

"Well, someone paid the hospital bills. It was an accident, and they admitted as much. They sent an envelope to my parents. I was not supposed to see it, but I did. It was a lot of money, and I heard them talking about it one night. But that is not the end of it."

"How so?"

"I started working at APHINT as a junior intern, one of the youngest the company had ever had. I was twelve years old when I began to get paid by them. Now, I was just going to school and spending an hour there after classes one day a week. A development program, really. But they were *interested* in hiring me long before that."

"They heard about the incident?"

"They did," Vero said, nodding. "But more than that, I discovered many years later that the grandson of a high-ranking APHINT executive lived in my parents' neighborhood."

"They were the actual target, weren't they? The gang wanted to hit that guy's grandson."

"Yes, exactly. And that's not all—when I was hit instead, all five of the Dominguez members were never heard from again.

Their parents fought for a while to find them, but the police were not interested in helping out. And then my parents received the money, but it was not from Dominguez."

"It wasn't?"

"No," she said. "It was from APHINT."

CHAPTER 56

"So it was APHINT?" Jake asked. "The real reason for the Dominguez attack?"

Vero shook her head. "No, not Dominguez. A *subset* of Dominguez. Like a smaller gang within a gang. And obviously the leaders did not approve of the tactic, of shooting at innocent civilians, even if APHINT was their ultimate target."

"They forced APHINT to apologize to your family, and the kids who did it were sent packing." Jake thought back to the young men who had been "disappeared" by the local police force. Apparently Dominguez was no stranger to forcing people to do things their way.

"Correct," she said. "And it eventually led to my getting a job at APHINT. I am, of course, a brilliant enough chemist to have achieved this alone, but the incident may have helped." She winked at Jake.

Jake smiled back at her. "I'm sure. So did this little feud between Dominguez and APHINT end then?"

She shook her head again. "No, not really. It morphed into something new. Changed direction. Some may say it became much more subtle."

"How so?" Jake asked.

"Well, for example," she explained, "the preferred method of inciting fear in the public is through these targeted and planned bomb explosions. But the preferred method of making things happen behind the scenes is through kidnapping. They do not drive up to a child's home and shoot them—they simply kidnap them. But the more effective way is to kidnap the parents."

"Why?"

"Because it's quiet, and they can then make demands. After I was accidentally shot, I noticed a shift in this direction. Rather than brutal, seemingly random attacks and kidnappings of children that would have the entire country screaming for justice, instead there were people who simply did not show up for work the next day, or any day after. People would just assume they did something wrong, did something to anger Dominguez. Only because I was paying closer attention did I start to realize that some of the reports of kidnappings were related to pharmaceutical employees and their families."

"Did you know anyone?"

"Not directly. There were rumors of course, rumors that other gangs were trying to gain power or that the police were colluding with executives and other companies to remove certain political enemies from power, but I believe the answer is much more simple."

"Usually the simplest answer is the actual answer," Jake said. "I never considered that angle, either. I wonder…" He pulled his phone up to his face and started typing. He knew the date; it had been emblazoned into his memory. Most of his research had been US-based. Jake hadn't known at the time that the Boston attack had been of a terrorist cell, nor did he know that it was from a Puerto Rican-based gang. With that knowledge, he typed a string of searches along with the date and waited for the results to populate.

"What are you looking for?" Vero asked.

He didn't look up. "My ghost," he said. "If Dominguez was behind the attack in Boston, there's a chance the target was someone they had been focusing on for some time. And based on what you said, there's a chance the guy may have fallen off the grid somewhere here first."

He glanced over the results, the first three showing nothing of interest. The fourth, however, seemed promising. He clicked the article, a Spanish news headline that had been translated into English by the search engine.

The article was dated the week before Mel's death, and it was a simple missing-persons report from the online newspaper of a local town. He recognized the town as the same one APHINT was headquartered in, the same town Vero lived in.

"This is interesting," he muttered. He scrolled through the report, seeing the pictures of the individuals alongside a simple biography and where they were last seen. There were fifteen or so people, and Jake was beginning to get discouraged until he reached the second-to-last person on the list.

That's him. Jake stopped, his thumb hovering over the tiny screen. He breathed slowly, trying to prevent himself from getting excited. He swallowed, examining the image.

Unlike the screenshot image McDonnell had sent from the café's in-store camera footage, this picture was in brilliant high quality, likely taken from a fancy phone camera by a loved one or friend.

"What is it?" Vero asked softly. She leaned over in the boat.

In the distance, Jake head the revving of another boat's engine, echoing over the waves from somewhere behind the tip of the land protruding out toward the east.

He ignored the sound, focusing on Vero's question and the image in front of him. Not wanting to chase a dead end, he moved to the email app on his phone and pulled up the image of the man McDonnell had sent over. He pinched outward to zoom in on it, trying to let his eyes unfocus and see if the resemblance was still there.

Vero was apparently watching, as when he did so she gasped. "Jake, that is the same man!" She pulled the phone out of his hand, and Jake found himself now leaning over her.

"I think so," he whispered.

"There is no doubt." With a deft flick, Vero navigated between the web browser and the mail app once more, comparing the images herself. "Yes, this is him. Ezekiel Manuel Santos III."

"You know the name?"

"Yes," she said. "He was an executive at APHINT for a while. I have never met him. Looks like he disappeared on…" Vero searched for the date of the incident and mentioned it to Jake. "June 7."

Almost exactly a week before Mel's death in Boston.

Jake read the biography of the missing person. Ezekiel Santos had been the Director of Strategic Relations for Allied Pharmaceuticals International, and he had served in the role for two years after spending most of his decade-long tenure at the company climbing the ladder. He had been forty-seven years old when his family had filed the missing persons report.

"I think I remember this," Vero said.

"Really?"

She nodded. "There were more kidnappings that week. Maybe ten, eleven in total? Obviously a Dominguez move to gain power, because they were all from pharmaceutical companies."

"Ten or eleven kidnappings in a *week*?" Jake asked, incredulous. "Wouldn't someone have investigated? The police did nothing?"

"The police were probably paid well to keep their investigation tied up in paperwork, and any of the families of these people were silenced."

"I see. But this is my guy." He held the phone up closer, once again examining the picture of the man McDonnell had given him, then comparing it to the image of Ezekiel Santos. They were one and the same.

What were you doing in Boston that day, Ezekiel? Jake wondered. *Why were you targeted?*

"Oh," Vero said suddenly, her own phone close to her face. "Oh, my." She whispered something in Spanish.

"What is it?" Jake asked. He leaned over and tried to peek onto her screen.

"This man—Ezekiel Santos—is the nephew of Fitzsimmons' CEO."

"Wait, really?"

"Yes," she said, nodding in excitement. "Yes, it seems there is a family tie between Ezekiel Santos II and Charles Lafleur."

Jake was about to respond when the sound of a boat engine whirred into his ears. He looked up, trying to find the dark shape against the horizon. It was coming from behind their own boat, from the shoreline that stretched east of San Juan.

And he saw immediately the size of it—it was no small watercraft.

"Vero," he said. "Fire up the engine. I'll get the anchor. It's time to go."

He noticed that their trajectory would bring the boat directly over their position. Worse, it seemed as though they were speeding up.

And, worst of all, he saw a few dark silhouettes standing on the bow of the vessel, each holding long, dark, weapon-like shapes.

CHAPTER 57

The Dominguez boat was out of range to fire on them, but the distance was closing. Jake knew they wouldn't be able to hold them off, nor would they be able to outrun them.

"Vero, let's go!"

"Fast as we can, Jake Parker!" Vero replied, shouting over the drone of the tiny outboard motor. She held the tiller steady, pointing it toward the shore.

Jake could see a few pinpricks of lights from the marinas near where they were headed—San Juan's easternmost restaurants and waterfront cantinas, preparing to light up for the night crew.

He also saw a few boats, moored to the docks and piers, their masts becoming a visual maze of lines and sheets and sails against the darkened curtain of the blossoming San Juan nightlife.

"We have five minutes, maybe less," Jake said, eyeing the oncoming boat. It was also moving full speed, but it was a far larger vessel, with two inboard engines that were running at full tilt. They were gaining on him and Vero's tiny fishing boat, and their only hope of escape was to get to the shore before them.

The problem was that they weren't just outrunning the *boat*, they were outrunning the reasonable range of the men's semi-automatics. The dark would not hide them, as there was enough reflection from the city on the water that their absence of reflection would tell the other boat exactly where they were. And the Dominguez crew had already shot at them, so Jake knew they were obvious targets—these men, likely different members of the gang that had been patrolling the coastline—had been told by their counterparts onshore that there was a small dinghy with a man and a woman inside right around here. There was no doubt in Jake's mind they would start shooting as soon as they were within range, likely sooner. And he assumed they weren't going to run out of ammunition.

"We will not make it," Vero yelled, echoing Jake's fears.

"Okay," he said. "You got a better idea?"

"No, but I have a different one."

She yelled "Hold on," but Jake barely heard it over the whine of the engine. She jerked the tiller to the left, pointing the boat farther up the coast toward the mass of yachts and sailboats. It was a diagonal line toward shore, which meant the pursuing boat would be on them quicker.

But it was also a quicker way to the end of the docks, where they might find some respite amongst the larger vessels.

Jake pulled his pistol out, mentally trying to remember how many rounds were left in the magazine. *Three for the thugs back at the shore, plus…* he couldn't remember. That was a first. Obviously he was out of practice.

Still, he had the extra loaded mag in his pocket, weighing down the left side of his pants. He felt it, wondering if he needed to reload now or save it for later.

He opted to save it, just in case he needed the extra ammunition.

"Vero," he yelled. "Once we get there, let's split up. Ultimately they're after me, right?"

She nodded.

Good. Hopefully she could hear him clearly.

"I'm going to jump off and run down the docks as soon as we're close. You navigate around a bit, try to keep them focused on you." He hoped it hadn't come across as *I'm using you as bait.* He had seen her deftness with the small watercraft; he fully expected her to be able to stay in front of them.

She nodded again and pulled the tiller slightly right, aiming now for the space between the two closest docks. Jake could see the names of the boats lined up closest to their position, but it was too dark to make them out. Another few minutes and he'd have the darkness on his side.

Come on, he willed. The boat was slow, and the tiny engine had been working overtime. He was glad they'd taken the time to refill the gas tank as soon as they'd tossed the anchor. *Let's get there.*

The first dock came into view, the darkened wood planks popping slightly out of the water. Vero deftly navigated past it and turned down the narrow length between it, the boats tied off on it, and the boats across from it on the opposite dock.

Jake saw that the docks were arranged in a U-shaped pattern, with a floating island in the center to their right. On that island was a marina with a gas station and a single-window store on top of it. The boats to their right were tied off on the three slips on the side of the island.

Vero slowed the engine enough to glide past the island and farther into the cove, but fast enough to produce a nice wake behind them. When they closed in on a large luxury yacht on the left, Jake spoke again.

"Vero, I need you to figure something out for me. I'm going to lose these assholes and then I'll find you."

"What's your plan?"

He nodded. "Too much to tell you about now, but trust me, I'll fill you in. That okay?"

"Yes, of course."

"Thank you. I've got my ghost, but you've got yours, and I'm starting to think they look a lot alike."

Jake didn't wait for a response. He jumped off the edge of the small boat and onto the wooden dock. He immediately made his way for the closest yacht he could see that had an open deck gate.

CHAPTER 58

The boat full of Dominguez soldiers cruised by the yacht Jake was hiding in, tailing the smaller fishing boat through the U-shaped docks. They hadn't seen it stop long enough for Jake to get off, and he could see that Vero was crouched low in the boat, trying to stay out of sight. With any luck, the men would assume they were both still in the boat, hiding from them.

Vero's boat sailed past the single-room structure to its right, then started a wide arch around the last section of dock. The floating store and gas pumps were connected to the rest of the docks by a raised bridge, tall enough to allow the sailboats' masts to glide beneath.

Jake involuntarily felt for the Beretta tucked behind his back, feeling the reassurance of its presence, yet knowing that to use it would be a huge risk. It was smaller and lighter than the men's submachine guns, and he was the only shooter on his team.

No, the strategy now was stealth. He needed to stay out of sight, to get to the next phase of the mission without Dominguez catching on. It would be a long night, but he'd had plenty of long nights in his time.

He hoped Vero could lose the tail, and then that she would be able to return to either the resort or her parent's house unmolested, or at least book a motel where no one would think to check for her. He didn't need her getting any more caught up in his duel with Dominguez. Her brother, if he cared for her, would hopefully help keep his friends off her back for at least a night.

Jake pulled himself down the bow of the yacht on his belly, sliding forward on the pristine white deck. He rolled into the lowered main section in front of the bridge deck, then crouch-walked to the other side of the boat and prepared to exit. He was now fully out of sight of the other boat; it was his best chance to get away.

His boots hit the dock hard, and he took a few seconds to sense any movement from anyone who might be patrolling. Seeing and hearing nothing out of the ordinary, he aimed toward the edge of the docks where they met the concrete pavement and parking lot beyond. There were no streetlights here, so staying out of sight would hopefully be possible.

As Jake reached the end of the parking lot and found a quiet, dark street that followed the outline of the coast, he pulled his phone out and saw that he only had a few minutes of battery left. *First stop, buy a charger,* he thought. He looked to his right and saw a tiny corner store about three blocks away, its neon sign a beacon of hope.

He turned and jogged west, toward San Juan, seeing the lights of the old city in the distance above the tops of the buildings and cabana houses he was passing. The corner store's light was on, a young teenager working the first hours of the night shift.

He pulled the door open and nodded in the kid's direction, turning quickly toward the back of the store so the kid wouldn't have time to see his face. He couldn't be too careful. He grabbed a few bags of beef jerky, a soda, a cheap plastic phone charger, and a huge baseball cap with some unrecognizable team's logo on it. He put the hat on his head, pulling it down nearly to his eyes, then hauled everything else up to the counter.

"Buenos noches," he said, trying not to sound like a local, but also to not come across like a full-fledged tourist.

The kid grunted something unintelligible, clearly uninterested in the white guy who'd just stopped in for some munchies.

Fine by me, he thought. He peered down at the kid's wrists as he scanned the items. There was no tattoo on either one. He allowed himself to breathe a little easier. He wasn't sure how Dominguez spread the word about individuals they were tracking—was it a gang-wide order? Or were there soldiers, like the ones in the boat and back at the beach, whose job it was to find people?

He needed to figure out the bismuth thing—Dominguez was using it in their bombs, trying to call attention to themselves. He knew APHINT produced a lot of the stuff, but Jake wanted to see if there was a paper trail that pointed back to Dominguez.

He also needed to uncover whatever he could on this "Chemical X," and how it differed from the original product it was supposed to emulate. If it were actually causing Lewy body disease, did they know that? Or had they been duped somehow, eager to start production on a drug they thought was safe?

Jake grabbed the plastic bag after the kid loaded everything inside, then left the store. Using the last bit of juice on his phone, he hailed a ride-share driver and walked out to the nearest intersection to wait. The driver would be there in less than a minute, according to the app, and Jake used the time to figure out his destination.

There was a hostel nearby, but he was too old to get in and would stand out like an old man in a young man's world if he went there. The two closest hotels were cheap, but he wanted something a bit more secure. He found a large chain with a reasonable nightly rate—he intended to use the cash he had on him to buy the room, rather than risk a credit card purchase. If Dominguez was as powerful as he'd been led to believe, they'd easily be able to track him using card purchases.

The driver—a young college-aged female—arrived right on time in a nice-looking sedan, and Jake had the door open and was sliding in before the woman had fully stopped.

Fifteen minutes later and he had the plan in place. It would require a lot of careful maneuvering, it would require Vero to stay out of harm's way, and it would require a bit of good luck.

And it would require a bit of sleep.

CHAPTER 59

Cecil took a deep breath, held it, and finally released it just as his eyes started to burn. He started again, this time closing his eyes tight, waiting for the dancing sparks to replace the near-blackness of the backs of his eyelids. He opened his eyes, let out the breath, and repeated the process a third time.

He hadn't felt this uncomfortable in years. Since he was a boy, likely. He liked to feel in control, even if he was taking orders from someone above him in the organization.

This, he knew, was decidedly *not* what control felt like.

He had been given orders, and the person giving the orders had made it clear they had come from the top. From Mr. Diego himself.

Two times in less than a week he had received orders from the man who ran the entire Dominguez gang. Two times in less than a week Mr. Diego had pinpointed Cecil Romero and told him to get a job done.

He had never met anyone at his level who had been given two sets of orders that quickly, two reassignments. If they had been, he'd never heard of it.

What was worse, he was afraid the orders were a bit contradictory. The first—to intercept the letter from a certain Mr. Jaime Escalante Garcia that detailed the arrival of an FDA ambassador who was arriving soon to visit with Fitzsimmons' staff and leadership. For what? Why all the secrecy?

If the plan was for Dominguez to destroy this FDA agent, why hide that fact from their own membership?

There was obviously more to the game than Cecil was aware. And now he had become part of that game. His orders were clear, and direct.

He picked up the phone and tried his sister's number again. No answer. He sighed. *Vero, what have you done?*

He was sitting in his car, watching the front of the small beachside motel he'd seen Vero enter an hour before. He hadn't seen her leave.

He turned off the engine and got out of the vehicle, then crossed the parking lot, the entire time his eyes on the door of the room he'd watched her enter. *Room 125.*

Please, he thought, *do not be inside.*

He hoped she had somehow found a way to sneak out when he wasn't looking. Somehow gotten away. But he knew it was hopeless—he had *always* been looking. For one hour and thirty-seven minutes, his eyes had been glued to the door of the single cheap hotel room. He had seen his sister unlock the door, walk inside, and close the door behind her. He had seen the light turn on, and seventeen minutes later turn off again. It hadn't turned back on.

She was inside, and now he had to carry out the will of the organization. It was the only way.

He got to the door and knocked. "Vero," he called out. "Please open up. It's me."

There was no sound for a few seconds, and Cecil's heart rose. Then, shuffling. Like someone getting out of bed. He heard some heavy footsteps and the door's two locking mechanisms disengaged.

The door opened and his older sister was standing there, wearing a nightgown. "Cecil? What the hell—"

"Get dressed," he said. "We need to leave."

He had to force himself not to look at her face, to not peer into her eyes and see the little girl he used to know. Even without truly seeing her now, he knew this was no little girl—Vero was a woman now, but she was every bit as strong and stubborn as he remembered.

"Cecil, please. I am safe here. They don't know where I am, and if you—"

"*I* know where you are, Vero!" he yelled. "I'm *here*! Do you know what that means?"

He looked around to make sure there were no onlookers, but he also knew this was the sort of place that was often chosen because of its lack of onlookers.

He looked back at his sister and saw the recognition in her eyes. The confusion, the fear, and then the betrayal.

"How—why?" she said.

Cecil shook his head. "I am sorry, my sister. I have no choice."

"Of course you do," she snapped. "You always have a choice. That's what all of this is, Cecil. *Choices*. Choices you make, and choices you have made."

"And now I have made the choice."

"What is this?" Vero asked. "You are taking me where?"

"Away from here."

"For my safety?"

"For *security*. You will not be harmed."

She bit her bottom lip—a tic he'd seen of hers many times. She frowned, obviously struggling internally with all of it. "At what price?" she asked.

He smiled, then dipped his head. She always was brilliant. Whip-smart. Seemed to be a trait that ran in the family. "Get in the car and I will—"

"Tell me *now*, Cecil."

"Vero, please, I cannot stress how important this is to me—to us. To *you*. I need you to get in the—"

The door started to shut, quickly. Vero backed away as she went to slam it closed, but he was quicker. He stuck the toe of his shoe over the threshold, holding it open a few inches before it snapped shut. In the same motion, he grabbed the pistol he had tucked into the holster behind his back, affixed to his belt. He hadn't bothered to hide it—he had only worn a gun three times, and he wasn't planning on making it a habit. And Vero had done him the favor of choosing a motel whose guests would never bat an eye at what was happening outside of room 125.

He yanked the pistol around and stuck it into the crack of the door. He didn't know if the safety was on, or if it even had a safety. Cecil had forgotten the half-hour training he'd received from the gunsmith he'd bought it from—it had been another task given to him by Dominguez—an entry-level project all recruits were expected to go through, regardless of their future appointment within the organization. He simply hadn't thought it prudent at the time.

Vero's eyebrows rose, and her jaw clenched. But he was her brother; he had seen every facet of her personality, learned all of them almost as well as he'd learned his own. Beneath the facade of strength, of confidence, he saw the terror.

Her eyes watered. "You—you are going to shoot me, Cecil? To kill me?"

He clenched and unclenched his jaw. "I am going to do the job I was sent here to do."

"Then do it."

He didn't falter. "I *am*, Vero. I am trying. I am not here to kill you. I am here to put you into my car. To take you somewhere, so that you may help me and Dominguez."

"And if I don't? *Then* you will kill me?"

He closed his eyes, hung his head. "No. No, Vero, I will not kill you. But I have a very specific set of instructions that involves getting you into that car in the next ten minutes. And if I fail to do that…" His voice trailed off.

"I see," she said. She sniffed, holding back tears. The door opened wider.

"You are coming with me?" he asked.

"Do I have a choice?"

He shrugged. "No, Vero. No, you do not."

She nodded and allowed the door to swing open wider. "I need to get clothes on. Please give me two minutes."

"Fine," he said.

"Are you going to tell me what this is about?" his sister asked.

He considered lying, but knew she would be able to hear it in an instant. She would see right through it. "Dominguez needs the man you are with."

"I am not *with* any man, Cecil." She turned away, the nightgown fell, and she threw a t-shirt over her bare shoulders.

"The man you have been with the past few days. Do not play dumb, please."

She nodded as she sat on the bed, putting her shoes on. "I see. And what happens if I do not know where he is?"

He swallowed. *Always right to the point,* he thought. "Well, in that case, the gang takes matters into their own hands."

"You are saying they already—"

"Yes, my sister. They already know where he is. They have known it for a while. He is dangerous. But Dominguez is giving you an out: tell us where he is. If you do not, they will kill him."

She stood up, turning slowly. "And if I *do* tell you, they will *also* kill him. I am not stupid, Cecil."

After staring each other down for a few more seconds, he shook his head. "You are missing the point, my sister. If you do not cooperate, after they kill him, they will then kill us."

CHAPTER 60

Jake arose to the sounds of the coqui frogs, chirping their names outside the window of the hotel. He'd gotten a room that faced the road, but somehow the frogs had found him and camped outside his window all night. He didn't hate the sound—it was calming, reassuring.

But it brought back a memory that was as reassuring. *Honeymoon, Mel, the sound of the frogs in the distance…*

He sniffed away the sleep and blinked a few times, noticing that the sun was barely peeking over the horizon. *Good*, he thought. Today was not a day to oversleep. McDonnell had called him last night asking for an update, and he'd told the man there was nothing to worry about—the plan was good, and he was confident they would be able to foil the terrorist attack they knew was scheduled for that morning.

It wasn't a complete lie, but Jake was trying to balance his own insecurity about the plan with the need he felt to ensure McDonnell's mind was at ease. The man was forced to play silent partner, to watch from afar and wait for updates. To top it off, he had lost contact with his on-the-ground team, so Jake was his only point of communication with the happenings down here. He was determined to not let them down. He *wouldn't* let them down—not McDonnell, not Vero.

Not Mel.

Jake showered, dressed, and scheduled the ride-share drive he needed to catch into San Juan. He hadn't bothered to return to get the second rental vehicle, and besides, today's mission would be easier to pull off without his own vehicle. He called Vero, then when it went straight to voicemail, he sent her a text message. Jake didn't necessarily need her for the next step of his hacked-together plan, but he did feel obligated to at least keep her in the loop.

McDonnell's team back home had dug up information that Jake had used to hack together the beginnings of a plan, and unless they'd had bad intel or something changed, Jake was confident he'd have answers soon. Hopefully, in the next two hours.

The problem was that the attack could be scheduled for any time in the next two *minutes*. He needed to hustle.

The driver picked him up two minutes early and drove him to his first destination. He paid, got out, and walked across the street. He checked his watch, then his phone, ensuring both were synced up and working.

After another ten minutes passed, he knew that McDonnell's team had pulled through.

He was watching the building across the street in the busy financial and banking district, a twenty-story, glass-faced building that had an old-school brick first-floor landing. It wasn't the tallest building on the block, but the combination of old and new architecture done up to the nines seemed to give it some clout.

It was an impressive structure, and an impressive vehicle that matched the building's importance rolled slowly down to the street from a tucked-away parking garage. All-black, an SUV with sparkling rims and not a scratch on it, the windows tinted to perfect black opaqueness.

Jake swallowed, then gathered himself and his wits.

Here goes nothing.

He checked the Beretta behind his waist and under his shirt as he crossed the street at the nearby crosswalk. As he did, the driver of the SUV stepped out and appeared next to the door, his hands clasped in front of him. He was early by three minutes. Jake had been hoping for more time, but this would have to do.

He strode up to the vehicle and its driver, keeping on the wide sidewalk that ran in front of the building. There were a few people strolling by, and he slowed to allow them time to pass. When he got close enough to the driver for the man to sense his proximity, he rushed forward.

The driver's eyes widened, but Jake was there before he could react. Jake pressed the Beretta into the small of his back, his left hand gripping the man's left arm tightly. "Keep your hands exactly where they are. See the parking garage? We're going over there. Now."

He pulled the man forward before he could protest, and the man stumbled along while Jake walked by his side. He stowed the Beretta once again, not wanting to accidentally be seen by someone inside the building. Jake had needed it for the intimidation, to let the driver know he was armed. He had no plans to hurt this man, and he hoped the man didn't try anything abrupt.

"Wh—who are you?" the man asked in Spanish.

"Jake Parker," he replied, knowing it would be of no use to his man.

The man frowned just as they reached the dark interior of the garage.

Jake immediately pushed the man to his right, then sat him down on the ground. "You speak English?"

The man nodded, terrified.

"Good. Like I said, I'm Jake Parker. I'm with the US Army, Special Intelligence Division." He didn't have time to make up a better fake organization, so he just went with it and hoped the man didn't ask questions. "I'm not here to harm anyone. I just need to talk to your boss for two minutes while we drive around the block."

The man looked at him strangely.

"You don't have to trust me, but I'm telling you the truth. Two minutes. I'm going back out to your car to wait for him. I have no reason to harm him or you, but I *will* complete this mission. That means if I see your face, or you try to call him to warn him before two minutes is up, I shoot him."

The man gulped.

"Two minutes, then you call whoever you want. But it won't matter, because we'll be back, safe and sound. Got it?"

He nodded.

"Good. Sorry it has to be this way." Jake turned to leave, then stopped himself. "Oh, also—I need your keys."

CHAPTER 61

Jake waited inside the sleek leather interior of the SUV, but he had hardly caught his breath and slowed his heart rate before the thin, wispy-haired leader of *Fitzsimmons* walked out of the building and moved purposefully toward the car. Jake held his phone up, hoping the screen would be bright enough to be seen through the tinted windows and tell the man that his driver was slacking on the job.

It worked. The man opened the door, got in, and shut the door before chuckling. He addressed Jake in Spanish. "*¿No le abres la puerta a un anciano hoy, Raphael?*"

Jake put the SUV in drive and lurched forward onto the road, trying to get as much speed as quickly as possible. He flicked his eyes into the rearview mirror. "Sorry, Lafleur, not Raphael."

Lafleur, a Canadian who Jake knew spoke French and Spanish fluently, slipped into English without so much as a moment's hesitation. "What the hell? Who are you?"

While the man himself was old, his voice was that of a man thirty years younger. Deep, full, and booming, Jake felt himself straighten up in the front seat. He held the pistol up with his right hand, hoping it made the point. "Just want to talk, if that's okay. I told Raphael I wouldn't harm either of you."

"There are better ways to schedule a meeting," Lafleur said.

"I hate meetings. And lately, I'm not one to care much for the ways things *ought* to be done." He met eyes with Lafleur. "But I suppose you can appreciate that as well, can't you?"

"The hell is that supposed to mean?"

"I'm here to ask you about your nephew. Ezekiel Santos."

The man looked out the window, then nodded. "That's what this is. Private eye, I suspect? Some American hotshot she hired to find Zeke?"

Jake didn't flinch. "Something like that."

"Right. His mother always was addicted to drama. Couldn't just accept the fact that the clowns out here will do anything for attention."

"What clowns?" Jake asked. "Dominguez?"

Lafleur sucked his teeth. "I thought you were a PI. Don't you know anything about this place, or this case you're on? Dominguez runs the show here. Kidnapped him and three other boys from my company. Good employees, too. Zeke had a shot, even. Smart kid." His head fell, and Jake wondered if it was entirely an act, or if he felt remorse for Ezekiel Santos' death.

"I know he wasn't kidnapped," Jake said.

The man's eyes lit up. "Where is he?"

Jake shook his head, pulling into the left lane to turn and drive back around the block. "He's dead. Killed in a terrorist attack three years ago. I saw his picture recently, and I recognized him immediately." He paused, then waited for Lafleur to meet his eyes again. "My wife died that day, too."

There was a flash of recognition in the old man's eyes. "Ah, yes. I read about that bombing in Boston. It was such a terrible thing. I'm sorry to hear that."

"I was, too." Jake changed the subject back to Ezekiel. "Anyway, we think your nephew was the target—can you tell me what was he doing there? And why he might have been targeted?"

Lafleur shook his head, no doubt relaxing a bit to learn that his head was not on the chopping block, that the crazed gunman who'd just committed grand theft auto was simply an investigator trying to learn about a cold case. "I have no idea. Just like I told the police here, the investigators, everyone. I've been trying to do my job, but the infighting—the gang activity, the terrorist attacks—it's all gotten so damned out of control. I'd seen this sort of thing happen, but I never expected it to happen to Zeke."

"Sorry," Jake said.

"It's harming things here, you know," Lafleur added. "Cases like these, they're bad for business. You've got US and Puerto Rican relations crumbling, no one wants to come here for work or pleasure, and—" he stopped himself. "Sorry, you're just trying to piece this together about Zeke. Wish I could help you more, son."

"You've been very helpful," Jake said, placing the pistol on his lap as he pulled around the last corner, nearing the building where he'd left the driver.

As they got closer, he could see the driver standing, ghost-white, on the curb. He seemed to release a thousand gallons of air when he caught sight of the SUV.

"Well, I think this is your stop," Jake said. "Take care."

"Strange way to do business, son," Lafleur said. "But I get it. Hope you find what you're looking for."

Jake smirked as the driver helped his client out of the vehicle. "I think I've got a pretty good idea of where to go next."

CHAPTER 62

"What'd you find?" Jake asked, nearly yelling at the phone in his hand. He'd gotten into yet another ride-share, this one driven by a young, clean-cut man who seemed barely old enough to drive. He also could barely see over the dash. Jake's concern had lasted all of three seconds, however, as he had much more pressing issues to deal with.

"We're not sure yet," McDonnell said. *"Some old pictures, newspaper articles. Bolivar is working on getting into the company's intranet, to see if there's anything there."*

"Good," Jake said. "I'm on my way into San Juan." He hadn't yet told anyone about Vero, and he didn't think it wise to try to explain her at this point. He also didn't have a specific plan in place to meet with her yet.

There was a pause, and Jake heard shuffling on the other end of the line. He was about to repeat himself when McDonnell's voice came back on. *"Jake, Smith just found something. It might be…"* another pause. *"Holy crap. Hell yeah, that's it."*

"What is it?"

"It's the informant. The one who's related to Holland's guy?"

"Yeah, El Gordo. He's married to Delmonico's sister or something. On vacation on a company retreat nearby for the next week or so."

"Right, he's staying at the Encanto Beach Club at Dorado Beach. Anyway, it turns out he's been cheating on his employer."

"APHINT? How's that?" Jake asked.

"I'm sending over the article, but take a look at the picture. It's black-and-white and grainy as hell, but El Gordo's in it. Much younger, but it's the same guy. Bolivar just checked as well. But according to his file, he's only worked for APHINT during his career."

"And?"

"Well, this is a photo shoot of Fitzsimmons *employees. And Charles Lafleur's also in it."*

"Wait, really?"

"Unmistakable."

"Okay, that might change things," Jake said. "Hold on a sec." He pulled the phone down and looked over at the kid, who was blinking quickly and gripping the steering wheel tightly. The kid looked over and they met eyes, and Jake suddenly wished he had a driver with a bit more experience. *Oh well,* he thought. *When in Rome.* "Hey, how fast you think you could get around Puerto Rico?"

"Around?"

"Yeah," Jake said, snaking a motion with his hand. "Get on the highway. Head up to Dor… Dor Beach?"

"Dorado Beach?" the driver asked.

"Yep, that's it. Get there quick and I'll toss you another fifty."

The kid immediately gunned it and Jake felt his torso thrust backward against the seat. He maneuvered around three cars, finding the far lane, then took the exit and they sailed over the road onto a new, wide highway.

"McDonnell," Jake said, once again talking into the phone. "I'm heading there now. I'll find El Gordo and do the job Holland should've done a long time ago."

He hung up and started to pull up the browser on his phone, but another call came in the same second. He frowned, not recognizing the number. It was local—a Puerto Rican line.

"Hello?"

"Jake Parker." The voice was slow, menacing. Thick accent, but clear English. *"You have something I need."*

"I do?"

"Sí. You have it, and my employers require it back."

"I'm not sure I follow."

"You have information I need."

"I don't think that's true. Even if it were, I'm not sure I could give that *back* to you. Who the hell is this? You with Dominguez?"

"Retrieval of information is one of our specialties, Mr. Parker."

"What information is it you're looking for? And you never answered my question: who is this?"

"You will present yourself to my associates. Tell them where you are now, and they will meet you there."

"I don't really have time to wait around."

"You will not wait long. We are everywhere, Jake Parker."

So it is Dominguez. Jake tried to figure out why they were calling now. Why wait? If they thought he knew something, why wouldn't they just show up and take him by surprise? And why would they call him first anyway?

"Fine," he said. He needed time to think. He needed to get off the phone, to try to get ahead of this. He realized that he had a bit of a drive coming up; perhaps that was enough time to get a handle on the situation. "I'm in the car now. I'm not sure exactly where, but I can let you know a destination whenever I—"

"This is not a joke, Mr. Parker," the man said. *"We will find you. In one hour, if we do not hear from you, we will kill her."*

Jake pulled the phone down away from his ear, trying to understand. *Kill her?*

The blood drained from his face. He swallowed. They'd gotten to her—somehow Dominguez had Vero.

"Where is she?" his voice was filled with hate, and he did nothing to try to hide the vitriol. He kicked himself for not keeping her with him, by his side. "Tell me where she is *now*, or I'll—"

"You will do nothing but obey, Mr. Parker. Tell us where you are and we will get you. That is all."

"Why? What is it you want to know? You think I have information, and you want it? How does that make sense?"

"It does not make sense because we do not need information from you, Mr. Parker. We simply need to ensure the information you already have does not become information you give to anyone else."

Jake nodded, silent as he listened.

The driver glanced back a few times but averted Jake's eyes when he looked up.

"It is a simple trade, Mr. Parker. Your life. For hers."

"Where are you?" Jake shouted into the phone. "Tell me where, now!" He felt a surge of panic, then shoved it back down. He felt the training kick in, the years of practice and emotional control exercises. He wouldn't let his own mind best him, not now. He needed to stay calm, to figure out the last pieces of the puzzle. Only by solving it all could he ensure Vero's safety.

Or so he hoped.

"Fine," he snarled through gritted teeth. "I'll text you an address. Be there, with Vero. Alive."

The call disconnected.

CHAPTER 63

"McDonnell, I need backup!"

Jake was nearly shouting into the phone. The driver was racing through traffic on the highway, no doubt excited from the one-way shouting match taking place in the back seat of his car. He dodged a few box trucks and pulled into the open left lane, then gunned it.

Jake didn't tell him to stop.

He was heading for Dorado Beach, but he wanted to know what he'd find when he got there. Before he could even begin to come up with a plan, he needed to see if McDonnell had any support on the ground he could benefit from.

"Jake, I wish there was something I could tell you," his old friend's voice said. *"But Bolivar and Smith are out of ideas. Holland going rogue was the loss of our last asset—besides you—on the island."*

"Shit," Jake said. "Shit, shit. What the hell are we supposed to do?"

"You haven't heard from Holland either?" he asked.

Jake clenched the phone. "No, nothing. It's like after Delmonico saw me in the—" He stopped. Glanced around, tried to breathe deeply and steady himself.

"What is it? You there?"

"Yeah," Jake said. "I just realized… I'm not sure if it's a plan, but it's a start."

"What is it? Anything we can help with?"

Jake shook his head as he answered. "No, at least not yet. Unless you've got a small army here in Puerto Rico ready to start a war with Dominguez, I think I'm on my own."

"Right. I was afraid of that." McDonnell sighed, and Jake heard the sound of Bolivar or Smith speaking in low tones on the other end of the line. He couldn't distinguish the words. *"Okay, I've got to go. Call immediately when you know something."*

Jake confirmed, then hung up. Without glancing up from his screen, he dialed Holland's number. It rang twice, and then—surprisingly—Holland answered.

The voice was gruff and rapid-fire. *"Hello? Parker? That you?"*

"It is," Jake said. "I need you to do something. I need—"

"You need me to do something? For you? Are you out of your god—"

Jake cut him off before he could finish. "We don't have time, Holland. I know who you think I am, who you think I'm working for. You're wrong, but I don't have time to explain it."

"Tell me where you are, and I'll give you plenty of time to explain."

"I'm not sure that's what you want, Holland. We're supposed to find the next terrorist attack, right?"

There was a pause, but no answer.

"I know where that is. Have your team meet me at Dorado Beach. Encanto Beach Club."

"There?" Holland scoffed. "That's where you think—"

"I don't need you to trust me, Holland, but think of it this way: there are three options: I'm telling you the truth, and we'll be able to stop this thing before it potentially kills a lot of people, or I'm lying, and sending you on a wild-goose chase. If that's the case, what does it matter? Or, you do nothing at all, and we see how this plays out."

Jake could almost hear the soldier's wheels turning, trying to figure out whether or not he was getting played.

Finally, after a gruesome five seconds of waiting, Holland's voice returned. *"Fine. We'll be there. Parker, I swear to God if you're lying to me—"*

"Save it, Holland. We've already got enough bad guys after us—the least we can do is be on the same team for once."

He hung up before Holland was able to reply, and noticed that the exit to Dorado Beach was coming up in a few short miles.

Think, Parker. He willed himself to summon all the pieces, to visualize all the components of the puzzle in his mind at once. He closed his eyes. *Vero. APHINT. Chemical X. Bismuth. Dominguez. Fitzsimmons. Lafleur.*

It was all too much, and yet it all fit together. The common thread wasn't just that these things were Puerto Rican, that they existed in close proximity to one another. No, these things were all *intimately* related. They all went together in a very specific, very controlled—and *designed*—way.

That was it.

He almost had it.

He frowned, squeezing his eyes shut and trying to see the events of the last few days played out in front of him. Everything here made sense together somehow because everything here had been *designed.* Purposefully, all the pieces pushing toward a singular goal.

All for a reason.

Jake wasn't naive. He knew that things happened for a reason, and many times that reason was money. Someone on this island needed these pieces to fall into place—these *people* to fall into line—in order to make *money.* There was a lot of it at stake, especially considering…

He smiled. *That's it.* He knew now what he had to do.

It involved a bit of a leap of faith—he needed to trust Holland and his team—but every great prize required an equally great leap. This would be his, and everything would be on the line. His life, Vero's life, potentially Holland's.

But now, finally, he had a plan.

CHAPTER 64

Cecil Romero was tense. His body ached, his back ached, and his head ached. He felt like a tightly wound spring, ready to burst. He drove in silence, ignoring the deep-held instincts to turn around and forget about all of this. He wanted to scream, and at the same time he wanted to head back to his parents' home, the home he grew up in, and apologize for everything.

He wanted it to end.

Yet he also knew there were at least two endings. He could force an ending by giving up, by giving in. That would save his sister for the time being, but Dominguez would find him, and then her. And he would have only furthered their cause and gotten his family killed.

The other option was to see it through. To push on, persevere, as he always had. To accomplish this assignment would be to accomplish the impossible task that all the Dominguez leadership had at one time or another accomplished. He would gain by doing this, and that gain was his promise of future power.

I will press on.

He drove toward the entrance of the complex, the destination he had been given. He knew it was a risk coming here, but everything lately seemed to carry with it a level of risk. He was comfortable with that risk, normally, but now—with everything that had changed—that risk was starting to feel less like adventure and a lot more like crippling fear.

Cecil took a deep breath, held it. He parked away from the main building and closer to a smaller copse of palm trees that obscured a tinier structure, finding a spot at the location he had been given. He took his seatbelt off, let out another deep breath, and opened the door.

It was hot today, drier than normal. He blinked away the bright sunlight and pulled his sunglasses from his pocket and placed them over his ears. Cecil took a pause for a few seconds, studying his surroundings.

The parking lot was nearly completely surrounded by palms and ferns, the thick, dense jungle hiding their actual location. He could hear waves crashing nearby, likely only a few hundred feet from the edge of the lot. The larger building they had passed on the way in was back and to his right, looming over this lot and his car. He didn't see any employees, nor did he see any locals or tourists.

He knew better than to think he was alone, however. Cecil had been given this location by a trusted Dominguez agent, and that person would be here soon, if they weren't already nearby, waiting for him to arrive. He would not be alone, either.

Cecil looked around and tried to spot any cameras mounted on trees, the corners of buildings, poking out from above roofs. He saw none, but that meant nothing. Surveillance technology was far more advanced than ever before, and the fact that he'd been allowed in meant that no one yet had a problem with his being here.

And why should they? The vast majority of people here had no idea what was taking place just feet from the beach, and none of them would. He intended to keep it that way.

Cecil tugged at the unbuttoned Hawaiian shirt he was wearing on top of a white T-shirt. He wanted it to look natural, to hide the holster and pistol he was wearing beneath the outer shirt. Satisfied, he then walked around the rear end of the car and opened the passenger door.

She was sitting there, eyeing him, her mouth closed and quiet, but her face screaming at him. Her hands were bound by ties around her wrists.

"Get out," he said.

Vero stared at him, not complying.

He didn't have time for insubordination. He grabbed her arm, pulling her hard out of the car. She didn't fight him, but she also didn't make it easy.

"Vero," he said. "They will *kill* you. They will kill—"

"You?" she replied. "You are worried about your own life, yes? You are worried about your own status with Dominguez, so much so that you will kill innocent people. Your own family. Cecil, this is not—"

"Quiet," he snapped, dragging her to the edge of the parking lot. He had been given the coordinates of a spot near the main hotel, on the resort's grounds, where they could enact their plan in relative peace. Jake Parker would be stopped, here and now. Cecil had been assigned the role of arbiter for this mission. He was not sure if there would be other Dominguez members in attendance, but it didn't matter. Cecil had a job to do, a plan, and he had time and resources on his side. He would prevail.

He pushed his sister to the curb, and then onto the sidewalk, toward a narrow break in the forest, a nearly invisible path. "Walk," he said.

She stumbled forward, gained her balance, and then walked slowly up the path. The coqui frogs chirped in delight as they drew near, their singsong voices welcoming to Cecil's ears.

"Where are we going?" Vero asked. Her voice was low, barely audible over the growing cacophony of the frogs.

"To see your friend, Mr. Parker."

Her head snapped around. "He—he did not accept your offer," she stammered. "He *would not*. You are being deceived, brother. Jake Parker is too smart to—"

"He thinks he has us fooled, yes," Cecil replied, his voice calm and steady. "But I assure you, he does not. He gave up his location to his team of American soldiers, but they do not know what you and I know—Dominguez is everywhere. Including there."

"There's a spy?"

"I would not call it that. Simply someone interested in furthering Dominguez efforts, as we are. You will see—when we get to your friend and his Americans, I will introduce you."

He saw Vero's jaw tighten, her chin raise. She was defiant, just as he was. Stubborn, a Romero family trait.

But he knew that no matter how stubborn one could be, Dominguez was not a force that could be stopped.

CHAPTER 65

The entrance to Dorado Beach was every bit as flamboyant and over the top as Jake's own resort accommodations for the week, yet Dorado seemed to be even one step higher. Founded by Laurance Rockefeller in 1950 and now owned by Ritz-Carlton, the resort sat on the northernmost edge of the island, just west of San Juan.

The driver dropped Jake at the front entrance and was zipping off to grab his next ride before Jake could thank him. Perhaps the kid was scared of who he might have been chauffeuring around.

Jake didn't pause to glad-hand the bellhops standing around the entrance—he had a target, and that target was somewhere inside. He strode up the front steps through the massive, immaculately appointed entranceway and atrium, and steered around groups of tourists and hotel employees, aiming for the back hallway that led to the beach outside. From there, he could turn around, examine the main buildings of the hotel and see, for the most part, all of the rooms at once.

He pulled the phone up to his ear. "Anything?"

"Yeah, maybe," came the reply. *"Bolivar's in, I think."*

"I'm looking at it. Just tell me which way to point."

Jake wanted to find the man before Holland's men and Dominguez each got there. He had never told the caller who had Vero where he was headed; it was part of his plan to get here, confront El Gordo, and *then* see if he'd been right. He'd know he was right if they showed up.

He had called McDonnell and told him the first half of the plan—the half he'd need McDonnell's help with, and Jake knew this task was easy for a man like Bolivar.

"Okay, got it. He must have left his room around 9 a.m., because it looks like hospitality came through about 9.15 for morning cleaning."

Jake checked his watch: *9.47.* "Where is he now?"

"Hasn't used his key to unlock the door since then," McDonnell said. *"But it looks like he did use it to check out a couple of beach towels."*

Jake smiled. "Perfect. Seems like I'm already close."

He turned a half-circle and faced the beach, wondering if he'd be able to spot his target from here. He started walking toward the water when McDonnell started talking once again.

"You told them where you're headed?" McDonnell asked.

"No, I didn't."

"Okay, then—"

"Consider it a bit of a test. I'll explain later."

Jake hung up the phone and started jogging along the path. The coqui frogs were singing harmoniously from the thick, densely packed forest along the path's left side. The resort had created an appropriately believable facade of rainforest, giving visitors the effect of being boxed into some island paradise. It was beautiful, and Jake could imagine how the place might sparkle at night, the tiki torches lining the paths lit up and the waves twinkling back at the shoreline in the moonlight.

When I find Vero…

He really hoped he was right about all of this. He *needed* to be right. If the man who had called him earlier was telling the truth, her life was in his hands. If he was going to end this, he needed this end game to run without a hitch.

There were a few cabana-style beach huts scattered along the sand, between the buildings of Encanto Beach Club and the water, and on the second one in Jake saw his target.

285

A tall, thin man, sipping something from a straw jutting out from the top of a coconut, sunglasses on and wearing an unbuttoned Hawaiian shirt.

Jake slowed, walking up and standing beside the hut.

The man didn't respond, nor did he look up at Jake.

"Morning," Jake said.

El Gordo finally looked up, frowning. "I know you... you—" he snapped his fingers. "You're that kid from Holland's investigation."

Jake nodded.

"What the hell are you doing here? I'm on vacation, and—"

Jake sprang forward, grabbing the older man by the collars and pulling his head close to his. "Listen, asshole. I've got half a mind to smash *your* coconut with *that* coconut and leave you face down in the shallows, but I need to get some answers."

"Wh—what are you talking—"

"Save the act, Garcia—El Gordo, whatever you're called. Whatever you're planning, I need to know about it. Now."

"I really don't know what—"

Jake yanked hard on the man's shirt, pulling him completely up and off the lounge chair. He yelped in surprise, nearly garnering the attention of a nearby bellhop who was delivering some food to the cabana next door.

"Get over here," Jake said, pulling El Gordo along and toward the path. He stepped between two immature areca palms, their fronds forming a nearly impregnable wall of green, lush leaves. Jake pushed hard into the fortress, hopping out the other side and finding himself standing in knee-deep grasses. He and Garcia walked uphill until they were a good distance from the path and buildings on each side.

The sound of the coqui frogs rose in excitement, delighted or frantic about the newcomers. Jake pushed El Gordo forward once again, who fell to his knees, landing in a thick, goopy mess of mud. He turned, his eyes pleading.

"Hear that?" Jake asked.

"What? The frogs?"

Jake smiled. "Let me tell you a little story."

CHAPTER 66

"I need to make sure things are happening on schedule, so I figure we've got a few minutes."

El Gordo looked at him strangely.

"I was married," Jake began. "Best person I've ever met. I miss her more every day. But we got married in Hawaii—Big Island, actually." Jake paused, not expecting any input from the thin man.

Instead, he began to complain. "What the hell is this about?"

"Shut the hell up for a second and you'll find out," Jake said. "Anyway, these frogs? The coqui? They're *everywhere* out there. These little guys are some of *your* island's national treasures. But these same frogs were there, too—brought over in the 1980s on nursery plants from Puerto Rico. However, out there, there aren't any predators for them, like there are here. No bats, no monkeys. So they're considered a *nuisance*."

The calls got louder, as if the coqui frogs were listening to Jake's little presentation.

"You hear that? They're like thousands of distress calls. Each one of them trying to be louder than their friend. Drowning out everything that's about to happen out here."

El Gordo's eyes widened further, terrified.

Jake saw the tiny coqui tattoo peeking out from the inside of the man's wrist. "Jaime Escalante Garcia, owner of a massive plot of land just outside El Yunque National Forest. Is that correct?"

"How—how do you know that?"

"You were careful, but not careful enough. Not everyone around here might do their homework, but I do. I wasn't just trained to be a soldier—to take orders and wait for more information. I was trained to *dig up* the information. And it seemed like when I was poking around that land there was a *lot* to dig up. You know?"

El Gordo swallowed.

"People like your brother-in-law. He never knew you were *actually* the guy who bought the land and put your sister's maiden name on the deed, did he? It was a cash purchase, so no one's going to come knocking, and you pay your taxes on it just like a good citizen. But that doesn't mean your brother-in-law's off the hook, either. Am I getting warmer?"

"No, you are mistaken. Your information is wrong. I am just—"

"I don't have time for more lies, El Gordo. Our friends should be here any second."

Jake didn't let the man's act get to him. Instead, he pulled out the Beretta from his waist. He held it at his side, tightly but swinging it slowly, trying to make it seem haphazard, as if he weren't afraid to fly off the handle and use it.

"I know you're playing both sides," Jake said. "You're Holland's informant because of that fact. You work for APHINT, right?"

He nodded.

"So what do you do for them, exactly?"

"I am just an administrator. Mid-level management stuff. I make sure the FDA regulations that come through are passed around and approved. It is… truly boring work."

"And is the work you do for Dominguez so boring, as well? Like buying land, setting up a compound out in *Campo de Almas?*"

Garcia frowned, then followed Jake's gaze. He looked down at his own wrist. "I—This tattoo? Is that what you mean? I have it, so you think I am helping Dominguez? The coqui frog, as I said. It is a symbol of—"

"It's a *gang* symbol, Garcia. Everyone on the island knows that."

"I am no longer participating in that organization."

"Ah," Jake said, raising his chin. "So you can do that? Join, swear loyalty, then just back out when it no longer suits you?"

"No, I mean—"

"How did you know Ezekiel Santos?" Jake asked.

Garcia looked around, as if searching for help. When he couldn't find it, he began to speak. "He—he was a hotshot. Hot*headed*, too. Wanted to get Dominguez to expand to the States, even took a meeting with a US contact in Boston without getting approval from the leadership. Shame that he died the way he did."

"And what way was that?" Jake pressed. "I thought he just went missing? Everyone—police, media, papers—they all thought it was a kidnapping, right?"

El Gordo's eyes widened even more. "I—I don't know, truly. I think you must have the wrong—"

Jake brought the pistol across his face, hard. It wasn't a lethal blow, as Jake made sure it would only scrape the man's cheek, but the effect was the same. Garcia fell backward, stunned. "I need you to stop lying, Garcia. This ends here. *Now*."

El Gordo looked up at him, and then his face changed. He seemed to understand something now, about his role in all of it. Jake had seen the expression before, when a criminal knew he was caught. He wasn't about to admit to anything, but he knew that in order to keep the status quo, he would need to buy himself time.

"Start talking, asshole." Jake hit him again.

El Gordo started to laugh. Slowly at first, just a slight chuckle. He coughed, still catching his breath, but the laughs fell out more rapidly by the second.

"What's funny, Garcia?"

"You—you are naive." He turned and spat a chunk of blood and tooth, one that had become dislodged by Jake's blow. "You come here—all of you—thinking you know this place, that you can *help* this place."

"You don't think I can?"

"It is not what I think, Mr. Parker," El Gordo said. "It is that no matter *what* you do, it will never *end*. Dominguez—you think it is a group of men and women who like making money from drugs. That is true, but it is also so much more. It is a heartbeat. The coqui frog—you know it to be true. 'The voice of a people.' You say that it ends, but you are mistaken."

"That so?"

"Indeed, Mr. Parker," El Gordo said, holding his bloody cheek. "It *never* ends. It never has, and it never will."

CHAPTER 67

"Parker!" Holland shouted. "Freeze! Hands in the air!"

His voice carried through the trees and into Jake's ears, judging by the way Parker's back straightened and his arms went stiff.

Caught you, you bastard, Holland thought. *Time to end this, and get some answers.*

The last few days had been hectic, but the last twenty-four hours had been insane. Holland had spent most of the time trying to follow the locations of his men, each of which he'd sent in as many directions, trying to uncover suspicious Dominguez members they thought might be involved in the attack to come, or trying to get a lead on Parker. All of it had grown to a fury of confusion, chaos, and double-crossing. He had never expected a man like McDonnell to turn on him. He had never expected to be playing against his own team like that, to be led on a false chase that would end with him or his team getting killed.

And he was *not* going to let that happen. He could only trust himself now, that much was clear, and that meant he shouldn't trust Jake Parker, McDonnell's golden boy. It had been too strange that McDonnell had sent the kid here right before an expected massive terrorist attack, and now it had culminated in discovering that Jake was working for the same gang Holland had been trying to bring down.

Parker turned, slowly, and Holland could see that he wasn't alone. There was another man there, his nose bleeding and eye puffy, and—

El Gordo? Holland almost couldn't believe his eyes. He didn't *want* to. He had suspected that his informant, Delmonico's brother-in-law, had been involved when Jake had called him with the location to meet up. The same resort El Gordo had told them he would be staying at this week. It was well-deserved time off, and Holland had had no problem with it.

But seeing his face, seeing the damage Parker had done to the man, Holland now knew the truth. Jake was working for Dominguez, and he had decided to take out the best link to the American soldiers—to the mission—Holland had.

It was a blatant, overt attempt at sabotage, and the fact that Parker had called him beforehand, told him where he could be found, meant the kid was every bit as cocky as he'd initially thought—

Or, it meant something else entirely. Something Holland wasn't quite ready to accept. Something he didn't *want* to accept.

"Holland," Jake said, his hands in the air, the Beretta dangling from a finger. "Glad you came. I was just—"

"Drop the gun, asshole." Thompson and Delmonico were flanking Holland as they moved as a unit toward the opening in the foliage. Krueger and Jacobsen were back in the car, listening in and ready to provide backup if things got out of hand.

Jake sniffed, looked at each of Holland's men, then nodded. He carefully set the gun down on the forest floor. El Gordo didn't move.

"You called me to tell me where to find you," Holland said. "I half expected to find El Gordo here alone, sipping from a coconut. You nowhere to be found."

"Well, you're half-right," Jake replied. "He *was* drinking something fruity when I got here."

"Why tell me the truth?" Holland asked. "Why let me bring my team here? You're outnumbered, surrounded."

Jake nodded. "Yeah, well, it's not what you think."

"Damn right it's not what I think!" Holland shouted. He glanced around and saw that there was a couple, some European tourists, staring at him and his men. He lowered his voice so only Thompson and Delmonico could hear. "Get in there with them," he said. "We don't need an audience for this."

They all stepped through the thick flora and into the small clearing. The humidity rose, and Holland heard a few croaks of the coqui nearby.

He continued, "It's not what I thought at all, Parker. You—McDonnell—all working against me. A Dominguez plant, on my own team? What kind of fool do you take me for?"

Jake shifted, his head lowering. "Well, thing is, you're right. There *is* a plant on your team. That's why I called. That's why it had to be done this way. You wouldn't believe me otherwise. You wouldn't trust me, I knew that already."

"The hell are you talking about?" Holland slid his right hand slowly around his waist, preparing to grab the pistol. He didn't know what other tricks this kid had up his sleeve, but he was not about to be taken off guard. Thompson and Delmonico held their ground as well, both now aiming pistols at Parker.

"I told you where to find me," Jake explained. "Because I needed to find an answer to a question *I've* been asking myself for a few days. I was pretty confident about it already, but this would seal the deal."

"What would?" Holland asked. But Jake was peering over Holland's shoulder, not even looking at him. *Asshole*, he thought. "You got someplace better to be?"

Jake smiled. "I knew it. Heads up."

Holland couldn't help himself. He turned around, noticing movement in the foliage and seeing a woman and man step through. The woman's hands were bound, the man behind her pushing her along. They had similar features, and Holland immediately noticed the tattoo on his wrist.

"What the f—"

Before Holland could finish the thought, Thompson whirled and aimed at the Dominguez man.

"Thompson, no!" Delmonico shouted. "Easy, easy. Let's just—"

"Who are you?" Holland shouted.

For his part, the younger Dominguez man standing behind the woman seemed equally confused. He didn't falter, however, and instead brought a pistol up to the woman's head.

"Whoa, whoa, hold on," Jake said, stepping to the side, and began moving toward the newcomers.

Holland pulled his own pistol and pointed it at Parker. "Take another step and I put one through you. I'm done playing games, Parker. Someone here better start talking. Now."

"Right," Jake said. His eyes flicked toward the woman and man at the edge of the clearing. "Cecil, I presume?" There was no response. "Yeah, as I thought. You didn't expect this either, did you? And I apologize, but my Spanish is not great. I am hoping your sister can translate—"

"My English is fine," the man—Cecil, apparently—said. "What is this? Who are these people?"

Holland wanted to intervene, to take control. He wasn't opposed to letting bullets fly, but he wanted to know more of the game here before pulling the trigger.

Jake addressed the woman. "Vero, you okay?"

She nodded.

"Holland, this is Vero. *Sister* of the guy holding her hostage. He's typical Dominguez trash, as I'm sure you can see."

The man sneered at Jake, but didn't respond.

Holland watched on, his interest piquing.

"I was telling you the truth a second ago," Jake continued. "You wanted proof? About why I'm not the one you're after? Here it is: *I* didn't tell Cecil and Dominguez about this little rendezvous."

"No? Then who did?"

"You did."

"All right, Parker. Enough with the games. I'm not—"

"I'm serious, Holland. It was a test, and your team failed. I didn't mention this meeting to *anyone* but you. I gave *you* the location, and no one else. So that means you've got more trash to take out, in your own ranks. Vero's brother, a Dominguez member, knew exactly where to find me—but I didn't say a word to him. I'm assuming you didn't, either. But you told your team, didn't you?"

Before Holland could react, Delmonico took a few steps forward, his pistol swinging around and aiming up at Jake's chest.

"Delmonico—no!" Holland shouted.

But it was too late.

The shot fired, the unsuppressed pistol cracking loudly.

CHAPTER 68

Jake had expected the shot—he was surprised it had taken Delmonico this long. He dove to the side, narrowly dodging the point-blank shot only because he knew it was coming. He fell to the dirt, his own pistol up and already looking for its mark. Jake found it and fired twice.

One shot hit—Delmonico wailed in pain and fell, the round striking his left thigh. Blood immediately gushed out of the wound.

Vero ran forward, toward Jake, and he saw her brother standing empty-handed, no doubt trying to figure out what had just happened. His mouth opened, his hands coming up to protest, but before he could move, Thompson and Holland were there, holding him back.

"What the *hell*, Delmonico?" Holland shouted.

Delmonico was holding his thigh, no longer interested in shooting Jake. The large man looked up and met Jake's eyes with a searing rage, the vitriol clear on his face.

"You—you *asshole*," Delmonico whispered.

"Sorry, man," Jake said. "I had to do it."

"Seriously, what the hell is—" Holland said.

"This guy's been playing you," Jake interrupted. "He's been playing all of you. Both sides, actually. You think El Gordo's the informant? There's a reason he couldn't get you any more information, Holland. Because Delmonico stopped *giving it to him.*"

"You're saying—"

"I'm saying Delmonico is working with Dominguez. He has all along. He—"

"That's not true," Delmonico protested. "He's—"

"Save it, Delmonico," Holland said. "Run your mouth like you run your piece and it's going to get you killed this time."

Jake continued. "I was curious about the relationship he has to El Gordo. Brother-in-law, right? Meaning he married El Gordo's sister?"

"Yeah, but El Gordo's sister's never had anything to do with Dominguez. Her brother was involved with some low-level stuff for a bit, but she's clean."

"She is," Jake confirmed. "I had McDonnell look into it. But that doesn't mean they still couldn't use her. She and Delmonico bought some land here, a while ago? Up near El Yunque National Forest?"

Holland swallowed.

"That's *Dominguez* land, Holland. Backs up against a place called 'The Field of Souls.' Sounds ominous, right?"

"There was a Puerto Rican cop that died out there, not two nights ago. You know anything about that?"

Jake nodded. "Yeah, I knew the guy. Good officer, too. Damn shame."

"What are you talking about?" Thompson said. "*You* killed him."

Jake almost laughed. "Is that what you think? Is that what *this* guy told you?" He motioned down at Delmonico, his eyes now bloodshot, tears forming around them. Jake assessed him in a split-second. He was about a minute away from going into shock, and possibly three away from blood loss-induced death. "I didn't kill *anyone*, Thompson. I simply did my job. It took a bit to find someone who would help me out, and a bit more legwork to dig up answers, but it seems Delmonico here has been taking you all for a ride. He had El Gordo use his sister's maiden name to buy the land. Seems like using family members is something pretty typical for these Dominguez guys?"

He saw Cecil's eyes narrow, but Thompson and Holland held him tightly. Vero was standing between him and Jake, near El Gordo, who was still sitting on the ground, watching and listening with interest.

"Anyway, when I saw Delmonico in the market at the same time as the other Dominguez guys that attacked us, I started to put things together. How El Gordo here was getting his information, how the Dominguez gang has always been a step ahead of you guys. It's not because they're some massive organization with spies everywhere, Holland. It's because you've been infiltrated."

"That's not true!" Delmonico wailed. "He's lying. He's—"

"Shut the *hell* up, Delmonico," Holland said. He walked forward, stepping up closer to Jake. His eyes were slits, his pug nose sniffing for anything fishy. Jake saw the soldier trying to decide whom to believe. "I've got more questions, Parker. Like why you were in the marketplace?"

Jake nodded. "I know. And the answer to that is simple: I was investigating. Why were you watching *me* in the market?"

Holland sniffed. "I wasn't, until Delmonico told me you were there. But don't be naive, Parker. After that, I was curious. I was going to have one of my guys tail you, and Delmonico volunteered. I'm starting to understand why."

"He's been burning the candle at both ends. Played it well, too. If I hadn't seen him down there, I never would have thought to check into him."

"And you also know that we don't have time right now. This attack—" Holland pulled his wrist up and looked at his watch. "This attack is supposed to happen any time in the next two hours."

"Actually," Jake said, looking at his own diver's watch, "it was scheduled for three minutes ago."

Holland's face fell, and Thompson glanced to his left and right. Even Cecil, still being held at gunpoint by Thompson, fidgeted.

"Three minutes ago?" Holland asked, his voice ratcheting up half an octave. "Then what are we still doing—"

"Relax, Holland," Jake said. "I called it in. Port Authority found it fifteen minutes ago. I had McDonnell's team back home coordinate the sting."

Holland's mouth opened and closed.

"It's not your fault, Holland," Jake said. He motioned with his head toward Delmonico, now breathing steadily on the ground, holding his thigh. His hands were slick with dark blood. "This guy didn't want you to figure it out. He even convinced you that I was in on it, so that you'd cut off McDonnell and be out of the loop completely. When I visited the docks, I noticed that the piers normally reserved for the biggest operations—Fitzsimmons and APHINT—are right next to each other."

"So?"

"*So* I did some digging, with Bolivar's help. He found that there was an FDA ambassador scheduled to arrive on APHINT's pier 5 today. The PA team found him—along with an entire metric ton of explosives—onboard."

"Shit."

"Yeah. But it gets better."

"It does?"

Jake nodded and smiled at Vero, then winked at her brother. He glared at Jake. "I think it's best to get these guys locked up first though—then we can talk."

Holland nodded, and Thompson moved a step toward Delmonico.

In that moment, Cecil Romero decided to act. He pulled a pistol from beneath his shirt and fired, quickly.

One round, aiming for Jake, caught Thompson in the back. The man fell to the ground. Jake saw Cecil moving from the corner of his eye, but he wasn't looking at him.

Instead, he was focused on the *second* person who had just fallen to the ground from Cecil's other shot.

Jake screamed, lunging forward, but he didn't get there in time.

Vero fell to the forest floor, the blood already started to spill around her.

CHAPTER 69

"Krueger, Jacobsen—Get in here, now!" Holland shouted. He didn't bother pressing the small in-ear device to his ear. His two other men waiting in the back lot would have heard him. They'd already be on the move, ready to come in guns blazing and prepared to fight.

Holland whirled around in time to see the younger Dominguez man, Cecil, dash through a thick wall of ferns and disappear.

"Shit," he said. He wanted to yell for someone to follow him, but both his men had been shot. Delmonico was no longer on his team, anyway. Thompson had been hit at point-blank range in the back, and he was likely already dead.

Holland gritted his teeth and started running, just as he caught more movement to his left, above Jake's head.

He frowned, expecting to see his teammates bashing through the forest and joining him, but instead the men who entered the cleared space were darker-skinned. Worse, they were aiming directly at him.

They yelled in Spanish, pointing submachine guns at him, but Holland was already on the move. He dove forward, hoping that putting the two thin tree trunks between him and the attackers would do something to stave off imminent death.

But Jake was there, too. He rolled back, pulling his own Beretta and firing up into the three oncoming Dominguez men. He hit one head-on, grazed another one in the shoulder, and the third at least stopped to reconsider his attack.

El Gordo sat up and crawled toward the third man, obviously hoping the ally would help him out.

"Come on!" Holland yelled.

"Not without her," Jake said. His eyes were direct, piercing, and Holland knew there would be no persuading him of anything otherwise. He watched as the third man pulled El Gordo into the thicker part of the edge of the clearing, both men disappearing.

"There will be more," Holland said. "You can't fight them all off."

"Dammit, Holland," Jake yelled in response. "Watch me try."

Holland grunted in frustration but started toward the fallen woman. Jake was already lifting her head and shoulders, preparing to roll her over and pick her up. Holland grabbed her feet and helped. "We need to get out, *now*."

"We'll put her in your car," Jake said, his voice not allowing any discussion. "At least we'll have a chance to get her to a hospital."

"They're going to be everywhere," Holland said. He fumbled Vero's feet with one hand while aiming the pistol over Jake's shoulder with his other hand, waiting for the third Dominguez member to pop back out into the clearing. Thankfully, he didn't see any movement.

"They've *been* everywhere, Holland, all along," Jake answered. "That's what you have to understand. Delmonico, El Gordo, this guy Cecil—they've been around, watching us. Watching *you*. Waiting for an opportunity."

"An opportunity for what?"

Jake didn't answer, and Holland didn't need him to. He got the point.

They carried the bleeding woman through the forested area of the resort's perimeter, finding Krueger and Jacobsen waiting for them, guns drawn, at the parking lot. Both men sprang into action when they saw the trio, helping with Vero and watching the edge of the rainforest for any motion.

When they got to the car and carefully placed Vero across the middle seat, they piled in and Jacobsen started the engine. Holland was in the front seat, Jake and Krueger in the back.

Krueger looked from one man to the other, finally finding his words. "Wh—what the hell?"

Holland shook his head. "Delmonico. Damned traitor. Working against us all along. He even had me believing McDonnell was the enemy. Stupid."

Jake spoke up. "*You* weren't stupid, Holland. You were just a pawn in their game."

"Yeah, well, I'd like to figure out how I might *win* this little game before another one of my men gets killed."

"Easy," Jake said. "You have to figure out how to become more than just a pawn."

Holland frowned, turning in the seat as Jacobsen navigated the SUV out of the resort's parking lot just as a convoy of Puerto Rican police cruisers piled in, lights blazing. "Yeah?" he asked, watching the officers spread out and head toward the edge of the parking lot, near the clearing. "And how do we do that? All this stuff is, like you said, a game—if we're just going back and forth as smaller pieces on the table, that means the best we can do is check the opposing player. Dominguez is too big, too spread out. They're decentralized, even, which means I don't see a way to get to checkmate."

Holland turned back around, watching the highway and scenery pass by on the way to the nearest hospital. Krueger was on his phone, likely typing out an update to McDonnell, explaining their absence and silence for what it was: subterfuge and sabotage.

When he looked back in the rearview mirror, Jake was smiling.

Holland shook his head. "That damned smirk of yours, Parker. So cocky. I'm guessing you're going to be telling the rest of us just what the hell you've been up to these past few days? And how we might checkmate this gang once and for all?"

"Yeah, we'll get to all that. But the problem you're running into isn't one of *how*—it's *who*?"

Holland frowned again.

"You're not trying to beat Dominguez, Holland."

"I'm not?"

"Nope. And that's why we've been feeling like pawns in someone else's game. It *is* someone else's game. We're not going to be able to checkmate Dominguez because we're not *playing* Dominguez. We're playing against someone else entirely."

CHAPTER 70

"Okay, Parker, tell me what I'm missing."

Holland stared at Jake, who was watching the massive USNS *Comfort*, a Mercy-class US Navy hospital ship, docked at the port Jacobsen had driven them to. Holland had decided that the best place for Vero, and the rest of them, to recover, regroup, and debrief, was safely inside the hull of a United States Navy vessel.

Jake smiled back at him. The pair was standing near the parked SUV, waiting to talk to the port entry guard about the black SUV that had rolled up and was awaiting entry. While Krueger and Jacobsen tapped away on their phones in the parked car, McDonnell and his two teammates were also hard at work remotely, dialing numbers and trying to gain Holland and the others entry.

While they waited, an EMS team was attending to Vero, preparing to move her into the ambulance. If they were allowed entry onto the ship, the ambulance would bring her the final two hundred yards to the floating hospital.

"Sorry I've been vague," Jake said.

Holland snickered. "Understatement of the year, kid."

"I had to be—I wasn't sure who it was on your team. I suspected Delmonico after I saw him in the market. The way he looked at me without waving or trying to communicate. Seemed fishy."

"Smelling fish in a fish market isn't anything to be proud of."

"Trust me, I'm not proud," Jake said. "Vero—the 'date' I was with at the market? She didn't deserve any of this. She was doing just fine until I showed up."

"Why her? What did she have to do with this?" Holland asked.

Jake looked at the water, unable to prevent himself from thinking of Mel, and then of Eliza. Eliza had been in a similar situation thanks to Jake. Shot and injured, hospitalized. Vero would also make a full recovery, he was sure of it. Yet he couldn't help shake the feeling that he was the reason these women had ended up in harm's way.

He looked back at Holland, focusing on his dark sunglasses. "She's… something special. I don't know. I like her, but she's not hard to like. From a professional standpoint, she seemed like an ally. She works for APHINT, knows the ins and outs of what they're trying to do."

"And that is?"

"That's what I was going to tell you," Jake said. "She was working on a new compound, a drug they would use to treat Lewy body disease."

"Lewy body?"

"It's like Parkinson's. Not important though. The thing is, APHINT was trying to get the jump on Fitzsimmons, who's *also* been trying to work on a similar drug. But APHINT's drug—and Vero was positive of this—was actually *causing* the maladies the drug was supposed to help."

"Interesting," Holland said. "Sounds like a bit of double-dipping. Make a drug that causes users to need more drugs."

"Precisely. But here's what's *really* interesting: El Gordo works for APHINT, right? Well, I had McDonnell's computer geek dig into El Gordo's emails. He was able to hack in, and he found something interesting."

"Do tell."

"Vero told me that her company was basing this new drug—the stuff she was testing, they call it 'Chemical X'—off of a new chemical compound they somehow acquired from Fitzsimmons. A little corporate espionage, nothing abnormal."

"Right."

"Well, it turns out it was El Gordo himself who handed over Chemical X to the R&D team at APHINT."

Holland's chin raised a bit, and Jake could see that his eyes narrowed slightly behind the sunglasses. "El Gordo himself, huh? That's convenient."

"*Very* convenient. Since we know that El Gordo's in bed with Dominguez, I predict that if Bolivar did a bit more digging…"

"He'd find that Dominguez planted it. They were the ones who told APHINT where to look to create their new drug."

"Their new *miracle* drug everyone's been hush-hush over," Jake said. "A miracle drug that's so miraculous it doesn't even heal—it *hurts*."

"Got it," Holland said. "But in the car you mentioned that we're not actually fighting Dominguez, right? Who's the culprit then, ultimately?"

Jake smiled again. He watched the EMTs moving Vero into the back of the ambulance, working methodically. From the open door, he could see Krueger in the back seat, his head down, looking at his phone.

And he could see something else, too. Since both rear doors of the SUV had been opened, Jake had a clear view *through* the vehicle. About a hundred feet past the parked SUV, across the street that led to this dock, he saw another car parked.

Three men were standing outside of it.

And one of the men was holding something.

"Holland, I—"

"Jake, get down!" Holland yelled. He had seen it at the same time, put a meaty hand on Jake's chest to push him back.

But it was too late. Jake was sprinting, heading for the open rear end of the ambulance.

The EMTs were oblivious to the man running up on them from behind, just as they were oblivious to the fact that from the other side, from the front of the ambulance, one of the men from across the street had just launched a grenade.

The rocket-propelled explosive device shot through the air with a tiny, dense line of smoke trailing from it, heading for its target.

It was making a beeline for the SUV, but Jake knew the problem even before the impact.

The ambulance—with Vero inside—was in the way.

The shockwave hit him first, the thousands of pounds of pressure picking him up and tossing him back like a piece of cloth that had been caught in the wind. He was nearly back at Holland when the ambulance went up in a gaseous explosion that took out all the windows of the SUV, along with Krueger and Jacobsen inside. The SUV kicked and rolled, the smashed and smoking hulk bouncing twenty feet and coming to a stop near the edge of the water.

Jake heard screams, saw the sailors and pedestrians running in every direction. He saw the ambulance, just a charred skeleton of metal and black, billowing smoke. He saw the EMTs laying face down, arms sprawled at their sides.

And he saw the men, dark-skinned, wearing sunglasses and Hawaiian shirts, getting back into their car. The man with the tube tossed the weapon into the trunk and then walked to the front of the vehicle, opened the door, and looked at Jake. It was a Dominguez grunt, but not one he recognized.

There was a small, menacing smile on his face.

CHAPTER 71

"They—they killed her!" Jake screamed. He couldn't hear his own voice. He couldn't see, either. There was blood, or sweat, or something, covering his eyes. He swiped at them, pushing whatever it was aside, and his hand came away smeared with red. Jake couldn't feel it, and it wouldn't have mattered if he could.

Holland was there, standing over him, his gun drawn. His head was moving back and forth, his mouth moving, but Jake couldn't hear anything.

"Bastards killed her," Jake said again, trying to make sense of what he'd just seen.

Holland reached and scooped Jake up, placing him on his feet. There was a *whooshing* sound, and finally the noise and cacophony reached his ears.

"... police and SWAT are on their way," Holland was saying. "We need to get you to the ship."

"Bullshit," Jake said, pawing again at his face, now feeling the searing sting of sweat *and* blood, running together through cuts and scrapes on his face. "I'm fine."

"Yeah, well you *won't* be if we're not on that ship."

Jake tried to parse the sentence. Had the explosive been meant for him? For Holland? Or Vero? Had they known they were all together? Why had the man looked at him like that afterward?

He shook his head, allowing himself to be pulled along by Holland, toward the ship.

No, he thought. *She's still there. She's alive. She has to be.*

He was arguing with himself again. The anxiety was there, too, bubbling just beneath the surface of his consciousness, trying to meddle with his mind's active threads.

You killed her, the voice said. *This is your fault.*

And then, *No. no, it's not my fault.*

He shook his head again and saw stars, felt himself spinning. He clutched Holland's arm tighter, hoping the old soldier was strong enough to carry him on.

Holland didn't flinch. He walked straight, as if holding nothing but a bag of laundry under his arm. He didn't talk, didn't try to ask if Jake was okay. He had a mission—get this man to safety.

Jake appreciated that. He knew the blood on his face must have been covering some injury that was much worse than it looked, but then again he didn't even know how it looked. He might actually be okay, he might be unharmed…

His body seemed to react to that thought with a vengeance, trying to prove him wrong. He felt the adrenaline and dopamine subside to allow the *real* pain, the stuff his internal chemicals had been dispatched to mask, return. He stumbled, his leg suddenly not working.

Two sailors ran out to the dock to help Holland, and Jake suddenly felt like he was floating. He saw his legs dangling, but couldn't feel them anymore. The pain was gone, replaced by a comforting calm and cloudy murkiness. He felt warm, but the hairs on the back of his neck were prickly.

The ship's massive frame blocked out the sun, and Jake felt a blast of cool air from inside the open hatch as they marched him up a ramp.

The darkness loomed, and he felt himself drawn to it. He wanted it now, the cool and the dark and the safety it would provide.

He let himself fade, seeing a few more hospital crew running around inside the ship, just before his eyes shut completely.

But it wasn't the last thing he saw. There, on the inside of his eyelids, he saw their faces: *Officer Luis Quintanilla, Krueger, Thompson, Jacobsen.* They drifted up at him, like bodiless heads floating in the abyss. Eyes open but not looking. And yet staring at him all the same. And then they faded away and were replaced by three more.

The faces were blurry, but came into focus one at a time.

Vero.

Eliza.

He was almost asleep now, he could feel it. He *longed* for it. Didn't know if it was the forever kind, but he would take whatever he could get.

And finally, just before everything went black—

Mel.

CHAPTER 72

"Tell me something, Parker," Jake heard. The voice was close, but it sounded like it was going through a voice distorter. It was warbled, like it was being amplified through a tin can.

He opened his eyes and saw Holland sitting there. The man's overshirt was off, a white tank top snug against his body. Jake saw a stain of sweat around the top of it. His hair was a mess, his eyes bleary and hanging.

"You look like shit," Jake said, his voice croaking. His throat hurt, but as he assessed his body and the pangs of fire running up and down his extremities, he realized his voice was most likely the thing that had fared best.

Holland chuckled. "You should see yourself, mate."

Jake tried to swallow but found a lump there. He could breathe, but it was uncomfortable. He struggled to clear it for a moment, then gave up. Finally, after another minute of pushing around in the hospital bed, he sat up and faced Holland. "You want me to tell you something? I'm guessing it's about our conversation that got, uh, cut short…"

"Yeah," Holland said, his voice low. "I'm… I'm real sorry, Parker."

Jake nodded. It was all Holland needed to say. Vero was gone. Nothing anyone could say that would change that.

But he didn't want to think about that right now. He couldn't. There was still work to be done, so he allowed himself the grace of denying his emotional state and focused once again on Holland.

"You want to know about Fitzsimmons. About how they set all the dominoes up, to fall on their command."

"That's reaching, isn't it?" Holland asked. "They set *everything* up? I thought Dominguez were the ones launching the terrorist attacks. Like the one in Boston—the reason you're even here?"

Jake nodded. "Sure, yeah. They technically are the culprits, but—as always—it goes deeper than that. Fitzsimmons is ultimately who we have to blame."

"How so?"

"Well, I started by playing an old game called 'follow the money.' Vero was right about the bailout—a few years ago, the FDA secured a bunch of money from Congress that was disseminated around the island's pharmaceuticals depending on size."

"Which means Fitzsimmons and APHINT got the vast majority of it."

"Exactly. And there was a not-so-subtle hint that there was plenty more money to go around, if things got hairy."

"Things like a local gang terrorizing the ports of entry and shipping logistics of same corporations."

Jake smiled. "The more devastation that Dominguez brings to the pharmaceuticals here, the more *money* gets injected into their coffers."

Holland chewed his lip, frowning as he thought through it. "And in Boston? I talked to McDonnell—the café your wife was in? How is that related?"

Jake looked out the large porthole window of the hospital ship. He saw seagulls dancing through the air as they searched for crumbs of food on the boardwalk below. "The guy who was their target—my ghost—was Ezekiel Manuel Santos III, a suspected kidnapping victim who was upper management for Fitzsimmons. *And* he was Charles Lafleur's nephew."

"Wait a minute—*the* Charles Lafleur?"

"Yep," Jake said. "One and the same. The CEO of Fitzsimmons put out a hit on his own family member, because he needed it to look like his connection with Dominguez was one of victim and victimizer, not the reality that they were actually in bed together, planning everything. Nothing like having the gang off your own family member to earn pity from any onlookers."

Holland squeezed the bridge of his nose. "Now, wait. How do you know that?"

"'Cause I had a little impromptu meeting with the guy. I mentioned that he died in a terrorist attack, and Lafleur said he remembered that—he was sad to hear about the attack in Boston."

"So?"

"*So* I never mentioned Boston. Just said my wife died that same day. *He* filled in the blanks, slipped up. He was pretending Santos was kidnapped by Dominguez, pretended to not know he was dead."

"I see. That's not really actionable though, is it?"

"Not alone, no. But McDonnell's already got his whizz-kids working on getting into Fitzsimmons' intranet, trying to find something tying their Chemical X to APHINT's research. My hunch is that they'll find something. I think Fitzsimmons baited APHINT, and then they can blame them for corruption and foul play when they rush their new drug to market without FDA approval."

"Right," Holland said. "And then they can have Dominguez launch these attacks, making it seem like all the companies are the target, blaming them on some dream of freeing Puerto Rico."

"That's what I'm thinking," Jake said. "And they took it a step further—El Gordo works for APHINT, and we know he's with Dominguez as well. I'd bet he's the one Lafleur's been using to handle the inter-company deals. Like using APHINT-produced bismuth in the bombs."

Holland looked at Jake strangely.

"Bismuth—it's in the chemical residue in all the terrorist attacks. And it's one of the main things APHINT produces from local sources."

His eyebrows rose. "So it's yet another thing making APHINT look like the bad guy."

"Exactly. And yet another thing making Lafleur and his company look like the victim. He's been using guys like El Gordo to set up the terrorist attacks, strategically planting them in places where it will do damage without *really* hurting business."

"The FDA ambassador," Holland said. "He arrived at an APHINT dock in a boat filled with explosives, two hours before the scheduled arrival."

"At a dock *right next* to Fitzsimmons. Lafleur's own company would have suffered some losses, but they would have been minimal."

"And once again, APHINT would look like the bad guys." Holland sighed, then stood up and walked around Jake's bed. "Okay, fine. I buy all of that. But how do we stop it? We can't expect to take down an entire company by ourselves."

Jake shook his head. "We don't have to. We've got an entire overgrown, bloated bureaucracy dedicated to that sort of thing. We just need to write it up and turn it in, and McDonnell will pass it up the chain to Congress. The FDA will get a slap on the wrist, Charles Lafleur and his goons will get indicted for planning at least a dozen terror attacks, and—hopefully—people around here will start to see Dominguez for what it really is."

"It all sounds a bit simplistic, Parker," Holland said.

"Oh, it is," Jake replied, winking at the soldier. "But El Gordo told me something back at the resort that I've been chewing on."

"What's that?"

"He said it never ends. It never has, and it never will."

"He was just being arrogant."

"Yeah, definitely. But I'm not sure he's wrong," Jake added. "Our job wasn't to come down here and solve all the problems. *I* thought I could, but I'm realizing that by solving one, you end up with another."

"You came to settle your wife's death?"

Jake nodded, then swallowed.

"And then Vero."

Jake nodded again, his eyes piercing into Holland's.

"Still, it seems a bit nihilistic, doesn't it? You came here to find answers, you got them. You *did* solve it, Parker. Don't beat yourself up that you can't change everything and fix the country's problem in one visit."

Jake thought for a moment, and then noticed that his phone on the nightstand next to the bed was vibrating. He frowned, wondering if it was McDonnell. But the number was a Washington, DC number that wasn't programmed into his phone.

"Need to take that?" Holland asked.

"Not sure," Jake said. "Let me see who it is first."

Holland gave Jake the room as he pulled the phone up to his ear. "Hello?"

"Jacob," the voice said.

Jake's blood went cold. He recognized the voice, knew it viscerally. He gripped the phone tighter.

"I heard a rumor you've been dicking around in Puerto Rico. My report says you've been interfering with a little project of my own. Something I've been working on for years. Is that true?"

"What are you talking about?"

"Don't play dumb with me. I can see through your bullshit. Always have."

Jake swallowed, then looked up at the ceiling. "Good to hear from you, Dad."

A LETTER FROM NICK

Dear reader,

I want to say a huge thank you for choosing to read *The Patriot*. If you did enjoy it, and want to keep up to date with all my latest releases, just sign up at the following link. Your email address will never be shared and you can unsubscribe at any time.

www.bookouture.com/nick-thacker

I hope you loved *The Patriot* and, if you did, I would be very grateful if you could write a review. I'd love to hear what you think, and it makes such a difference helping new readers to discover one of my books for the first time.

I love hearing from my readers—you can get in touch with me by visiting my website at www.nickthacker.com.

Thanks,
Nick Thacker

AuthorNickThacker

www.nickthacker.com

CPSIA information can be obtained
at www.ICGtesting.com
Printed in the USA
LVHW011728080121
675851LV00004B/352